ALWAYS
A
GOOD
ENDING

A DIVERSE SHORT STORY COLLECTION

DAVID LEE HENLEY

All correspondence with author use:
brutushenley@hotmail.com.

Publisher's Note: This is a work of fiction. Names, characters, places, and incidents are a product of the author's imagination. One exception being "I DIDN'T HAVE A CHOICE", which is a true story. Also, stories in Chapter "FUN TIMES," which are remembrances of authors younger days.
Locales and public names are sometimes used for atmospheric purposes. Any resemblance to actual people, living or dead, or to businesses, companies, events, institutions, or locales is completely coincidental.

Book Title: ALWAYS A GOOD ENDING/ DAVID LEE HENLEY. 1st ed.

Contents

Chapter 1

I Didn't Have A Choice

One Girls story

Sub-*Chapters*

Preface

Before I begin my story, I have a brief comment.

There is a different attitude in society today, which was completely absent when I was growing up. I only wished it had been as it is today back then. Maybe I would then not have had a reason or need to write this book.

People at the time this all happened had an, I don't see, I don't hear, and I don't know anything attitude to things into which they did not want to get involved.

I found as all the horrible things that I had to endure, which were happening to me that everyone who, as I think back upon it, knew what was happening and had simply ignored it so they could justify their inhumanity and cowardice.

Their excuses were as many as the times they encountered me in my need for help. It is none of my business; I don't want to get involved, what difference could I make anyway, all false justification defenses for their lack of common decency and unwarranted and unjustifiable fear.

It has always mystified and frustrated me as to how absolutely everyone for the whole time I was a captive to the person whom I will call a monster in this book that not once did an ounce of help come to me.

Government officials, school officials, hospitals, all believed or accepted the lies told to them. Neighbors, who had to have heard my screams of pain, my family, my own mother; not one would investigate or lift a finger to stop or prevent the suffering and humiliation I had to endure from the monster I had for a step-father.

It has taken me a lifetime to get to the point that I could even attempt to write about this part of my life. It is still excruciating to remember it at all. I feel now that possibly by writing about my experiences, I might save a young girl's life and hopefully get others who know of or suspect these kinds of situations to show some backbone and get involved in stopping the horror.

I have spent years trying to block out the past to no avail. It is and always will be a part of me. I will see or hear something that triggers an instant recall and flashback to that time in life I most want to forget but am unable to. At times it causes panic attacks, of which I have no control, and I think I am having a heart attack.

I wake at night screaming from my nightmares. The monster did his evil on me, and it has left lifelong consequences.

Introduction

Society has always allowed complete changes in its commitments to marriage. Some stay faithful to their promise of unto death oaths even under extraordinary circumstances and situations of suffering. Many have dissolved the union at the first argument. Most run the gauntlet of betweenness.

Others have mostly had beautiful and loving relationships, though they are getting rarer and seen more as in the minority. Most live together just getting along for the children's sake, or that is the excuse of most.

It is not this writer's place to judge any particular set of rules to live by, nor to establish basic living together criteria. Every person designs their very own unique niche in cohabitation with their partner, husband, and wife, significant other, however, you define your arrangement.

There are, however, a few fundamental understandings that are never to be crossed. These are fundamental principles of a civilized society.

Never do harm to your partner and likewise never allow others to harm them. Basic and simple.

There is an understood obligation that from the uniting of couples who bring into the world the consummation of their union, the children, that they also are afforded the same love and care the couple should have for each other.

Therein lies a point where some have crossed that barrier for their own particular selfish wants and desires. It is where sometimes out in the open and sometimes in secret, these rules are cast away.

This is a point where most only do a small thing of little consequence, and from there grows to more severe acts of selfishness and misbehaving. Such possibilities are: by hitting in anger but not truly meaning to, cheating out of a desire for another, and feeling bad about it. Such things are terrible in the scope of things to healthy relationships.

But then you begin to get into more and more outrageous behavior, even unto murder at the extreme. Yes, people can run to extremes of mammoth proportions in their search for self-gratification.

The one thing that even the evilest-minded among us do not tolerate is the willful harming of the most vulnerable, the most innocent, the children.

You can prove that point any time by putting someone who willfully and with malice harmed a child into the ranks of the most ardent of criminals, and though they will tolerate each other among themselves, they will kill the molester without a second's hesitation.

It is something inherent in the more significant majority of us to protect the young.

This story is about a girl who was passed over in that protection. She was somehow never given the most basic of protections from all around her. To this day, it is not fully understood how this could have happened to this extent. But happen it did.

It is why this story has to be shared. To help in any way it can by hopefully getting others to stop helping continue this cycle of abuse and to end these horrific situations which are still going on somewhere and are known by others too afraid to speak out.

It must be in this enlightened and courageous time the abused come forward and tell their darkest secrets, which until now were kept buried within families as a shameful thing not to be opened to the light of day. We have to get people out of their comfort zones and speak out if suspicious of some egregious act that might be happening around them, to save the children.

This story is but one story, her story, exclusively unique to her, but its representation is repeated in too many other stories.

It is not this writer's desire to put into words the feelings of horror and suffering that would be inherently and profoundly lived and felt by the storyteller herself. She has had a challenging time relaying the story to me as it is.

I cannot even guess as a male the emotions and trauma a female must feel at the time of being accosted. I can only give the verbal accounting given to me by the victim.

It will be the reader who must fill in that portion as only a female can. If you're a male reader, maybe a small fraction of the real horrors can be revealed and empathized with from her story.

I give her a grateful thank you for her courage to come forward and expose the man who caused so much harm and try and prevent others from being victimized with the same fate as herself.

I also want to say how much she should be admired for the inner strength she must have to come out of all the horror with her sanity still intact

Sub Chapter:1

How It All Began

I have found from listening to other women who have gone through the horrors of abuse that no story is the same. Each circumstance was predictably on the same path, but how it happens is unique in each situation.

The bottom line is that once the man decides he is going to do the molesting, it is only a matter of time and opportunity before he acts on his inappropriate, disastrous, shameful, and painful to his victim's lusts.

Nothing is more harmful to a young girl who has given her trust to someone who violates that trust so abhorrently.

Nothing scars deeper than the faith one has in finding the most trusted to be so utterly devoid of respect and caring and be so barren of compassion and concern for the pain and humiliation of putting someone through such a horrific experience.

One that has endured these acts can never again fully feel safe in a man's company. Doubt will always linger in the back of their mind.

One example of this was when I was newly married, and my husband was getting a little too aggressive. It caused me to recoil in fear and spoiled the moment, even though I knew it was not meant in a harsh and insensitive way.

Just the force used in complete ignorance and playful fun by your loved one instigates past repressed feelings and brings them back to life.

This occasion happened only once with my husband, who was pretending to overpower me playfully. I just froze and began crying. He was shocked when he saw I was crying. He could not have known how such a simple thing would so adversely affect me. Honestly, I didn't either until it happened. I thought I had progressed past those moments. He never played that game again.

I think it took a lot out of our relationship in that there are times a woman wants a man to dominate her and not always have to tell them it's okay. That, of course, would be just one more thing the monster has taken from me.

**

My story should start somewhere, so, I think a point when I was simply another little girl growing up should be appropriate.

**

Before the monster came into our lives, we, as very young children, used to have a fun time. Mom would date some guys, and they were nice men. We always had fun with them and enjoyed their company. I was about four or five at the time.

Mom was hardly ever around. We stayed with babysitters most of the time. I suppose she was trying to find a husband to take care of us.

Mom eventually started taking us to see the monster in some prison. It was a long drive. To this day, I will never understand why my mother would want to have anything to do with a man in prison. We would play on the floor while she would talk to the monster through a glass wall. I never knew how mom had gotten to know him. Did she even know why he was there? I never found that out.

We didn't know anything as young children. He treated us pleasantly as he was courting mom. I remember he was always kind to me back then, at first.

He always wanted me around but did not seem to want my brothers around. I remember him starting to get mad at my brothers a lot, and I wondered why he was acting that way toward my brothers; they weren't doing anything wrong.

I think I was about five and a half when mom married him. We children never really liked him. We wished mom would have married one of the other men who were genuinely respectable to us.

There were several verbal fights between mom and grandma. I don't think grandma liked the monster any more than us kids. We were too young to know what it was all about. Mom and grandma never got along very well.

My grandparents told mom to watch out for me around the monster. So obviously they could see something was going on or knew more about the monster than we were allowed to know. I wished they had cared enough to help me more than they did. Mom just dismissed it as them not liking the monster.

It seemed when the monster would talk to my brothers, it was always in a derisory voice, and he would speak to me in a friendly voice.

Mom was never nice to me. I never got hugs from her, and when she combed my hair, it was like she was trying to pull my hair out. I think back on it now, and I think she learned to be uncaring from her mom, my grandma. Or maybe it was an inherited character flaw through her genes. Both were cold, demanding women. Not much love flowed in the family from the women toward the women. Mom always told me I should have been a boy.

She was relentless in her disparaging remarks.

The monster picked the perfect woman to marry for his needs. A woman that was desperate for a man willing to care for her and her kids. A woman who unmistakably wasn't particularly fond of her own flesh and blood daughter. He could no doubt see the similarity of my mother and my grandmother in that they both were alike in their lack of caring, the perfect situation for a manipulating molester to find.

I always thought I should have a mother who would love and protect me, but she never hugged me or said she loved me. She just told me I should have been a boy.

I always had fantasies about my father. I would be daddy's little girl. That was a fantasy in any little girls' dreams. It just didn't work out that way.

I remember mom married the monster in our grandparent's living room.

He could now start his slow and methodical power and control over everyone as he had always done to everyone around him to the point of blind obedience to his will. Making everyone scared to death of him seemed to be his goal.

When I was six or seven, things started getting worse. Mom was working days at a hospital, so she was never around when the monster mistreated us. That gave the monster a couple of years to work on my brothers and me, but especially on me as I would soon be cast as the only one able to stop him from hurting my brothers. That was the threat he would eventually come to use.

Mom would come home from work, and my brothers would tell her the monster was mistreating us, but she didn't ever do anything about it. She just said we must have been doing something wrong and probably deserved to have been punished for it. She just shrugged it off.

Sub Chapter:2

The Monster Is Here

Finally, the day came as it inevitably would, the day he could no longer wait to satisfy his lust for little girls.

I was in the third grade when one day he told me he was going to pick me up at lunchtime so I could go home to eat. I can still remember that day as clear as a bell. I must have been nine years old then, although I seem to feel I was more like seven and a half or eight years old.

I thought that was strange and puzzling of him wanting to take me home for lunch, but I was not feeling very well that day, so I did what I was told. He took me home and fixed me a sandwich.

After I ate it, he told me to go take a bath. That was really surprising and unexpected. I wondered why he wanted me to take a bath. But he was harsh to me then, and I was too scared to say no. So, I went and took a bath. Then he came into the bathroom, and I told him to get out. He just came in and sat down on the tub rim. He told me he was going to do some things to me. I wondered, of course, what things he was talking about. He said to me if I told my brothers or my mother anything, he would hurt my brothers really badly.

Well, I loved my brothers. I told him, I didn't want him to hurt my brothers, I don't like you hurting my brothers.

He said, then don't tell anybody about what I am going to do. That is when I started crying. Back then, you always did what your parents tell you to do, no matter what.

I didn't even know what he was going to do, but I knew I wasn't going to like it. I didn't want him in the bathroom, and I couldn't figure out why he would come in there anyway. I was embarrassed by him being there, and seeing me naked and unable to do anything about it was more than I could handle.

All I could do was cry and tell him to stop as he forced himself on me. I tried fighting him, but it was useless. He was too big and strong. He just kept telling me to be quiet and to stop crying.

I don't want to tell all the obvious things he did to me in the tub and later after he made me go to the bedroom. It is hard enough to even talk about it now. But, as I was too small for him then, he continued day after day, month after month until I could finally take him inside me. He made me do more and more things for him.

I can never forget the horrible pain and humiliation of those times.

I am sure the neighbors could hear me screaming and crying out in pain. But no help ever came.

Months went by. I was missing school so often now because the monster took me home almost every lunch period, and the truant's officers were starting to come around asking questions. I would have to re-take the third grade because of the missed time. That was when we suddenly moved to the south.

It was my grandparents that loaned the monster the money to move to the south when the school started calling at our house about me missing so much time. Mom had lied to them about the reason they needed the money. She said she needed the money to buy a house, but it was money needed to run away from the prying eyes coming around looking into my absence from school.

The monster simply could not stop himself from taking me out of school for his pleasures. Once he started on me, he could not stop, even to help himself stay out of jail. He was indeed one sick monster. So, we ran or moved away as it were.

Thinking back on that time, I think the only reason we would have suddenly moved was to save the monster from the prying eyes of the state looking into what was going on. I just wished they would have followed up on their investigation instead of dismissing it as, oh well, not our problem any longer. Mark up another failure by the government to do its job.

The first house we moved to was remote, deep in the woods, and it had all the privacy the monster could need. It didn't have anything but a roof. We had to use an outside toilet and take bathes in a metal tub. All of us kids hated it.

Now the monster could have me anytime he wanted with no problems.

As I look back now, I had thought my mom was supposed to be there for me, to be my friend, but she never was. She never cared to help me with my homework; she never cared if it was even done. She only cared if I didn't finish the chores. She was never there most of the time anyway. She was always working.

The monster got hurt doing some job and was electrocuted. He stayed in the hospital for a while. That was before my half-sister was born, I think.

When the monster got out of the hospital, things got really bad then.

Time seemed to stop then. I just lived from one day to the next, always at his side. He made sure I could never have a moment alone with anyone that I could confide in, just in case I tried to get help. But he had worked on me very well. I was totally under his control and did not even think of trying anything. I did what I knew I had to do to keep my brothers as safe as possible.

Once the monster came into our lives, my brothers and I lost a lot of our playtime together. It was always chores and angry confrontations. The monster was always on us about something, anything to keep us under his rule.

Even as I did everything demanded of me, it seemed he would still hurt my brothers. There was just no way around it.

Later in life, I remember when I finally did tell my brothers about what happened to me. They just started yelling at me. Why didn't you tell us? Why did you put up with all that from him for so long?

Everything is always my fault. I get the blame for everything that happens. I can understand how they felt and why they were so upset, but I had no control over anything. I did what I had to do.

It really hurt me to have them yelling at me. I couldn't answer a lot of their questions; I just froze up from all the verbal yelling coming at me. I was sorry I had even told them.

Now everyone was mad at me. I thought I would get a little sympathy and understanding, but all I got was anger. I never thought I would be viewed as the bad one for trying to keep them all safe from the monster.

I withdrew back into my shell again. Their hatred for the monster just went up ten-fold, but without my keeping them safe by doing what I did, they may not have even been there today. It was now my burden to bear alone.

When the monster opened up an antique sales and refurbishing business, I would go everywhere with him. We would travel to distant locations and always sleep in the truck.

I was allowed to only work in the back, or if customers came in, I would have to stand at his side. He had such a tight rein on me. I would just look at the ground while he talked to the customers. I could tell everyone thought it was strange how I acted, but they never said anything.

This was the south. I think a lot was going on in other homes as was in mine, and people just turned a blind eye to it. A don't get involved attitude.

Of course, there was no place he would not have me when he felt like it, even at the business.

I did get to go fishing with him. I loved fishing. It was the only fun I can remember having. Of course, I knew it was just another reason to get me away from the house for his pleasures, but by then, it was just a chore to me. I came to expect it as something that was going to happen, so I concentrated on the positive parts, like my love of fishing. I at least managed to find some fleeting moments to treasure.

I never felt any of the pleasure people claimed to have from sex. I suppose I had blocked out any feeling to it like a normal person. My body was dead to any senses. I just went through the motions as he would ask of me. If there were any time, I had felt the sensual side of the act, I must have blocked it out. My mind would never allow such things.

Later I will tell of my eventual awakening to the feeling of pleasure, but it was never once with the monster. The monster never thought of making me feel good. I was only around for his enjoyment, his gratification.

After my oldest brother got dad to let him come live with him, it was just my younger brother, and I left to suffer the monsters' wrath. I was glad at least one of us was able to escape. I used to wonder why dad would not take all of us away from this constant terrorizing by the monster. I was sure my brother would tell him how bad it was for us here. But I guess it was not a concern of his.

Of course, my half-sister was there, but she was the monsters' little darling and was spoiled rotten. It was my job to see to her every want and need.

As a punishment for not doing what the monster wanted, he would send my younger brother to bed and lock him in, as usual, to make me more cooperative with his wishes.

I remember I begged the monster to feed my brother before he was locked in his room at night. It was just another torture he inflicted on him to make sure I did what he wanted. He had to pee out the window because he could not go to the bathroom, locked up as he was.

It made me feel so bad for him. I knew I would be responsible for anything that happened to my brother if I did not put out for the monster. I always tried hard not to go to sleep until my half-sister went to sleep, and I could go to his bedroom to satisfy his needs.

Mom would never stick up for the boys when the monster would hurt or mistreat them.

The day my last brother, the youngest, left to go live with our father, he had gotten into a fistfight with the monster. He was older now, and he would not take any more beatings from the monster. He beat him up pretty good. The monster was backing up from the fists coming at him and tripped over something. When he went down, my brother got on top of him and pounded him good. But the monster got up and was saying he was going to kill my brother. I yelled for my brother to run. The monster was going into the house to get the shotgun. I knew he meant to kill my brother.

My brother waited in the gulley by the road until mom came home. The monster was sitting on the porch for my brother to come back. He stopped her and told her what had happened.

I was sorry then that I had not poisoned him on the many times I dreamed of doing it. I always did the cooking, so my fantasy was putting poison in his food, but I never acted on it. I don't know if I could have anyway. The fear of failing and his surviving the attempt kept me from trying. I think it was also that I am not a murderer even to save my own life; it didn't stop me from thinking about it, though.

My brother had run to save his life, and eventually when mom came home, and she got the monster to agree to send my brother away to his father to live, which saved his life. I was so happy that both of my brothers were now free from the monster.

Mom would have horrible fights with the monster. Then she would tell me we would leave him after my half-sister was older. I would beg her to leave him now, but she never did. She never left him, ever.

I could never figure out why my father did not ask for me to come live with him. Of course, thinking about it, he never asked for any of us. The boys had been forced back on him. My oldest brother had constant arguments with the monster, and mom finally sent him to live with dad.

My brothers I am sure had told of all the horrors the monster had put us through, except of course the part about the secret only the monster and I knew.

I used to wonder why dad had not thought to ask for me to be also sent? Never once did I hear from him. No letters, phone calls, nothing, it was only later when I finally was able to talk to him that it came out. He never wanted a daughter, just boys. I can't tell you how much that hurt. It was like stabbing me in the heart. I wished I had never asked him.

My brothers had been sent away to live with our birth father before my first pregnancy, so they never knew what was going on. If they had been there at that time and found out what had been going on, I could not say if any of us would be here today. I think the monster would very quickly and with no guilt have killed us to protect himself from prosecution.

The prophylactics he used were always breaking, and it caused me to become pregnant twice by him in the time I was there.

The most heartbreaking thing I can remember was coming home from school one day and finding our home had burned down.

We were having trouble with a leaking hot water tank, and the reason given as to why the house burned down was because it had lost all the water and exploded. The house was so old, and the wood so dry, it just burned too fast for anyone to stop. It was gone before anyone could even get to it. Every one of the few things I had was gone. I had nothing left but the clothes I had on. I just cried and cried.

We had some neighbors that let us sleep on their screened-in porch until we could rebuild the house, but as it was rebuilt on the old foundation, it always smelled of burned wood, a constant reminder of my loss.

As I said earlier, I was never allowed to have friends. I never even got to play with my brothers. I had to take care of my half-sister. She did get to have her friends over to play and was allowed to go to their house as well. The monster would take me to the shop and leave my half-sister with mom.

As I said earlier, once mom had found out about us, she never stopped him from doing anything with me. I was his to do with as he pleased.

I remember when I was older, my oldest brother, who I hadn't seen in years came to visit with his wife. He finally got a moment alone with me and asked me if I wanted to leave with him. I was shocked, and in response, I told him I had to stay and take care of my half-sister.

It was so sudden and so unexpected I didn't have time to think about it. I was so sad when he left, and I was back to my old life again. I regularly cried, outwardly, and inside. I sometimes wonder if he had been more determined and persistent in getting me to go if I would have gone.

Mental chains are harder to break than steel ones.

After my brother left, the monster told me to quit crying, slut. He always called me that. The monster and mom both would call me that in front of everybody. I was a slut in mom's eyes, and I was a slut in his eyes.

People would just stare at him and look at me. But again, no one helped me, ever. It was so embarrassing. I didn't want the public to look at me in that way.

Here I was trying to protect my half-sister or thinking I was at the time. I found out later after I left, he started doing her as well. She was twelve years old. I had thought she would be safe because she was his little darling.

I always tried to find a way to escape, but the monster was continuously close by. I couldn't even go to town. I never went to town with mom. She didn't want me around her.

I don't know how I made it to the eighth grade. I was always failing everything. I had no help. I didn't have time to do my homework or study. I would start my day by waking before anyone, and cooking breakfast for everyone, then doing the dishes, getting my half-sister ready for school, then I could think of getting myself prepared to go to school.

Mom had gotten a job in town working in a retirement home and got home after midnight, so it gave the monster all the time he wanted with me at night. I was left to do all the work around the house myself.

When I came home from school, I had to clean the house, milk the cow, churn and strain the butter from the milk, take care of my half-sister, cook for everybody, do the dishes, wash the clothes, clean the barn, pick up the cow droppings, do the gardening.

Of course, those were just a few of the chores I had to do. As the tasks were needed, I did them until they were all done. Then I had to wait till I could service the drunken monster before I could sleep.

Many times, my half-sister would wake up when I tried to slip out of bed to go to the monster, and I would tell her to go back to sleep, and I needed to wait till she was asleep. The longer I took, the drunker he became, and that made my job a lot harder.

Many times, she would wet the bed, and I would have to get up and change my clothes, and hers, and the bed, before she would finally get to sleep. This was my life.

I never had a mother who talked to me about anything. I was never told about a period, and when I started, I was so scared. I thought I was broken somehow inside.

I wrote to my father about three times, begging him to come and get me. I never got an answer. I found out later that he never received them. I finally figured out the monster had checked the mailbox and took the letters. I didn't think about the possibility he would take them. I was so naive.

As I think back on it now, I realize the monster must have taken my letters because he would tell me my father didn't want me, he never writes you, he doesn't care about you. I think if my father did write to me, the monster would have destroyed them as well. He did have absolute control of me.

I will say, the only truth the monster told me was that my dad really didn't want me. I will hurt from that truth until I am dead.

I had asked my mom to send me to dad's, but she never had the money for that. My dad had been a policeman, and I wondered why he never wanted to know how I was doing. It probably would not have mattered anyway. My father told me later that he never wanted me in his life. He never wanted a daughter.

No one wanted me. I was all alone in the world. I wondered many times why I should keep on living. This was no life. I was reaching my breaking point.

There came a time I guess the last one or two years I was there. I would see the public from the back of the antique store staring at me. I was so big and old. At least that is how I thought of myself. Girls my age were usually married, and I was so fat and homely because of how I was made to dress and cut my hair. I was still forced to use the bowl on my head to cut my hair above the ears.

I would stand around the shop just waiting for the monster to tell me what to do. I was getting older now and finally starting to realize just how controlled I was. I had to go to the people's houses to do work on antiques, and I saw the way the people would stare at me and ask me why am I still at home? How old are you? Don't you work? I would have to go into these people's homes and strip the furniture and cabinets, and they would just stare at me, wondering why I was doing all of this. I was older now, and everyone knew the monster was married to my mother.

It was apparent now to them what was going on. At those times right in front of all those people, he would call me a little bitch or you little slut, or whore. I didn't know what those words meant except I knew they hurt. I was so embarrassed.

I started thinking, is life really so bad out there that I need to stay here putting up with this. Could there be anyone out there that might want me? There's got to be someone out there that wants me. I just could not do this any longer. I could not keep living like this. I would either find a way to escape or die trying; I was done. I had reached my breaking point.

Even the times when I got sick, I had to go to work at the shop or do my chores at home. The monster never gave me any sympathy. I would sit there, stripping furniture and throw up. It didn't matter to him.

For a year and a half before I left, I felt a lump in my breast, like a golf ball. I told mom I had a lump, and she asked me how long I had it. I told her a year and a half. She put me in the hospital where the doctors removed my nipple and took out the lump and put back my nipple. I was fine after that.

Sub Chapter:3

The Escape

I became so sick one day. I was throwing up frequently and had a high temperature. I could not get out of bed. So, the monster, for the first time in my life, left me alone at the house. I suppose he thought I was too sick to try anything.

I don't know why I did it, but I remembered where the monster kept a jar of money under the sink. For the first time in my life, I was alone without the monster around. I was scared to death. I was twelve miles out of town with no way to get there, and I was sick as a dog.

I had never been out in public alone.

Imagine if you were put into a room and not allowed out for sixteen years, that was what it was like. I never got out of the chamber of horrors. I was twenty-four years old. It was time to do this or die trying.

I knew the monster's parents lived 7 miles away. They knew what was going on with me by this time, I am sure.

I called them up and told them I have to do this. I have to do it now. Would you please drive me to the bus station? I was so petrified they would say no because they were afraid of the monster as well, but they were my only chance of escape.

I was to the point that I said to myself, I am going to either kill myself, or I will just do this. What did I have to lose? There was a gun in the house to end it all and a jar of money under the sink. I chose the money. I told myself I have been used and humiliated long enough.

This world cannot be as bad as the monster has told me it was. If it is, someone can just come and kill me if it was.

So, what I did was, I got under the sink and took $288.00. I was more scared than I had ever been in my life. I thought the monster would drive up at any moment. He had the truck, so I reasoned, or more like hoped, he thought it was okay to leave me sick at home.

I remember one time he had an argument with his parents, and he called his mom a bitch and his father a bastard and told them he hoped they burned in hell.

I called up his parents and talked to his mother.

I said, "I am all alone. I stole $288.00. Could you please come and take me to the bus station?"

She said, "I will be right there." She immediately hung up.

What wonderful people. It was like they were just waiting for me to ask for their help. I thought, had it always been just that simple. Just ask?

True to her word, they were there in minutes. I was so afraid when I saw them because they had to go by the shop where the monster was to get to the house. I was scared he would be right behind them.

I had earlier called the greyhound bus station and asked them if they had a bus that went nonstop to Huntington Beach, California?

They said, "we have a bus that was going to leave here at three o'clock."

I threw a few clothes into a little suitcase. I was scared, I was shaking, and adding to all of that, I was sick as a dog.

I watched for the monster's parents, and when they came, I ran out and jumped in their car.

I said, "would you please hurry? If the monster knows!"

Before I could finish my statement, she said, "honey, I know."

I said, "would you please hurry? Just get me on the bus."

Okay, here I was, having never been to town alone before, running as fast as I could toward the cliff of freedom. Just take the leap, I was persuading myself. As I grabbed the ticket, I was thinking, oh God, please don't let the monster come and get me. I was wondering if he had come home yet?

Well, they left me at the bus station. It cost me $110.00 for the one-way ticket. I got on the bus, and I was panicking and crying. The bus driver looked at me, but I was afraid of the bus driver too. I said again to myself; I've got to do this. I have got to do this if it kills me. At least I can say I went, I tried.

The bus finally left the depot. It seemed like it was never going to depart. I was crazy with panic, worry, and dread.

I think about that moment, and it reminded me of a movie I once saw. It was a man that had jumped from an airplane, and his parachute did not open properly, and he was falling to certain death.

His only recourse was to cut the lines from the malfunctioning parachute and deploy the reserve parachute before he hit the ground and died.

Those few moments, he was working to save his life were exactly where my mind was when I decided to run. Time was not on his or my side. Both scenarios were life or death, and it was our moment to succeed or fail. Live or die. I believe the emotions were the same as well.

The first place we stopped was in Memphis, Tennessee.

I asked the bus driver if he could help me. " I need to get to Huntington Beach, California."

The bus driver said, "I tell you what, you stay on this bus, and if you need to get off to get something to eat or use the bathroom, you have twenty-five minutes before we leave."

I didn't know then we had bathrooms in the back of the bus. I would be too afraid to walk past all those people anyway. I sat in the seat behind the driver. I suppose for whatever security that would be, and I could make sure he didn't leave without me.

I was so afraid to get off the bus at that time. I was fearful it might leave without me. But eventually, I got famished and needed to go to the bathroom, so I left just long enough to go to the bathroom.

On the way back from the bathroom, I saw a food concession stand. It was selling sandwiches. I asked the girl how much a sandwich was, and she said something close to $2.00. She asked me if I wanted one and I said, no thank you.

I didn't know how far it was to California and how much it would cost me to eat on the way. I was used to sandwiches I made at home with a big slice of bologna. This thing looked like you could see through it.

I went back to the bus, and at the next stop on the journey, the driver said we would be there for thirty minutes. I saw him going to a restaurant. I thought, well, I would follow him, I could be sure not to miss the bus. The bus driver noticed I was following him and asked me again if I was okay.

He said, "I noticed you have been crying most of the trip."

I told him I was fine.

He said, "well, okay. I am going in here to eat."

I uttered it! "You are?"

So, I went in and watched him just to be sure he didn't leave without me.

The waitress came over and asked me what I wanted. She gave me the menu, and I looked at it. The prices were three to four dollars for sandwiches with chips. I was used to eating big meals, and I finally ordered a hamburger. I ate it so fast. I was starved to death.

So, I rode the bus for three days and two nights. I was thinking, was I ever going to make it to Huntington Beach? There was a point in Los Angeles where I had to change buses. So, I went to the counter and asked the girl there; I am supposed to change buses to get to Huntington Beach, can you help me?

She said sure. Take bus 86 it is leaving in about twenty-five minutes.

I freaked out, twenty-five minutes? I asked her quickly, twenty-five minutes? Where do I go to catch it? She told me, and I went to the bus. I usually sat in the second seat, but I didn't want the driver to see me. I was having a hard time controlling my fear and crying.

Luckily, I had sat alone all across the country. Or maybe it was because people just didn't want to be bothered or get involved with a crying young girl.

When I had gotten into L.A., I saw people sleeping in the bus terminal, wearing dirty clothes, talking to themselves. I saw women wearing weird clothes. I didn't know what to think. It scared me.

I went to the bathroom and said to myself, hurry up, you need to get out of here. It stunk so bad. I straddled the toilet. I wasn't going to sit on that nasty seat for anything, and I had to pay ten cents to get into the toilet.

When I finally got to Huntington Beach, there was a little place called Terry's cafe. I decided that it would be better than staying in the terminal.

So, I went in, sat down, and said to myself; I have to get my strength up.

I had my younger brother's old phone number. I didn't even know if it still worked, but I had to wait till he got off work to call it.

When he finally answered the phone, I said: "Hello Paul, this is your sister Janet, I am in Huntington Beach, and I am trying to find dad, do you know where he is?"

He yelled, "Janet, did you say you're in Huntington Beach, California?"

I said, "yes."

I questioned him again. "Come on, Paul, where is dad?"

He said, "he is right around the corner."

He gave me dad's number.

I called, and dad could not believe it was me.

He said, "where are you?"

I said, "I am in this little Terry's cafe Paul said was right around the corner from you, but I don't know how to find you."

He said, "you stay right there."

I said, "Okay."

So, I walked out in front of the restaurant, and down the street, I saw walking on the sidewalk, my oldest brother Jim, my dad, and his wife.

I had not seen my dad since I was a little girl.

But when he rounded the corner, I started crying. I said to myself; I know that is my dad. I am thinking, Oh My God, this is actually happening. My life-long dream was now a reality.

They came up to me, and dad hugged me, his wife said hi, and also hugged me.

My brother Jim said, "Damn Janet, you're really here," as he also gave me a huge bear hug.

We walked back over to where dad worked, and he went back to his job, and I talked to my brother Jim until it was time to go home. We went to dad's house, and we talked and got to know each other.

I stayed for a week. Then dad asked me where all my clothes were.

I said, "this is all I have. It is all I brought in my little suitcase, two pairs of pants and a shirt. That's all I could take. All my clothes and stuff are still back home. I just need to go get them."

I couldn't ask him to buy me any clothes. I wasn't going to ask him to buy me new things. I didn't know how his wife was. I know she raised the boys. Now she's got me?

My brothers used to tell me how they hated her. I wondered if she would even accept me being here.

I stayed that whole week, and I told dad, "I hate to tell you this, but I need to fly back and get my clothes and stuff."

He stated, "I thought you didn't want to go back."

I said, "I don't have anything. I don't have any clothes. I don't have but one pair of shoes and a couple of changes of clothes. What am I going to do? What else can I do?"

He said, "Okay."

Here he is not offering to buy me any clothes. I had thought when I got out to California; dad would buy me clothes. He raised the boys and made sure they had clothes, surely, he'll take care of me.

Well, he wouldn't. That kind of shocked me. But I didn't know how to ask him for help. I didn't want to have to ask him. He didn't want me anyway; I was always told. What was I supposed to do?

He said, "are you really going back?"

I was devastated. I had no choice if my dad wasn't going to help me.

I told him I needed $300.00.

He gave me $300.00 for a round-trip ticket.

I flew back to get my stuff, and the flight back would be the next day.

I still don't know how I was able to do it. I was stuck with no alternative.

I called mom, she met me at the airport and brought me back home.

Well, the monster begged me to stay, promising to get me my own apartment. Then the monster started crying. I could not believe it. The monster was crying!

I told him, "I only came to get my clothes, and I am leaving."

He said, "oh, you're not leaving; you're staying."

I mustered every ounce of courage I could.

I said, "look, I only came to get my clothes, and I am leaving."

He started crying again and said, "I kind of figured for the last two years you were going to leave."

I said, "you're married to my mother, okay? My mother doesn't want me here."

I said, "I can't stay here; I have to go."

I could not believe this was happening.

He said, "well, I'll get you an apartment."

I said, "I have to go tomorrow, and I am packing."

I went upstairs and was scared to death. It took every ounce of courage I could muster to show them I meant to do precisely as I said I was going to do.

I took two trunks upstairs and started packing. I packed everything I could. I didn't know if the monster would even allow me to leave.

I had walked back into the prison, but I didn't think I had a choice. Dad was of no help. I had to do this all alone, as usual. But this time, I had my brothers who knew where I was and would come if I didn't make it back.

I think the monster knew it also, and the jig was up for him. He didn't have a choice now. He didn't know how much I had shared with everyone about him. He was gambling I would not tell and keep him out of jail. But that didn't stop him from trying to get me to stay. Control is hard to give up, I supposed.

I didn't know at the time dad and his wife didn't want me there, but it was the only place I had to go then, even if I had forced my way onto him, and after all, he was my dad.

The monster kept crying. I didn't sleep all night. I could not believe he had cried. Wet tears were clearly running down his face. Mom started crying, and my half-sister started crying. They all started crying. I could not believe it. They all treated me like mud on their shoes or worse, now they are crying like little babies.

The next morning, I told my mother to take me to the airport now. Take me now.

Come to find out when I had gotten to dad's house; there was a letter there from the monster telling me he had gone to all the bus stations in a hundred-mile radius of the house looking for me. I had made it to the bus station and left just before he got there. If he had gone to Memphis, he probably would have caught up with me. Lucky for me, he went to all the other stations hoping I was still there waiting to board.

The monster somehow found out his parents had taken me, and he didn't speak to them for years afterward.

I am pretty sure that it didn't bother them in the least. It was probably a blessing from God for helping me escape.

They took me to the airport, and I flew back to dad's house. When he picked me up at the airport, I pinched myself and said I couldn't believe it. I did it. I'm actually gone for good. I got out of prison.

I never spoke to my mother ever again. I don't know the proper way to prepare it, but verbally I disowned her.

She was never to exist as a part of my life again.

Sub Chapter:4

What Will I Do Now?

I now had to deal with my dad and his wife. No matter what, I did exactly what his wife told me to do. I still had stitches in my breast from the lump I had removed. I stayed with dad for about a month, and he would take me over to the jewelry store he owned. I asked him if he wanted me to sweep the floor for him. He said no.

I look back now and think he just took me along to get me away from my stepmother.

I was so naive, and they saw that. After all, I had an eighth-grade education at best. I never stepped out in public alone in my life; I had zero communication skills; I knew nothing about anything. They were sophisticated, upper-class high society. I was simply an embarrassment to them. A fat unladylike country bumpkin with a bowl haircut. How could I possibly fit into their cultured lives?

Dad's wife was getting jealous. She did not like me there, taking time from her husband.

I finally said I needed to get a job. Dad thought that was a good idea. It would get me out of the house and hopefully out of their lives. Well, not out of their lives but out from under-foot.

My dad worked in jewelry. He sold and gave appraisals to a vast clientele. He gave a party one night at his home, and not knowing what to do with me; he put some of his jewelry on me to show off to his guests. I was told just to be quiet and show the jewelry. But that was a disaster. I was an embarrassment all night. An overweight backwoods country girl with no societal skills, with a bowl haircut? The daughter of the host? That would never happen again.

Dad suggested I try the fast-food restaurant a mile and a half down the road in seeking a job. I walked down to it as no one would drive me there.

I went in and asked for the manager. I told him I needed a job badly. I told him I had never had a job before, but I did work refurbishing antiques for years. I said I didn't know how even to make a hamburger. I thought that was dumb to say as I really did know how but just not the way they did it in the restaurant.

He looked at me and said, you know what? I am going to hire you. I have a bunch of people here that feel like they can call in sick every time a good beach day shows up and leave me without a complete crew. I don't see you doing that. I am going to give you a chance. Also, I can train you the way I want things done without having to break any bad habits you might have learned elsewhere.

Three months later, I was made assistant manager over all the other employees who didn't like that one bit. One of them told me he had been there for a year, and he felt he should have gotten that position.

I told him he needed to talk to the manager, not me. He was the one that gave the job to me.

He didn't talk to the manager. I needed only to be taught one time, mostly on how to do something, and that was it. I took the job very seriously. I wanted to prove to everyone I could be needed and wanted. I was not going to bow down to any threats or misdirected attitudes from anyone ever again.

I was free, and I planned to stay that way.

Dad never did take me to my job or offer to buy me a car, so I saved my first two checks and bought a bicycle to get to work and back.

Eventually, my hair grew out, and I lost my fat from working, walking, and riding the bicycle. I never knew I looked so good. It shocked me to see the woman I had always been under all the deliberate hiding of my beauty the monster had put on me.

I started caring about my appearance and having respect for myself. I learned how to dress in beautiful clothes and how to apply makeup to accentuate my face best. I still had a heavy southern accent in my speech, but that just seemed to make me more appealing to the men I met.

After a while, the manager said he wanted to make me the supervisor of my very own restaurant. That petrified me. I had no education to do a position like that, nor had I ever held such responsibility.

I did not have the confidence at that point in my life to even consider it. It was apparent he saw my potential, but I didn't.

I was still just barely free from being a slave, and now I was being asked to take on such a dominant, authoritative position?

My lack of schooling left me at a significant disadvantage, and I knew I was over my head at that time in doing the books required for that position. I could work at any job in the restaurant, but the bookkeeping was out of my comfort zone and my education level.

That offer, I am sorry to say, was too soon in my self-awakening period. I was still too uncertain of myself and my abilities.

It would take a lot longer for me to finally break through my inner-most secret fears of whether people would accept me and find me worthy.

My brainwashing had gone on for seventeen years and would take a lot more achievements and resolve to break that hold, especially without help from anyone.

I would eventually come to realize I had skills, talent, and intelligence, which put me at the top of every job I worked at, but it was certainly not at this time in my life. I was soon to realize some places were male-dominated and was hindered, or should I say down-right blocked, in getting past a particular position.

But at this time in my life, I was still a fresh new delicate seedling flower just starting to grow after coming out of a terribly difficult winter.

I was still learning what a genuine real life was to be. How wonderful and exciting things happening all around me were. It was truly mesmerizing in their moment of reassurance and comforted me that I had made the right choice to live and escape.

To have freedom, to answer only to myself. To maybe someday share myself with someone I wanted to share with, and who would love me as I would love him!

That man would eventually come into my life. And through him, I was to finally experience my first orgasm. I never knew what it was.

He had me relax and close my eyes. He put my most favorite CD on, and I listened to it with earphones. All I had to do was relax and feel the sensations he was giving me; I had to do nothing for him, to him, with him. I had nothing to do but immerse myself, my mind, my body, in my own world of music and sensations.

Everyone knows what it feels like to have orgasms. But for me, it was indescribable. I never knew it existed up to that time. I cried from the exquisite pleasure I had never known before; it was so beautiful. From that moment on, I was able to feel the pleasures sex could bring.

It had opened me up mentally and physically, letting in all the senses I had forced down to the bottom-most depths of my being. All the things I would never allow the monster to have me feel were finally open to me.

It was no longer just another chore.

I do not want to spoil this moment, but I have to keep going on my story.

There was a big problem I never saw coming. It was a devastating blow. I had given birth to two children by the monster. My husband and I tried to have a child of our own, but after failing for so long, I finally went to the doctor, and he said I had too much scar tissue in my tubes, and the sperm could not get through to impregnate me. I could have my tubes cleaned out to remove the scar tissue, but that meant I could possibly have a tubular pregnancy. The only way was maybe using in-vitro fertilization. A slim chance back then.

My father would not loan us the money. He said there were too many kids in the world anyway. He was always saying no to me anytime I asked him for help financially. He was wealthy and spent his money on fine things, but tight as they come with me. We could not afford it ourselves, so we just gave up on the idea of ever having children of our own.

My dad died many years later, after having sold a big company and made millions. He never gave us anything except a three-thousand-dollar loan one time, which I paid him back.

He lost his mental faculties, which none in the family knew was happening, and lost or gave away most of his money to unscrupulous people that had surrounded him at that time. He was almost penniless at the end.

I heard he would walk around with a briefcase full of money, just handing it out to whomever he felt.

I was still sad I could not be with him at the end, but he was just too far away, and I could not afford to go to him.

My brother took care of him for all of us.

Dad had called him and asked if he could come and take care of him as he was getting worse health wise and my brother told him he would need to help him financially. Dad said, no problem.

So, my brother left his home and went to take care of dad just to find out he was, broke. Dad could not help him because he was basically penniless.

It cost my brother a bankruptcy in the process of doing that for dad. He lost everything he once had, but he still took care of dad until the end.

Sacrifice appears to run in the family, but martyrdom pays a heavy price.

I received word from my brother that mom had called and told him that the monster had died from a massive heart attack while he was doing a sermon at a local church.

I could not believe he had died while preaching. He never set foot in a church in his life. I can only surmise even God had tolerated enough of the monster at that point

Sub Chapter:5

It is Great to Be Alive

I have many moments in my story that would eventually define and portray who I have become as a person.

The many girlfriends, a few boyfriends, co-workers in the many varied occupations I have learned.

The skills I have learned that helped me grow, learn and expand my knowledge and abilities.

The moments I treasure most are the times when something new comes along. I can experience a whole new set of joys and laughter and thrills. I have had a lifetime of negativity, and I want only to live the rest of my life looking on the brighter side.

Traveling across the country, I get to see and experience the wonders it has to offer, meeting the people, hearing their stories.

Yes, and also tasting the multitude of flavors from so many diverse cultures and cuisines bursting with their own uniqueness.

I can hardly believe I have been able to do so much. In my darkest hours, I could only imagine such an existence as I now have! I am so thankful I was able to keep from taking my life; to have the chance to become all I ever wanted or dreamed I could be.

I can only imagine who and what I would have become if I had been allowed to live a normal healthy life growing up.

But I am content now at this moment because it is of my precise, with free-will, choosing.

Life now is what I have made of it. It is a manifest reality of my personal creation. I am going to enjoy it for as long as God allows me.

CHAPTER 2 ●

VIRUS PANDEMIC

Sub-Chapters

Preface

As in all things, there is constant uncertainty. Things you take for granted can be shattered in a moment. Everyone has lived through these calamities of disarray. One can only take what is presented and deal with the consequences.

So even though we live in an ever-changing and tumultuous world. We strive to make the best of any given set of circumstances. It is simply human nature to try overcoming the tragedies and adapt as best one can.

Once in a great while, something catastrophic comes along that involves everyone. It leaves the world in chaos and changes the way we all live. It is hardly ever anything we had expected, at least at that moment, and blindsides us with little or no chance to prepare, and so the label of catastrophe is applied.

Such moments do however bring out in us the good and the bad of our responses. Some take advantage of the situation, some think only of themselves and their survival, and yet many are helpful and sacrifice themselves for the greater good. Helping in any way possible to keep society running and assist those affected by the catastrophe to endure.

Yes, it is this mix of society that emerges in these times that helps to guaranty the survival of humanity. Each having a different role in assuring a successful subsistence and continuation of life scenario.

No one can claim it is fair and just, it is merely the way we are moved to respond. Surely some feel guilt-ridden as they are immersed in their selfish and abhorrent behavior but are still driven for unknown reasons toward that response.

Society has long known of these responses and accepts them as a given and acknowledges them to be unfortunate but inevitable.

Thankfully the givers outnumber the takers, and so allows humanity to endure.

It is in this manner of conduct so crucial and essential to our survival, we must honor those who dedicate themselves to key critical and vital services, for all our sakes.

Introduction

As in all stories, there has to be the villain and the hero. But this story may not fit that idea. There may not be a hero. It may also be just how you might want to perceive each to be.

Certainly, there is an abundance of evil and bad people throughout the story. and yet, surely one would have no problem in asserting the heroes to be the many who helped while putting themselves in danger.

Those helpers are not the ones being highlighted at this time. But the ones who caused the problem and the ones to fix it have a blurred line. Can you address blame and salvation all on the same people? Is only one party to blame?

This story twists the perception and impression of this hypothesis to a new level.

A maniacal military commander and a dedicated research scientist are on a collision course to alter the world in a catastrophic and possibly forever after transformation.

But others had a hand in this as well. There are many to blame. Who should eventually face punishment? Will we be around to wonder?

Sub Chapter:1

The Plan

General Chu, contemplated his strategic project as it was unfolding in his plush government-supplied office. His objective was purposeful, intentional, and direct. He had worked for years planning his attack, and the method of delivery to best have cover to its origin. Yes, it would be a masterstroke of design. No one could claim it was deliberate. A fluke of nature once again raises its randomness to deal a blow upon the world at large. Another freak crossover of an animal to human contagion that no one could have seen coming.

Searching for the perfect candidate to get the ideal virus from the arrogant stupid Americans took a little longer than he had planned but once he had her he knew it was worth the effort. Americans could always be played by him and his countrymen. Had they not almost totally taken over the world already?

If not for that last man who became President. He came out of nowhere and spoiled a perfect winning game of controlling the Americans. So close. They had been so close.

But they will pay dearly for that setback. That is all it is as of now. A temporary setback.

He thought back to how he had originally had the brainstorm idea of using a virus much like the other ones they deliberately unleashed on the world to test how the people and governments would react. And those tests had shown how the world ultimately responded to the different scenarios each unique calamity would present. How long it took to find a cure! What the governments did to contain the problems! How far they were willing to go to address the people's rights versus overall health concerns!

He knew the world would eventually find a cure or vaccine or treatment. That was not his objective to kill everyone. His objective was to cause global chaos economically. To shut down the whole economic system and create pandemonium in every country. To turn everyone against each other. To make America fall to its knees. To make them lose their powerful world dominance. To get China back in control of everything once again.

They almost had complete dominance of the world through its different controls of rare minerals, pharmaceuticals, antibiotics, multiple indispensable products. The manufacturing monopoly on phones, or at least the internal workings and control of parts for almost every necessary industrial use. Yes, they were nearly at a point where they could control the whole of the world through its need for the things China had acquired dominance over.

They had been able to persuade governments and businesses to follow in their direction through coercion, manipulation, or simple threats of China withdrawing its materials and support.

Yes, also becoming a member of the world trade organization was a major turning point for China. It made them a force to be dealt with.

And making businesses give up their rights to their own intellectual property to do business and force them as a cost saver to move to China to manufacture was a stroke of genius. They could learn all they needed about an industry and then manufacture it themselves with knock-offs. No patent infringements here.

All of that was coming to an end if China did not do something to cut the world down to size and allow China to get back its dominance that the stupid American President was trying to destroy. What was America thinking to put him into power? We had all the politicians we needed to control the government. Both parties were under our thumb. All past Presidents were useful fools for our goals. Then it all started falling apart.

One lone man gets a little power and decides to ruin everything we have worked for so long to achieve by making America self-sufficient and bringing many of the hard-won businesses China had manipulated back to America.

Well, his time is over. He will soon see how determined we are. This plan will not fail.

He called his party unit into the office to go over the detailed orders one last time.

Sub Chapter:2

It Was All So Easy

Virologist Ying Fan Lung was a smart, loyal, and dedicated member of the party. She had to be. No one was free to do as they wished if the party leaders wanted something of you. You just did whatever they requested unless you didn't want to continue living.

Her father had tried to speak out once and after his re-education camp experience, a short but intense period of time away from home, he came back a much more docile, in line with party doctrine and philosophy attitude.

He also was warned of his family's safety if he stepped out of line again. That had the expected effect on him they knew it would. It had worked for many other dissidents.

Some had been stubborn and they were dealt with and made examples of for others who dared to think for themselves and try to live as they wished.

Conformity was an absolute must in Chinese society. The government never had a problem in controlling the masses if need be. They had many locations for housing those who dared to speak out in protest.

Of course, the people were allowed to have some personal freedoms, it gave them the illusion of self-direction. As long as it was appropriately aligned with the collective, it was permissible.

Ying had always been fascinated with biology. She would love to look through the microscope at school and watch all the little never before seen world of tiny creatures living their lives unaware of her watching them.

It also reminded her of her own situation with her government always keeping a secret eye on everyone.

She reasoned that no one was ever alone and watching the creatures through the microscope gave her a little window into how the government must feel watching the citizens under their supervision. She actually felt a little pleasure from the controlling power, silly as it was in fact.

Maybe it was a factor of nature to want to be in control. But the government had taken it to a greater level of absurdity.

Oh well, it was what it was, and thinking about it would only cause trouble for her.

She had been honored to receive the support from her school to receive higher education studies in the field she loved. She was allowed to go into medical virology studies after receiving a master's degree and a doctorate as well as completing medical school, gaining her multiple degrees in microbiology and related fields. Many following years of study at Yale in America gained her international acceptance as an authority on virology-related topics.

She was a world-class expert research molecular virologist by the time General Chu contacted her.

After all, all good things have a price, right?

Ying had been happily working at the prestigious Wuhan institute of Virology researching bat viruses by seeking out and collecting samples from many different locations across China. She was worried that sooner than later a possible cross-over of a virus was coming and she wanted to be on the leadership team to find a cure if and when that occurred.

She was very aware that past viruses had already crossed the animal-to-human barrier and the consequences had been terrible.

Besides the most obvious viruses that humankind had finally conquered through vaccines like mump, measles, smallpox, and many other diseases, all of these horrors became as nothing due to the diligent work and evolution of dedicated scientists into the new field of virology.

Ying wanted passionately to be a part of that historical evolution. To find cures to known and as yet unknown diseases. To leave her mark, her legacy, on the world. To be more than just a drone worker for the party elite.

Then seemingly out of nowhere General Chu visited the lab and after touring the grounds and research facility he asked that Ying meet with him in a private room.

"Ying Fan Lung is a powerful name, General Chu stated flatly. Your parents must have known you would be a force of nature. I have been watching you for a long time and I like what I see. I think you would be perfect for the exchange program I am overseeing with America.

"You would go to America on an exchange joint venture as a representative of our country to work and collaborate within a lab at Fort Detrick, New Jersey. We could all learn from one another and maybe in so doing advance all our efforts in the field of microbiology.

"I will be frank with you. It is also a great opportunity to also find out what they know and how advanced they are compared to us. Not to mention what a wonderful opportunity it would be for you as well. It would boost your standing in your scientific community and give honor to China as well."

Ying was not a stupid woman. She knew General Chu had other motives. It was always a given with the government. Nothing comes without a price. She simply waited silently knowing the favor would soon come.

General Chu still talking in a flat tone as was his way began.

He said, "as you work with the Americans I would like, as a favor to me, for you to, if possible, focus on the work they have accomplished on the coronavirus and collect as much data as possible on it.

"Actually, it is one of your pet viruses is it not? It would be a perfect reason for you to show interest in it as your field of study are the bats which harbor the virus, is that not true?"

Ying realized he knew he had her. It would be the perfect cover story to want to discover what the Americans knew of her studies and if they had made any progress in her area of study.

She was just not yet able to understand why he had such an interest in it. But she was certain it would manifest itself eventually. And frankly, she was very happy about the opportunity.

After what seemed an eternity, Ying had finally arrived at Fort Detrick. It was all he had said it would be for her. She could not refuse the offer even if she wanted to. It was too close to her personal ambitions and goals. Maybe there was something to her name after all. A smart and dangerous dragon. Maybe, General Chu should remember that.

***

Ying knew she was beautiful. It was never something she bothered with. Her studies and work kept her satisfied and had no desire to seek other avenues of entertainment. Much to the consternation of the men around her. Her co-workers had given up on even trying to get her attention. She was cold to anything but her passion for knowledge and her research.

The American researchers had yet to learn that fact and were constantly vying for her attention during their work periods. But nothing moved her. She was focused on her mission of knowledge and would not be sidetracked from it.

She likened herself as not much different from her beloved viruses. Single-minded and focused on their mission. The very reason for their existence.

The Detrick lab was all she had imagined it to be. Everything, state-of-the-art technology. Any and every piece of equipment you could ever hope for just for the asking. No price tag to hinder you. Everyone was as dedicated as she was to infectious diseases. She loved finally being able to discuss her research with like minds with as much knowledge as she. It was a dream job.

The Americans went out of their way to accommodate the new celebrity arrival. It seems she was more famous than she knew.

The only person who was sorry she was there was the man who had to go to China as part of her exchange program. That was only because he would not be there to visit and work with her also.

Ying had gotten one of the less undisciplined employees trying to get her to like him to open up and share some highly secret research that was being conducted. It had to do with mutations from genetic sequencing of the virus which caused the SARS outbreak years earlier. They also were using bats and other mammals to evolve the virus to a stronger version.

That was a big no-no in treaties and laws. Ying knew she had to get a sample of that strain.

She acted very obliging toward the traitor who confessed to her about the progress of the research and using her wiles as a female got him to show her the vials containing the virus.

She pretended to be so grateful at getting to see the vials she molded herself into the unsuspecting fool, kissing him passionately as she switched one vial of the virus with another she had hidden in her pocket. He was so thrilled at her sudden and brash actions he never saw the switch.

A few days later she was recalled back to China carrying the vial with her on a Chinese airline.

Another week went by and suddenly the Fort Detrick bio lab was closed by the CDC after it had finished its inspection. The report stated breaches were found but the breaches listed were blacked out.

There were no infectious diseases found outside of the compound so the public was satisfied with no contagion release possibility.

But internally all hell was happening. What happened to the vial of the virus that had been switched? Eventually, one employee found he was to spend a long time away from home.

" I hope that the kiss you received from Ying was a good one. It will probably be your last," said the government agent. They were always so serious.

Sub Chapter: 3

The Release

General Chu was elated though one would never guess as he always remained in his most composed stature. But when Ying came home with the virus, he almost grinned.

"Excellent work," General Chu said with a little more emphasis than he had wanted to use. "Now we must see how strong of a contagion it is. Let's see how far the Americans have gotten with the virus."

Ying did not like that one bit. She did not bring the virus home just to have it used as a weapon. What a fool she was. She should have known General Chu would use it in such a way. She had wanted to bring it back and study it in hopes of finding a cure if it ever was used by the Americans against anyone. Now it was all her fault it was going to eventually be used by her own country. That was obvious.

She felt sick at the thought. The only thing to do now was to try and do what she had intended from the start. Find a cure.

General Chu had several "volunteers" from the many dissidents and political prisoners to test the virus on.

It was learned that it was not deadly to most but most certainly was to a great many in the elderly group. Those were acceptable losses. They no longer were contributing much to the greater need of society and so were a drain of resources. Better to thin them out. The country was way too overpopulated as it was and this virus would work to solve two problems at the same time.

He was a pragmatic man after all.

Ying did not want to help General Chu but knew if she was to find a cure, she needed to also have access to the victims of his testing program for her research.

General Chu was willing and glad of her desire to find a cure. In case it got out of control the cure would be necessary. Also, as the only ones to have the cure or the first to find a vaccine, a great price could be asked from the recipients of the medical treatment. He, or better put, his country could be hailed as the savior of the world's epidemic crisis.

But first, it must run its course throughout the world so that his initial plans could come to fruition.

All was in readiness. The only thing as yet to be done was to find the vaccine to stop the virus. Ying had been disappointing on her mission up till now and he was getting tired of waiting.

He thought at first it would only take a short time to do the nearly impossible. Not being a scientist, he just assumed it could be done easily and quickly. He was weary of all the excuses Ying was giving him.

He decided to set his plan into motion and maybe that would give her more incentive to work harder and finish her job.

General Chu, on the last night before the operation was to begin, sat alone at his desk. He had gone over all the preparations with his team and had been given the go-ahead from the high command.

The military had outgrown the need for politicians to control them and decided they were unnecessary for their global domination plans. Politicians always got in the way of the greater victory the military saw coming. Global control with China as the world leader. Now that was a worthy goal.

His plan would bring the world to its knees and then China could rebuild it in its image of how things should be

He envisioned how many deaths it might take before the job was done. It would undoubtedly take millions. It did not matter. It would be better with a virus than with conventional war which could not be fought with a certainty of its outcome. Not to mention the destruction variables. This way was not as messy and everything would be left untouched and unspoiled for the victors to claim.

Sub Chapter: 4

The Time Line

DAY ONE:
An agent of General Chu went to the open-air market in Wuhan and sprayed a small vial of the virus into the air at the site where the bats were being sold.

It was a virus originally contained in the bats so the cover story would be a crossover of the virus the bats had contracted had evolved and mutated and crossed over the animal to the human genome and so the virus would spread from that initial one in a trillion chance, into the epidemic soon to follow.

It was simple and direct. Plausible deniability and misdirection from the Chinese government propaganda machine as to what and how and when it happened.

Just another innocent inevitable crossover of nature.

WEEK ONE:
People were starting to get ill. It was at first thought to be the flu but as time went on the symptoms gave another thought. Not the flu. What was it? Another outbreak of Sars?

MONTH ONE:
Panic was rampant in Wuhan. The virus was spreading much faster than expected and the city was crying out for answers. The government closed the open markets as the virus was publicized apparently to be bat-related. It was suspected that the markets had sold infected bats and the people had contracted the virus as a consequence.

America as usual reached out to offer aid in trying to contain the outbreak as they did in many other pandemics in past years. But China refused the offer and continued to try and fix the problem themselves.

MONTH TWO:
China had to seal off the city of Wuhan due to the fast spread of the virus. It stopped all flights out of the city of Wuhan into the rest of China but for some unknown reason allowed international flights out to the rest of the world to continue.

That one act was why the world would suddenly find itself in the middle of the pandemic as well.

It was as if it was a deliberate act by China to infect the rest of the world while containing the virus within China to just the Wuhan area.

General Chu was elated. It was working better than he could have ever hoped for. The stupid fools of the world were listening to the experts that were controlled by China saying to the world how the outbreak was no big deal. Just go about your business.

MONTH THREE:

Now everyone was seeing the truth. The virus was a big deal. The experts were all wrong. But they just pivoted their story and said we now need to lock ourselves into our homes and shut down all businesses and commerce. We had to wait out the virus. Give it time to die out without infecting more people.

The President finally stopped all air travel from China and soon after that from the rest of the world as well. It was too late. The rest of the world continued to allow air traffic and as a consequence would suffer many more casualties from the spread of the virus. Eventually, they also stopped air traffic from China.

General Chu had succeeded. He now had the world's biggest pandemic in modern history underway. And with just a simple tiny spray of the virus.

His goal of the collapse of the world's economy was coming. He had taken steps to procure all the masks and equipment he could find and bought it all for his own country to use thus allowing even more infections to continue growing.

He also knew the world would shelter apart from each other and help to curve the contamination until a cure or vaccine could be found. It was really starting to annoy him that Ying had not yet found a vaccine. But still, there was time yet to do as much damage as possible.

He had his doctors at WHO and the scientists in his service convince the world at large that the virus was not manmade but was a fluke of nature and also continue to beat the stay secluded mantra to give the much-needed time to destroy all the world's economies. That was the real goal.

China could still work and produce as it only had isolated one city. This gave them the ability to come to the rescue of the world desperate for masks and pharmaceuticals and much-needed medical equipment. The world's heroes.

The compliant media gave cover to all the obvious mistakes made by China like how the virus was transmitted from animal to human and not by a lab invention. Why China refused to allow any inspection of its labs in Wuhan was still unanswered.

Just blame the American President for everything. It was all his fault. China's disinformation arm went into hyperdrive deflecting the blame to everyone in the world but themselves.

MONTH FOUR:

It was working, the world's economy was on the brink of collapse. The roads were bare of people too afraid to step outside. The markets and stores left open were becoming empty of food supplies and essentials like toiletries and medicines.

The meats, vegetables, and fruits were becoming scarce due to supply chains being interrupted.

Ranchers had to start killing thousands of their livestock because they could not feed or process them since the plants were closed due to infections among the workers.

Farmers did not need employees to work the fields because all the businesses that usually bought the products were shut down due to the infections which were running rampant throughout the world. They simply plowed the fields over, destroying the crops.

Milk was poured down drains as the need was greatly reduced from school and restaurant closures. This caused ranchers to have to kill many dairy cows.

So many businesses were collapsing because of the government forced closures of industries, restaurants, and services of all kinds. Most would not be able to return even if a cure was found as it was already too late for them to economically reopen.

Million out of work were dependent on government handouts. Most would soon file for bankruptcy as no jobs would be available to go back to, if and when the government allowed the few left to reopen.

A sad consequence of the government shutdown and shelter in place order was that thousands were just killing themselves out of fear and despair.

The world was slowly dying as it tries to protect itself.

MONTH FIVE:

People were getting fed up with the way the government was handling the pandemic. How long did they think the people could just stay home with no income or means of paying their bills? It was obvious now to most that the virus was not so bad for the young. Just the elderly and those with underlying health conditions.

So, a new mantra was being established. Let those with a slim chance of harm from the virus get out and open the world back up. Keep the elders and compromised sheltered. This would allow for a condition called herd immunity to transpire. It would give everyone a better chance of survival in the long run and the world would get back to living again.

People were starting to challenge government authority as going too far in restricting their freedoms. They began pushing back against the restrictions imposed on them for so long calling them tyrannical and overstepping the authority which was given them, by the people.

The governments in turn claimed to know best what was good for the people and pushed back against the few who rebelled against their perceived authority.

The stalemate was getting to a point of turning violent. Some of the more aggressive protesters were arming themselves and openly defying police orders and cease and desist directives. Business owners were opening their stores to customers and the government be damned.

It was becoming chaos in the streets.

MONTH SIX:

General Chu was beginning to regret his implementing the virus program before a vaccine was found. It was proving to be harder than he first thought it would be in getting one manufactured.

The virus had escaped the containment in Wuhan and had spread across China. No enforcement or control could stop its spread. That put his country in the same situation as the rest of the world and so had all but wiped out his plans of coming to the rescue of the world.

His country now had no advantage. They forced workers to stay at their jobs but that only spread the disease faster.

They would eventually have herd immunity but so would the rest of the world. Nothing was gained except the fact the world was now blaming China for the virus.

They did not believe the open-air market theory for the most part.

The fact China also helped spread the virus with air travel while restricting it within their own country thereby saving themselves during the first stages of infection convinced many as to China's true goals.

Also, there was how China had tried to blame everyone else for the virus was a bit much, and countries being blamed were insulted by such nonsense.

And at the last was the fact China would not allow any country to investigate the lab in Wuhan. What were they trying to hide?

MONTH SEVEN:

Countries were starting to cancel orders and to close businesses they had built in China, bringing them back to their respective countries.

The empire that had once been mighty was slowly dwindling away. Everyone was shunning China as punishment for its actions against the world. China would soon decay into a third-world country with little influence.

All the industries that had been meticulously brought into China through coercion or manipulation were disappearing from the country.

All the medicine manufacturers that had been built there were now being considered as dangerous to national interests.

Discussions and plans to start companies in other countries were being considered and would ultimately find drugs and antibiotics to be produced in other more trustworthy countries.

MONTH EIGHT:

Ying had developed a vaccine. She had worked as a person possessed.

It was all her fault. All the deaths. She was so guilt-ridden to know that fact. All her years of study to what end? Only to give the world its worst pandemic in her lifetime?

General Chu and his group of military commanders were going to get away with it. It was all for nothing and China would fail as a global power in the process. Senseless power-hungry egomaniacs with maniacal world domination designs literally destroying the fabric of the world. Its organization and foundation. She could not allow them the satisfaction of this on her conscience.

She had a member of her research team seek out a western American spy. She knew they were there, always trying to gain information. She had learned of one especially interested in keeping tabs on her work. General Chu had even warned her about him. She had to take the chance.

Her team member had lost his family to the virus and was aware General Chu was responsible. He wanted payback. So, he did as Ying requested knowing full well the consequences if caught.

He was true to his word. He gave the vile of vaccine Ying had given him to deliver to the American spy who quickly left the country.

Ying gave herself and the team member who delivered the vaccine a shot of the vaccine. Keep this between you and me for now, she said.

Ying waited for another week until General Chu came to get an update on her progress as he always did once a month. From there she knew he would go to a meeting with the other high command generals to discuss and plan new strategies to implement.

General Chu arrived and was brought to the room where he always met with Ying. She was short and direct. There was still no vaccine and she gave him the usual report on why it had not happened yet.

He said, "I am beginning to think you are the wrong person for this job. Maybe I should find someone a little more reliable and efficient. You have one more month to find a cure that is all. Is that understood?"

Ying acted frightened knowing he loved to see that in those under his rule. His superiority complex was pinned to his vest along with all the other phony ribbons he displayed.

"I understand," Ying replied with humility and showing the greatest of respect. " It will be done."

One thing that General Chu did not see was Ying breaking a vile with her foot on the floor under the desk. She had been fanning the air toward General Chu the whole time he was with her. He had been breathing in the virus for long minutes at a very concentrated dose.

Ying knew he would be contracting the virus and hopefully carry it to the other Generals he was going to meet next. Though that would be more than she could hope for.

After he was gone, she and her team member sterilized the room so no trace could be found of what happened there.

MONTH NINE:

General Chu Died a very hard death. The same death he had released upon the world nine months ago. He never understood how he and half the Generals he worked with contracted the virus. They had always been so careful.

An American pharmaceutical manufacturer had finally developed a vaccine, amazingly and seemingly out of nowhere. It looked promising in sped-up clinical trials. American ingenuity and innovation saved the day again.

Other drugs also helped when given early in the infection. There was hope again.

YEAR ONE:

It was sad the world had lost so many people to the virus. A vaccine was finally produced. But like the flu vaccine, it only worked on a percentage of cases. The young and healthy decided it was more effective to just get the virus and suffer through the mostly mild symptoms, be done with it, and get on with their lives.

The elderly and those with underlying conditions took the vaccine and hoped for the best.

Countries were getting back to living and working at a new limited pace, keeping social distancing to help protect the weak, and because the government would never let things go back to the old normal.

It seemed they liked the control they had on the population. Still clinging to the worn-out mantra, "it is all for the good and wellness of the people."

Schools were finally opened as it was found children had very little problem with the virus and also because the parents could not go back to work as long as the children were at home. As young teachers were now the educators the chances were good for all.

There are still many people unemployed and the government had to extend benefits to allow for that. A large portion of the businesses did not rehire when the government finally allowed them to reopen because they had closed and went bankrupt or were forced to cut the number of employees due to the government restrictions on social distancing.

Some countries just opened up everything and let the virus do what it would do to attain herd immunity.

They fared better than most thought they would and are better off than most now. They did pay a price in deaths but not in numbers as severe as everyone had previously imagined.

The vaccine helped save many lives for those going that route.

YEAR TWO:

The virus has all but died out as most have gotten immunity to it and it is not yet known if it will mutate and come back again in the fall.

Most similar viruses do not reappear. But time will tell.

It will probably never be known for certain how the virus originated as with so many others of unknown origins. But with modern virology labs and pharmaceutical companies we can only hope if they do, we will be able to tame it.

The End { For Now}

CHAPTER 3 ●

A DAY IN THE LIFE OF SERGEANT SMITH

A COMMON MAN

PREFACE

Do you ever get the feeling you're being watched? That eerie raises the hair on your neck kind of creepy, unnerving feeling? This story just possibly might have an explanation for that.

It might not be as ominous as you thought. Well, in this case, it isn't anyway. It is merely some unknown to us entities doing research. It is still weird though that we haven't been privy to any knowledge of their existence.

What form of life are they? Are they like us in shape and intelligence? Are they a different species from a different world or dimension?

How long have they been around watching and hiding from us? What is their purpose in our lives? At this time, all is a puzzle. Maybe at some other point in history, all will be revealed. It seems for the moment of this story, though, now is not the time.

So, as we don't know anything is even happening, it is undoubtedly something not to worry over, even if we knew about something of which to worry. Confusing enough already, isn't it?

So just relax and enjoy the story. There is plenty of time to ponder later as to who they are.

INTRODUCTION

Sergeant Smith is a common ordinary individual that has been selected by a dedicated investigative body of which is unknown to humans at this point. It is evident that no malice is aimed at Sargent Smith or us.

It seems we have an unseen force behind the scenes directing some sort of surveillance operation on the world apparently to gain knowledge as to our behaviors. It is also obvious these beings as we will call them are not willing to inform humans of their presence. At least for now. They are doing things on a rather large and broad scale.

It is only coming to our attention now because someone decided to write this short story about it. We don't know if this story is true or just a fabrication of this someone's imagination. We may never know.

All we have the power to do is read the story and wonder. Maybe throw a laser light toward a star at night and see if it winks back. Who knows what is real or not real anymore? Perhaps imagination is just another form of reality.

A DAY IN THE LIFE OF SERGEANT SMITH

ORDER: This council is now in session. Order.

It has come to our attention this subject has been long thought about but has never been acted upon has finally found its time. We the council have decreed this matter be looked at so it can finally be put to rest.

Have you studied the issue at hand from the documents we have furnished to you?

"Yes," we answered.

The council has authorized funds for this project and wishes to hire your research team to address this issue. We see from your prior reports; you have been very thorough in your investigations, and analysis. Do you accept the job?

Yes, we think the subject matter would be something worthwhile in pursuing. It has always been a field of study that has been skirted around forever, and candidly, not given much attention. So, we will accept the job with enthusiasm and will depart immediately and try to find a perfect candidate for our study. We will search high and low in our pursuit of understanding.

A while later, the research team has concluded its search.

Looking over the whole world, we think we have finally found a subject to examine, probe, and explore all his qualifications as to being, and what makes him, a common man. We look in.

***

It was finally morning, and everyone was waking up. Well, some were waking up, others had gone to their last sleep in. It wasn't as good a night as say a fancy hotel might offer. The accommodations were at best adequate, and it did provide a roof over your head if you can call a tent a roof. The winter was exceptionally frigid, but of course, any winter is cold if you live outdoors.

This one particular fellow who we have picked out of this menagerie of men who, as a whole, from the lot of them is let's say average. That is what we are looking for. We didn't want the dredges of society nor the highly educated participants. But an average kind of Joe. One like the boy next door. Your friend or brother or cousin. Just a pick from an average litter. Nothing special about him, nothing that stands out.

We just want to spend a day with an average person, in this case, a soldier, to see what goes on in his head. See what he does, where he goes, and what matters most to him. To see what makes him tick.

As we look in on him, we find he is writing a letter to someone. It doesn't matter who it is at this time as we are just seeing what is going on in his world.

Let's look over his shoulder and see what it is he is writing.

His letter starts!

Some days it just doesn't pay to get out of bed. Like this morning, here I was all snug as a bug in a rug in my tent when some jerk thought it would be a good idea to drop a bomb on it. Lucky for me, it hit three tents over.

Well, that just ruined my morning. I was hoping to sleep in. It was still thirty degrees outside and just starting to get light, no rest for the little guy. Everybody got all upset and started yelling and carrying on like it was a big deal. I thought so what! You lived, so what's the beef? The guys in the tent it landed on, now they had something to bitch about. That is if they could have. Not so much anymore, you see my point?

I had to get up because I couldn't sleep anymore anyway, seeing as it was just too noisy and we were told we had to move to another area. Somebody out there had our location down pretty darn good and who knew when the next barrage was coming.

I saw the logic in that and figured why not. The ground I had pitched the tent on was not very flat anyway, and something kept sticking me from underneath. So, I wanted to move anyway.

I was thinking! So, this is what it is like to be homeless? Every time you settle in someplace, get yourself a cozy sweet spot and fix it up just right, someone comes along and starts pushing you out. You got to go. You can't stay here. You need to look for greener pastures.

That looking for greener pastures would be nice about now. It is nothing but snow and ice around here. The best thing about the homeless as I see it is that they can move wherever and whenever they want to. I have to go where I am told to go. At least for now.

My enlistment is almost done. I will be coming home soon. So, I am just chilling, for now, literally chilling right now, it's so darn cold. But seriously, things don't bother me as much anymore as they once did. I guess it's because I'm a short-timer. You know almost out. A short-timer!

I have watched a lot of guys getting to be short-timers, packing their gear and shipping out, going to that elusive place called home. I sometimes wonder if that is really a place or just a figment of my imagination. Maybe when they leave, they just disappear into thin air. I guess I'll find out when my turn comes. They never write me and say everything is great, just nothing at all! They totally forget all about us dumb suckers still in the service, no need to worry about us anymore. They're home, right?

It has been a long hard road in the service, always doing my duty for God and my country. I just wished it paid better. Maybe when I'm finally out, I can find a job somewhere warm. In Florida, perhaps. I never want to feel this cold ever again. Some of the guys have lost toes to the cold. That would just suck. Is it worth that simply to get out of the service? I sometimes wonder if they let that happen deliberately so that they can get out? OK, I'll close for now. I will write more later. I need to post this now. Happy times.

Well, well, it seems John is a little disappointed in the way his military career has been going. Are we sensing a little animosity or resentment toward his fellows for leaving him to continue on?

No! He really wishes them the best. He is just an ordinary average guy that is feeling the normal average emotions of watching day after day, the leaving of his friends; his comrades in arms, his confidants. This would make anyone show some semblance of self-pity to his predicament.

No, he absolutely wants those who have left before him to attain the best life has to offer. With dreams fulfilled and wishes complete and love within their hearts or something along those lines anyway. Maybe throwing in a couple of good-looking babes wouldn't hurt either.

We seem to have forgotten for a moment our objective of keeping up with John, so without further ado, we return.

We find the outfit has gotten their gear together and are ready to head out to parts unknown. Well, somebody knows where they are going but just never seems to inform the enlisted ones of anything. Falling back on the essential need-to-know basis is always their excuse. Not that it matters much. One place is usually like the rest, just as unpleasant as the last!

We catch up with John marching in single file through the woods always complaining to himself about everything that comes to mind. And there seems always to be something to grumble about. So, you could say John likes to mutter to himself, which I think we have covered thoroughly enough already.

Maybe we should listen in and see what the average man mutters about? It perhaps concerns world affairs, the price of beef, and how it has gone sky high recently, or maybe, it is the latest in the ranking of his favorite ball team. Let's listen to his mind in action.

"Bummer, John's mind said. Why did we have to leave so quickly this morning? I mean what possible difference does a couple of hours make. We could have gotten some of the wood just lying around everywhere and built such a warm and cozy fire!

"I got this delicious rabbit I snared last night and would love to cook it before it spoils. I just hope it doesn't have any diseases or worms.

"I know we can't build a fire, yea, yea, I know. That would give away our position, and all hell would break out. But man what a few glorious moments of pure warm air and hot toasty toes would do for morale. "The smell of burning shoe leather from feet to close to the fire, your fingers thawing out from days of cold numbing stiffness. And your ears, man, just to be able to feel them again would be fantastic.

"Dang it, there he goes again. I really do pity that guy in front of me. He obviously got a bad C-Ration. Sometimes you get a contaminated can, and if you don't smell it good and sample it right, you just might get what this poor shmuck has got. A bad case of the runs and gas galore. I wouldn't wish that on anybody. Wait a minute; maybe I should take that back. There are a couple I could think of to give this to.

"But I mean, really! Why did I have to be the one stuck behind him? I know I have to keep close and stay in line because there are reportedly land mines in the area and we all have to follow in the last guys' footsteps or risk, well you know. But hells-bells how it smells. Just a one-man walking fart factory. And then we all have to stop and wait till he craps every few minutes, like the smell of his farts wasn't bad enough. This is not turning out to be one of my favorite days.

"Yea, there are a couple of people I would love to send a bad can of rations to. My wife and my best friend. My wife, who is as cold and heartless as the ground I woke up on this morning, just sent me a Dear John Letter. No pun intended, thank you very much.

"She said she and my Best Friend have hooked up and have been doing the toe-curling boo-gey'. The twice around the park, bark. The roll in the hay twice a day, while cooking a filet. Well, I got news for her. If he takes her off my hands, he truly would be My Best Friend!"

Maybe we should give John a little space for a while. He seems to be going through some hard times, more than usual, even for him.

After a while, everyone had gotten into a quiet slow-moving train of bodies, each mimicking the other, everyone thinking their own thoughts. John was finally reconciled to his fate of being behind the sick fellow and accepted his lousy fortune as just part of the job. How brave he is.

Just as we are getting back into his head for more reporting of his thinking.

BOOM! "What the hell was that?" John said as he and everybody else hit the ground and covered. John peeked up from his prone position and saw the blast had come from the front of the line. So that was it he said to himself. Another guy who didn't know how to use a metal detector properly. Moving too fast, no doubt. Taking too big a step and not completely covering the area before moving up. That mistake won't happen again, not by him. Just doesn't pay to get in a hurry.

I guess it's time to take a break and pick another who's on first replacement. John thought. Man, I hope it's not me. They know I am set to rotate out soon. I kind of feel a little guilty thinking this way, but having lived through all the hell up till now, and with just a week to go? Nope, it looks like they got a volunteer. I just love volunteers.

I remember my brother, who as a marine, went out of his way to emphasize one vital lesson to his little brother just joining up.

He said to me, "whatever you do, don't volunteer for anything."

I took that piece of advice and ran with it. I recall the first time the Drill Sergeant asked for volunteers to drive some vehicles. Man, the hands that went up. Many hands went up, but not mine. The Drill Sergeant said, "OK; all you volunteers, step forward."

They all believed they were going to get out of our usual regimen and drive a shiny new jeep for someone. It was not going to happen. Instead, he told each and every one of them to report to supply and secure a push mower and start mowing the grass all over the area. They mowed till midnight. Thank you, brother.

Wasn't that enlightening. John has some common sense; after all, it seems. What more is this character hiding? Maybe he's not the average guy we had first thought. He just might have some gray matter between his ears. That could be why he has received a few decorations, citations, and awards. We thought he just got lucky.

It seems we're back in line again. This time John found a different guy to follow. Yes sir, maybe he is smarter than we had first given him credit.

A little later, the company stopped to take another rest period. Packing all that gear turned it into more of a drop-in-place moment. But John, our average guy had to pee. So, taking advantage of the respite, he and another soldier went to the edge of the forest and started doing their business. Let's listen in. You never know when average guys will talk.

John, standing and relieving himself next to the soldier, said, "man, I almost didn't make it. That was too long a wait between breaks; I must have drunk too much water this morning." The man next to him started to say something and, CRACK, a shot rang out and the guys' head just exploded.

John hit the ground for the second time that day. He looked around quickly, trying to pinpoint the location of where the shot came from. It was across the field he told himself. The gunshot came from the other side of this field. "Sniper," he yelled to the company.

I hate snipers, John was thinking. You never know when they are going to get you. Damn, you can't even take a pee anymore without worrying about this----. Looking at the guy next to him, he couldn't finish his thought.

The luck of the draw, John thought. Sometimes he wondered why another guy gets it and not him. Not that he wasn't grateful, he definitely was.

So, as we contemplate his reflections, it seems the average man just accepts his lot in life and hopes all will work out in his favor in the long run. It was just the luck of the draw.

John contemplated, I wonder what these snipers think about when they see a person in their sights and know they are going to snuff them. Just say it's your turn, and pull the trigger? No conscience, no feeling of fair play, no wondering if the guy they're doing has a family! Do they care?

John understood the ways of war as he considered their options and resigned himself to what would happen next. We are going to try and hunt this guy down. Sometimes we get lucky, most of the time we just get more dead soldiers! This one was personal for some reason. It really shook him to watch the guy's head next to him just explode. He had seen plenty of dying. But this was too close and too graphic. This one will haunt him for a long time.

John was thinking, this is why soldiers don't come home and talk about what happened to them in the war, why they only talk to other soldiers on the few times, they do talk. Only another fellow soldier would get it and understand what he was truly saying. John knew that civilians could never grasp the horror of that moment. It was not like the movies. This you could see, touch, smell, and feel.

The worst part of it was that you would remember it all, at any moment, at the most, inconvenient times. Not even wanting it to, it was just there in a flash. Something just triggers it. Reality was a bitch, John thought.

We, the ones looking into John's thoughts are troubled by what he has just thought. It never occurred to us before at the impact on a person such as he, in having to deal with the horrors of war. It never entered our minds that the soldier standing here was not capable of just taking what came and upon returning to civilian life could not just forget it all and go on with his life. Being of those who have never had to deal with these tragic moments, it is hard to grasp the emotions that must be running rampant in John's brain.

How can society not help these men when they return, expecting them to go about their business with these things haunting them.

This sheds new light on who John really is. What a gifted man he is that can hold up to these moments he has to live with, fought through, day after day, and retain any semblance of sanity, a truly remarkable human being. We who have listened, salute you for your courage and devotion to your duty. We wonder if those amongst us could do the same and retain our sanity as well.

But enough of this retrospect for we have a job, as John does also, to learn what we can from an average man.

So, back to the moment. We see John and several fellow soldiers heading out to, hopefully, track down this killer of men, and seek justice for his fallen comrade in arms, and also praying they all come back alive. After all, this is not the game, we first envisioned. This is reality; this is war.

John speaking quietly to the team accompanying him, said," keep your eyes and ears open and your mouths shut. Use hand signals when necessary. Let's get this guy and come back safe."

We watch as the team fanes out and covers a large area as they walk toward the last known location of the sniper. John had done these jobs before. It was not a pleasant job, but somebody had to do it. As we listen to his thoughts, we are allowed to hear, the plan. It is a good one. One that sometimes worked. Sometimes? Well, we will see.

John hears the CRACK of another shot being fired. Another soldier dies. Then another CRACK, another shot fired. But this time from another location. Then you hear a paced-out three rounds fired, the all-clear signal.

John stands now. "OK, he said out loud. We got him. Let's report back."

We who watch are aware of the plan. It did work, after all, this time.

The plan John had set up was for him and a small group to go fishing. That is to try and get the sniper to show himself or find him, whichever came first. Then snipers from Johns' company would wait and if possible, try to pinpoint the enemy sniper before any real damage could be done and take him out. It usually meant one or more casualties more, but it had to be done, or that sniper would just keep picking the company's men off one at a time.

We now can conclude war seems to be a numbers game. Whoever is left standing in the end wins! They are the ones who get to write the history books about what happened. Who were the most just in their cause!

We seem to have been reflecting again about the situations we are witnessing more often lately. So, let's once again get back to our mission.

John is moving along with the company at a leisurely, pace, and just covering the ground, trying to make it to the next rendezvous point before dark. Everyone is pleased and relieved they had gotten the sniper.

John's thoughts settled into reminiscing about his time in the Fire Department before he joined the fight. Let's listen in.

Mark, it's been a long time since I have thought about you. Remember how we used to go on double dates to the drive-in. I still can't remember what movies we went to see, too busy in the kissing department.

Then on a dare, we joined the volunteer fire department. You took to that like a duck to water. Man, that got intense once in a while.

I remember one occasion we were called to a house fire and found some kids trapped in the second-floor bedroom. You didn't even hesitate; you just ran for the ladder, and after placing it, you climbed up that ladder and brought down three little kids from their burning house.

We all watched as you crawled into the window and came out with each kid, how you kept going back in until you thought there were known left to save. Then the mother yelled that one of the kids was not there. You climbed back up and disappeared into the smoke-filled room. We waited for a long time. We had just about given up on you when you popped your head out and yelled, "it's ok; I got her." The little girl had been so scared she had hidden in the closet. What a hero you were that day. You always took the risks that others shied from.

I also remember how you pulled that lady from her burning car. It was crazy how you just ran up to it and broke the window out and dragged her through it just before the whole thing exploded in flames, what a guy.

I sadly remember also your last attempt to do your job faithfully. The Fire Captain said someone needed to get on the roof and hack a hole through it so we could get a hose into the interior of the building.

You didn't even hesitate. You just climbed up that ladder, got on the roof, and started hacking away.

Maybe if we had gotten proper training, we might have known of the possible danger that the situation entailed and been more cautious in our approach to it.

I will never forget the moment you got the hole open and just fell through it. The fire had evidently eaten away at the underside without us knowing it. And the whole thing just caved in. As you fell in, the flames rose from the hole. We knew there was no hope.

Yea, you were always the one I looked up to. The one I wanted to pattern my life from. You were the best of the best. I guess you're the main reason I joined up. I wanted to carry on your legacy of honor and bravery and service. I sure do miss you.

We are very touched by what we have just heard. John is really a nice guy. He values friendships and holds to a high standard of morals. He seems to be someone who you would be proud to call a friend. Some woman is going to be lucky to have him as a husband. He appears to value all the decent parts of humanity.

Once again, we start listening in on John's thoughts. He is wondering when someone is coming to take him for processing out of the service. He should be heading the other way by now and not going toward the front lines. This can't be good; he is thinking. Are they going to put me into battle just before I am set to go home? Man, that's a bum deal. That will read just fine on my tombstone. Here lies John. He died on his last day of service. Somebody screwed up his paperwork.

It looks like the company has made it to the rendezvous point. Time to set up camp again and wait for the next continual set of orders to move out to whatever hell hole the brass can figure out to send them next.

John has settled into his tent and is writing another letter. We feel kind of uncomfortable now. Having gotten to know him so intimately in looking over his shoulder, it is like now we are intruding into his privacy. We feel guilty. But a job is a job.

His letter says:

Mamma;

I want you to know that I love you. I know it has been hard without my brother and me being there to take care of you. But hopefully, the money we send is helping out. I want to apologize for all the different problems I caused you growing up. I realize I was a handful. But this war is just something I had to help out with. I just could not let that tyrant come into our country and do to it what he was doing over here. It is better to keep the fight here than at our home.

I guess you were right about my wife. You always told me I should have married Barbara. I should have listened. Maybe when I get back, if she is still single?

I am supposed to ship out of here soon. I practically have my discharge in my hand. The guys are all calling me a short-timer. I love that name now.

I sure do miss you. And I sure do miss being home. Not that being here wasn't great. All the best four-star accommodations, exceptional cuisine, wine, women, and song. Not to mention the best friends a guy could ask for. All of us just sitting around the lounge talking about all the fun we're having and how much we're going to miss it all. It almost makes you want to re-enlist. I said ALMOST.

So, take heart and say a prayer for big brother and me. And I will see you soon. Love you.

Your son,
John.

***

We, as the ones taking notes on the average man soldier, are genuinely moved by John's devotion and caring for his family. A real American through and through. And such a swell guy. We hope he finds this Barbara unmarried. He deserves a break.

Well, it has been a long day, and we have seen and heard much. We have learned that the common man is really not so common. He is almost everybody. The common man is in the majority. He is not of the few; he is of the many. He is not unusual or unique. He is pretty much like most everyone else. We finally grasp why he is called the common man.

He is not of the unique few individuals who attain power, riches, and fame. Those would not be common at all. But neither did we think the common man to be so plentiful.

He is the everyday run-of-the-mill guy you would meet on any corner; in any bar, in any home, and in any Church. He makes your cars; he delivers your mail; he is your Police, your Firemen, and of course your Soldiers fighting your war.

So, we end the day of looking at our random pick into what makes up a common man and thank him secretly, as he never knew we were there, and bid a fond farewell.

And if you have a need to find out what happened to John from this point on. Sorry, we are just doing our job and have no clue what will transpire after this moment.

If we looked farther, we would not be following our directive by looking into John's destiny. That would be a different report altogether. And we weren't paid for that service.

But we can sincerely hope that life deals him a fair hand and would see him home safely.

CHAPTER 4 •

ALONE:
A WAY OF LIFE

Introduction

This short story starts with a monolog from the main character describing his view of life as he has lived it. He is convinced he does not need nor want any connection to or even have any desire to be associated with humanity in general or at large.

That is a tough thing to do as the world is filled with people. So, he finds solace in getting away for short periods in an isolated environment where he can live his desire to be alone.

He finds though that even in a far-removed location, it is never quite far enough. There will always be some who will discover him, and whether he likes it or not, draw him into their conflicts.

This time it will force him to deal with the ramifications of their intrusion. It will cause him to disregard his own wants and needs for his self-appointed obligation of helping to return the intruding couple back to civilization.

It is strange that a man who wants nothing to do with people is thrust into such a predicament.

They do not make his mission to help easy at all. There is a constant threat to his life and theirs, the whole way back.

ALONE: A WAY OF LIFE

Since my earliest recollections as a child, I have never felt the companionship others seemed to enjoy. It has always eluded me in my interactions with family and friends.

Even while surrounded by a multitude of people, there was never that feeling of belonging or acceptance expected from these encounters.

In retrospect, I have to admit I never really put myself out there as one probably should have, and there was never a desire to do so.

So, here I am out here now, living my life as one separated from everything. Absorbing and partaking of all that is around me, which does not belong to the societal construct, and finally finding my peace, my wish to be alone is satisfied.

I have realized in retrospect; I was meant to be this way. My true happiness is within myself. My inner thoughts are all I have ever needed in the form of communication with the world around me.

Imbibing of the waters from the stream, eating the labors of my hunt. Caring only for myself, seeking only to be alone.

I suppose I was born too late. I would be better suited to have been born during the mountain man days when men sought to go alone into the wilderness and create a life alongside nature.

I looked at the wall calendar and said to myself; I guess I should go home now. The time I allotted myself to dream my fantasy of getting away from the world and being all alone is over.

A couple of days walk, and it would be back to the grind. The never-ending, never free, always busy doing something, grind.

While walking out of my self-imposed isolation from the outside world, I decided to stop at the waterfall one last time. It had always been my favorite spot to sit and reflect on life's little joke on me.

My purpose for being and lack of fulfilling any predetermined destiny was an enigma. It posed a combination of a challenge and a mystery.

What if anything at all was I to do about myself, and if I were to decide to change, how could I? It was incomprehensible to me that I would have a desire to change nor a will to do it at all. As I stated earlier, I have no aspiration to be a popular or famous person as everyone else thinks I should be.

Then breaking into my thoughts and self-analysis, I hear a scream. It was coming from the top of the falls.

As I was at the bottom near the actual cascading water, I could not see up to where the yelling was happening.

Then I heard clearly a woman yelling," no stop, get away from me."

Then I heard a man scream back at her. "I will have my freedom one way or another. You're making me do this!"

Then another scream from the woman and I saw her then as she was falling from the top of the cliff. She kept screamed as she fell. I saw her hit the water at a bad angle and knew she was in big trouble. Not just from the unseen man at the top of the cliff but by the way she hit the water. That would be bad.

I waited for her to come back up, but after not seeing her for a few seconds, I knew she was going to drown if she had not already.

I pulled off my shoes and jumped in. I swam to where I thought the current would have taken her, and sure enough there she was. I pulled her as fast as I could back to shore and seeing she was not breathing. I did all the steps I knew about drowning victims on her.

Let's see now how did that go?

First, check for breathing. Nope, not breathing. Check for pulse. No, no pulse either. Start compressions on the chest on top of the breastbone. Compress two inches at a rate of 100 to 120 pushes per minute.

Let's see, now what else. Com on man think. Oh, yea. Do thirty compressions and then two quick breaths into the mouth while holding her nose closed with her head tilted back.

Two breaths and thirty compressions. Two breaths and thirty compressions.

I kept doing that, for it seemed an eternity until she coughed and spat up water. She choked for a while but finally got control and looked up at me and quickly looked around.

I told her the man is not here.

She seemed to relax a bit visibly.

She looked at me then, probably a million questions going through her mind.

I said, "I heard you and the man, whoever he is, yelling, and then you fell into the water. I got you out and did CPR on you. That's all I know about this. If you don't want to talk about it, that's fine with me."

I was hoping she would not. I wanted nothing to do with any of this.

I don't know why I even jumped in and rescued her. I had never done anything like this for anyone ever before. I just stayed as distant as I could.

I did it without thinking, I told myself. So, what prompted me to do it? I had no ready patent answer.

She finally said, "thank you for saving me."

That was it. Nothing more. She obviously didn't want to talk about anything that went on between herself and the man.

She said, "how do I get to a phone from here?"

I said, "well, I am assuming you won't have a car as I am pretty sure your friend would have taken that. And he didn't come down to look for you, so I figure he thinks you are dead.

She looked happy about that.

"Good, maybe I can get out of here safely, "she said with doubt lingering in her voice.

I added, "we are in the middle of nowhere out here. The nearest phone is days away walking. I hiked in myself, so there is no easy way out."

"Oh, that is just great," she said with disgust."

She started to stand and yelled, "OHH."

Falling back down, she grabbed her ankle. "That hurts," she gasped.

I looked at her ankle, and sure enough, it was swelling and turning color.

"It looks like you sprained or broke your ankle," I said.

She said, "damn, just what I need right now!"

I thought to myself, ditto for me too, lady.

We both sat there for a few more minutes, both realizing she was still helpless. I, knowing I was not through helping her unless I just abandoned her, and she not wanting to impose any farther on me, but knowing she had no choice was waiting for me to offer it.

I said, "I have a cabin just over the rise over there. I will carry you to it if you wish. There is no way you can walk on that leg. We can wrap your ankle and try to keep the swelling down and work on it there, okay?"

She looked at me as if deciding if I was a threat or not and decided her position was not a good one and had no choice anyway in accepting my help.

She said, "I hate to be a bother to you, but it looks like I have no choice. I thank you again."

I stood and helped her up. I let her climb on my back with her arms over the top of my shoulders and her legs wrapped around my waist, so carrying her would be much more comfortable, and took her to my cabin. She was not as heavy as I thought she would be.

I was aware when we finally made it and were inside the cabin, that we were both soaking wet.

I told her, "look, I am not trying to be weird, but we need to get out of these wet clothes. I have some spare clothes you can wear until yours are dry. I can give them to you, and you can change them in the bathroom over there."

She looked at me with apprehension.

I said, "if I wanted to do something to you here, you couldn't stop me, I said bluntly and slightly insulted. Do whatever you want. But when we wrap that ankle, you won't be able to get out of those pants you're in now."

She knew that was all true.

"I'm sorry, and I apologize. Yes, I could use some dry clothes. Thank you once again," she said.

I brought her a change of clothes and helped her to the bathroom where she changed. I could hear her as she worked the pants down over the swollen ankle. "OH, augh, damn."

Finally, she opened the door dressed in my clothing, oversized for her as it obviously hung on her frame.

I helped her to the couch and tended to her ankle. I first took a large cooking pot I had and filled it with cold water. It was the best I could do in place of having no ice handy.

Then after twenty minutes in the water, I wrapped her ankle in the prescribed manner I had taught myself, as a just in case I got myself into this same situation.

Starting with a point farthest from the heart, I wrapped it not too tightly and had her elevate the foot by lying on the couch with her foot above her heart. I gave her some aspirin for the pain.

Every three hours, I re-soaked her foot to try and help bring the swelling down. While she was resting, I went out and found a branch and cut her a staff to use to help when she needed to get around. It would keep her weight off of her foot and help with balance.

I suddenly became aware I was not alone. It is a feeling you get when you are tuned into your surroundings as keenly as I was. It had saved me on more than one occasion with wild animals.

I take such warnings very seriously. I could not see or hear anything, but I knew something was out there. The hair on the back of my neck was standing up, a good sign of danger from the subconscious mind.

I pretended not to notice and went about doing my chore with the staff, and when I was finished, I went back to the cabin.

I had another chore to do. And it would be done before nightfall. I had an unannounced visitor that did not want to be found out at the moment. That told me it was probably the man from earlier. I was not going to be a victim to anyone for any reason.

Whatever these two people had between them was not my concern. My only interest was what the man intended to do next? He was not acting as a reasonable person would, who had witnessed his lady friend going over a cliff.

He had not found his way down to show even the slightest worry over her well-being, nor did he come and introduce himself and attempt to help in this crisis. He was going to be a problem.

Well, he was not the only one that could be a problem.

I gave the lady the staff, and she was very grateful.

She said, "it will come in handy in helping me to get around."

She said, "you are a strange man. I have been here all day and not once have you wondered about me, or the situation I find myself in, not even my name."

I said, "it is none of my business.

"If you had wanted to tell me, I figured you would do so, being nosy is the least of my faults."

I guess she was getting bored, and as most women are, they need to talk. So, she started by asking me about myself.

"So, are you a hunter? I see you have a lot of heads of animals all around, so I suppose that was a dumb question," she corrected herself.

I didn't answer as she had already fielded the response.

I watched her mull over things in her mind. I knew then she was going to tell me about her friend.

She finally decided to talk. "I think you deserve an explanation for what went on earlier.

"By the way, my name is Jill, and my husband is Jack, and yes, I know that is a strange combination for obvious fairytale reasons, she added wanting to get the old clichés out of the way.

"I caught my husband, Jack, with another woman, and he has apparently chosen to divorce me. I didn't want that; I wanted to work things out. It seems, very plainly to me now, I should have gone that route myself.

"He brought me to this location where it is evident; he planned to kill me. I figured that out as he pushed me off the cliff into the water to drown.

"If not for you, he could have claimed it was an accident. But now it is attempted murder.

"He is a very dangerous man. If he knew I was still alive, it would be bad for both of us; I am certain of that."

I looked at her.

"Lady, I said, I think you still have a problem. I am almost sure your husband is lurking around out there somewhere, just waiting to get to you."

She was petrified. "What did you say? Is Jack out there now? How do you know that?"

"Just a feeling I have, I'm not wrong, usually," I remarked.

"What can I do, she cried out? He will want to keep me from telling on him, and you're in danger also as a witness."

"I said, well, this is a problem. I can't kill him because you have stated you wanted to get back together with him. I guess the only thing I can do is detain him. Or at least try. I never captured a human before in this way. It sounds like fun."

She looked at me with a puzzled look. She was wondering who was the real crazy man now.

I began to think, and then, to build my trap.

Late that evening, I made a point to get plenty of wood for the fireplace and let whoever was out there get the feeling I was unaware of him. I settled in and began the waiting game.

At around eight, I shut off the lights and pretended to go to sleep.

At ten, I heard the door. It was opening, and someone was coming in. I waited till he was at the right spot and released my trap.

"Son-of-a-bitch," he yelled.

I lit the lantern and got a view of the man finally.

I walked over and saw his knife.

I said, "let go of the blade, or I will use this spear on you."

He settled down as he saw the spear at his throat. He let go of his knife. This guy had meant to do some real damage. I was tempted to finish this now, but now I had a witness, and I was not willing to kill her too.

Instead, I turned the pointy end of the spear around and hit the man in the head with the blunt round brass ball on the other side. He went limp. I needed to get him out of the netting that had wrapped around him when the trap was released. It was somewhat amusing the way I had set it up.

When he had walked under the location where I had planned him to be, I released the string that was holding the netting up on rings on the ceiling.

That allowed the net to fall straight down and cover the man. As he couldn't see anything, he thrashed about and got himself even more caught in the netting until he fell. That was when I lit the lantern.

His wife was frozen in fear looking at him.

"Is he dead? Did you kill him," she asked?

"Do you care," I countered?

She didn't answer?

That probably made her question herself as to her own agenda for the man called Jack.

I took the opportunity to put a pair of handcuffs on him. Out here in the wild, you never know what might happen, and I always believed in being prepared. So, I had a couple of pairs of cuffs as a just in case. It looks like I was right; life follows you everywhere.

I told the lady, "you can watch him if you want, but I am getting some sleep. It has been a long day."

She said, "what am I supposed to do if he tries something?"

I said, "whatever you want to. Or just yell. Whatever works for you. I personally don't like killers, so whatever you do makes no difference to me. You do know what, whatever means, right? Goodnight."

I put a chain around the cuffs and locked the chain to a floor bolt with a ring, and went to sleep in the corner chair. He was not harming anyone tonight.

The next morning, I woke up and saw the man had sat up and was looking at the lady with a hate as big as Texas in his eyes. She was still asleep and didn't see it. Probably for the best. He saw me stirring and refocused his hate-filled eyes on me.

"I owe you one, mister," he said with a deadly tone.

I said, "oh, you talking to me."

I walked over and kicked him in the face.

He flew backward and yelled, "damn you."

I picked him up and said, "say you are sorry right now, or I am going to gut you."

He looked at me with a whole new respect.

He said, "ok, I am sorry," then stupidly added, "for now."

So, he was still not getting it.

I hit him again.

"No respect, I said. Now let's try it again. Say you are sorry."

He was getting the idea finally how this was going to play out.

He said, slowly and deliberately, "I'm sorry."

I said, "bright boy. You come inside my house to do me and my guest harm, and you think I should care how or what you think? You really need to stop and ask yourself, why would a guy want to live out here in the middle of nowhere all alone?

"Maybe I have issues, and you shouldn't push my buttons too hard, eh?"

He began to see that he was not the only hard-ass around these parts.

"So, what now," he asked?

I answered, "I haven't thought that far ahead yet. That depends on what you two work out. I know I will not just let you go with your attitude. I won't be spending my life looking over my shoulder for some ass looking for payback. Remember, you started this party."

Jack said, "what do you mean it depends on what Jill and I work out."

I said, "well you tried to kill her yesterday, and by the way, you actually did kill her, I just brought her back with some CPR. You can thank me anytime you want. No? I didn't think so."

"So, Jill," I said, "we're all stuck here until you get well enough to walk. So, what do you want to do?"

"I want to get out of here and get away from him," she said.

Jack said, "that is what I've been trying to do, you idiot, you just won't let me go. So, I did the only thing left to me. You did this to yourself."

Jill cried out, "how can you put this back on me? I loved you? I was willing to forgive you for cheating around on me. I never in a million years would have thought you hated me so much as to kill me. What sane man does that?

"You can have your divorce, and you can spend the rest of your life in jail for all I care."

"What do you mean, are going to turn me in," Jack said?

"You tried to kill me, what do you think," she said?

He got serious then. "Ok, if that is how you want it. Just know this, if I get the chance, I am going to finish it. So, your boyfriend over there, better watch his back."

I stood up and walked over to Jake and kicked him in the face again. That sent him flying back and out again.

"You don't learn very fast," I mumbled.

I told Jill, "while he's sleeping it off, I am going hunting.

"We need some food if we're are staying here for a while longer. Be back later."

She said, "you're leaving me here alone with him?"

I said, "same as before, if he acts up, do what you need to do."

I was happy to get out of there. People and their relationship problems drag me down.

I didn't know who wanted who to leave more. It seemed like a stalemate all around.

I could see why he wanted out of the marriage. The lady sure liked pushing his buttons. But his cheating didn't help matters much. Everyone has their faults.

I shot a deer, cleaned and skinned it, and brought back the meat for processing. I saw the killer and his wife were still at it. So, I just took the deer meat to my cleaning and cutting table and cut the deer meat up for use. I started a slow, low fire in the smoker shack and began turning the venison to jerky for more extended storage and use.

By the time I got back to the house, they were taking a break from the constant bickering and threats. Good, I didn't want to have to listen to all that.

"So, your jaws getting tired," I quipped.

The man said, "are you going to starve us, or do we get some food around here?"

I said, "we, you said, we? You mean you're thinking of her needs again? Well, well, that is progress."

Jack said, "that's not what I meant."

"So, Jill, do you like deer meat?"

Jill stated with horror, "you killed a deer?"

"That is what is running around out there unless you want me to bring you a bear," I said.

She said," I never had deer meat. I don't know if I can eat that!"

"Well, suit yourself," I said.

I got the fire in the cookstove going and started cooking a few deer steaks. The aroma permeated the cabin, and everyone smelled it and made them all hungrier. I knew neither had eaten for a full day or longer, so they had to be practically starving.

I put a plate of steaks on the table and said; "Pardon me, but I am hungry, and these steaks are getting cold."

I cut a bite and chewed it groaning aloud, "oh man, is that good."

The girl looked at it and finally said, "I guess I could try it."

I said, "help yourself."

She hobbled over and sat down. She took a cut from a steak and put it in her mouth.

"Oh, that is good, she said surprised, it tastes different from beef, but it is good." She continued to eat.

Jack said, "what about me?"

I responded, "say, please!"

Jack knew if he were going to be fed, he would have to grovel, so be it.

He would have his chance sooner or later.

"Please, may I have some food," he asked, holding his acid tongue this time.

"Sure," I said and tossed him a steak.

He caught it and said, "what about a knife and fork and plate."

I told him, "murderers don't get things to kill with, get used to it."

I could see the calculations in his head. He was figuring I would eventually make a mistake, and that would be it for me. He might have something there. I have to be sure of every move all the time, while I also only need to be wrong just once for him to kill me.

As the days slowly went by, I was feeling the pressure, and he knew it. The long walk out was going to be where he would make his play.

Jill had gotten to where she could stand on her foot again, and with the therapy I gave her, she was getting better fast. It would soon be time to go.

"So, Jack, I asked, where is the car? It would make everything a whole lot easier if we simply drove out."

He said, "I don't remember. I got lost following you here."

Well, I knew that was a lie. But there was nothing short of torture I was going to be able to do about it.

The next morning, I decided to try and find it. I went back to the waterfall and went along the trail that led up to the top of the falls and started looking around. Sure enough, there it was.

Good, I thought, this would make things much more manageable.

Well, I thought it would until I checked the car and found it was missing three plug wires.

Cautious man. I had greater respect for him now. He was thorough. Yes, but two could play that game. I took three more plug wires and buried them as I am sure he did the same with the ones he took.

If it worked out that he won this little game we had going, he was going to be surprised when he tried using the car.

I also took the vehicle registration with his name on it so that when we left the cabin, I would leave a note with a message and his registration on the table telling of the happenings around here and if I didn't return to destroy the message then Jack had probably killed the lady and me.

In the next couple of days, I was busy getting the supplies ready for the trip. I put all the heavy things in the pack killer Jack was going to have to carry.

That would at least have tired him out somewhat when the time to make camp came around. I figured it to be a three-day trek with the lady still not up to one-hundred percent.

They had been doing a lot of talking to each other. It was like a family therapy counselor would try. Get them talking, and maybe they could work it out. The only problem was that pesky; he tried to kill her thing, still hanging in the air. That was a kind of deal-breaker in my book. But who knows, time will tell.

We took off the next morning. It was looking like good weather all the way, warm but not hot days, and not too cold nights. The couple walked side by side, talking and laughing, remembering the good times.

They seemed to be falling in love again all over again.

I, for my part, had my doubts. If I was Jack and time was running out, I would turn on the charm just like he was doing and try to convince her not to prosecute. To maybe even give it another try.

Jack was even trying to buddy up to me, saying how sorry he was that he had acted so aggressively when he first came into the cabin. He sees things more clearly now. I played along.

Don't worry about it, I said. I don't have to live with you. Just get you out of here. I don't harbor any grudges. You got the worst of this deal as I see it anyway.

He looked at me then, and I could see he knew I wasn't buying his act one bit. So, he continued to work his magic on the lady.

I have to admit he sure knew how to charm the ladies. Jill was soaking it up. She looked like she was coming around to his side.

I might need to start keeping an eye on both of them.

That's the thanks I get. I save her life, and she helps the guy that tries to kill her take me out. Just wonderful.

So, once again, why do I like to be alone?

The first night was mostly peaceful. I wrapped and locked a chain around a tree and hooked killer Jack to it with the cuffs. Jill slept near him but not close enough that he could reach her. She wasn't that smitten just yet.

The jerky I had made was good. We all had some for our meal.

Morning came too soon, but it is what it is. I gave everyone some jerky to start the day. Jack was feeling the soreness from carrying the heavy pack all day but didn't complain. He wanted to show his good side at all times. Fine by me.

He saw I was not going to give him an opening to catch me off guard. His only option was his wife. He was stepping up his game on her.

Now he was talking about what-ifs. What if we could work this out! What if we could try again! He was starting to have deep feelings for her yet again. The baloney was getting cut thicker with each slice.

I saw what they didn't. A snake crossing just ahead of them. I always keep a watch for snakes. I hate snakes of any variety. Two-legged or no legs, they are all the same. If they can bite you, they will.

I pulled my pistol and ran up on the oblivious couple. Just as they were next to the snake, I could see it was rearing up to strike. The fools didn't even hear the hissing; they were so into each other; or were they.

I had just enough time to see Jack stop with Jill right in line with the coming strike. He was keeping her occupied as best as he could. Jack was keeping her focus on him. Yea, he had seen the snake and was setting her up for the kill.

I shot just in time. I am a good shot if I do say so myself. I practice all the time. I took the snakes head clean off with the first shot. Jill screamed and looked at me. Jack just looked at me. His gaze had a different meaning. I had spoiled his little surprise for his wife. Well, that was just too bad, I say.

Jill yelled, "what the hell are you doing? Are you crazy?"

I said, "that is still up for debate. But as for why I shot, look down at your feet."

She looked, jumped back, and screamed again.

"Snake," she cried out.

I said, "calm down. It is dead. But, on the bright side, at least now we have something new for supper."

Jack, never wasting a moment to get in her good graces. He grabbed her in a hug and said, "oh honey, are you, all right? That was a close one."

She ate it up. Jack cared about her; she no doubt was thinking. She hugged him back.

I thought she might be better off if I had let the snake bite her. Either way, she was a goner.

He looked at me from over her shoulder and smiled.

I just said, "well played."

Yes, the snake was a good change of pace for our evening meal. It was huge, and Jill wanted none of it.

"More for me," I said.

She ate the deer jerky.

We would be out of the forest tomorrow, so if, "Killer Jack," were going to try something, he would have to do it tonight. I stopped all of that nonsensical thinking.

I not only put cuffs on his hands; I also put a chain on his legs and locked it tight. I basically hogtied him. I wanted a good night's sleep.

Jill slept next to him, so I got up and went into the woods and hid, just in case. I figure he had gotten to her, and this was not going to end well for her. But I was not going down with her.

People can be so gullible, so trusting, so stupid. Gullible in that, in their innocence and naivety, they become trusting in any streetwise smooth talker that comes along.

You can sometimes get them to see the truth with facts, but you can't fix stupid. That is why I don't bother to worry any longer about Jill. Some people are just born victims. They seek out or simply put themselves into the most unwise positions.

She knows without a doubt that her husband was trying to kill her. And with just a few words of endearment from him, she's ready to forgive him and allow him the opportunity to try again, believing he is a changed man until the moment he tosses her over the falls once again. Just stupid.

I have to admit, though; it is fascinating watching it all play out right in front of me.

When morning came, I went back to camp. There they were talking as if nothing had ever happened between them. Now I knew how this was going down.

I asked Jill to walk with me. I left Jack cuffed to the tree. When we were out of sight and ear-shot, I got to it.

"Okay, Jill, I said. You tell me what your decision is! I am not going to waste any more of my time in bringing your husband back if you are going to let him go with no charges. I might as well let him go right now, and you both can leave and do whatever you want.

"But in good conscience, I have to warn you; he will kill you at some time. He is a good con artist, liar, and we both know him to be an attempted murderer. Whether you believe me or not, I am telling you he set you up for that snake to bite you, I saw it as plain as day.

"He will say and do anything to get you to change your mind about turning him in. And from what I see, he has done a bang-up job.

"So, what is your answer? I got things to do."

She looked at me for a minute and finally said, "you are probably right about him. He is a charmer. But I still love him. I know I am a fool, but I can't help myself. I can't explain it. I swore an oath when we were married, for better or worse till I died. Well, if that is what it comes to, then so be it.

"But I want to thank you for all you have done for me, even if it turns out to be for nothing.

"You are a good man. I don't think you give yourself enough credit in that regard. You saved me; you took care of me; you protected me on numerous occasions.

"I don't deserve all you have done for me with this stupid decision I am making, and yes, I know it is a foolish decision. But it is what it is, as they say.

"So, to answer your question, I am not going to turn him in."

I reached into my pocket and handed her the key to the cuffs.

"It's your life, lady, I said. Go ahead and enjoy it while you can. Just leave my stuff where it is, I'll be back later to get it. Follow the trail, and it will take you into town; if you make it."

I turned and walked away.

She watched me for a while. I am sure she had wanted to yell for me to come back but was unable to, probably because she had just convinced herself, or was it because she had trapped herself in her own bull story.

As an avid hunter, I was good at sneaking around unheard and undetected. As soon as I was out of her sight, I began to circle around in a wide ark and sneak up on the site where Jack was still cuffed to the tree.

She had made it back, and they were talking for a while longer. She definitely was having second thoughts now that she was all alone with Jack, or she would have simply turned him loose.

I am sure he wanted to know where I was, she would tell him I left, and she was deciding about his release.

She finally went over and uncuffed him from the tree. He was free and alone with her.

He looked around to be sure I was really gone, and he hugged and kissed her, smart boy, that one. Get her totally at ease for when he would do her in. Find another accident location.

They started down the trail then, hand in hand.

They walked for a long while; I knew he was making sure I was really gone before he made his move.

Then they came to a deep ravine. It had steep sides, the perfect place. Jack guided Jill over closer to the rim as they walked. I had to get nearer. She saw how close they were getting to the edge and stopped.

She looked at him, and they started talking. I couldn't hear yet, but as I crept closer, I was able to start picking up their conversation.

Jill said, Jack, "I told you I was not going to turn you in and prosecute you; why do you have to do this?"

Jack said, "I still want out, and I know you. You will never sign the divorce papers. This is still the best way. Till death do us part, right baby?

"I will tell them how horrible it was that you got too close to the edge and slipped. I didn't have time to get to you before you fell, such a tragic accident," Jack said, grinning at her.

He grabbed her then, and she began to fight for her life. She was screaming and thrashing. That was what I was waiting for, so he would not see nor hear me coming as he was now occupied with her.

I got to them both just as he was pushing her over. Damn, I was too late.

I grabbed him, so his push to get her over the cliff was not as strong as he had wanted or needed, but it was enough. She disappeared over the edge. Jack and I both went down to the ground together. Getting on our feet, Jack instantly began to fight me. We started swinging on each other.

This battle was close and personal for both of us. Jack finally knocked me down close to the edge, and as I was trying to get up, he lunged at me to try and shove me over the side. I dropped quickly, and as he passed by, he tripped on my foot. He stumbled, and not being able to stop himself went over the edge. I could hear him screaming all the way down.

I quickly got up and went over to the place where Jill had gone over and saw she was hanging on to a ledge about seven feet down. It was a small thing, but it gave her just enough of something to hang on to for a short while. I could not reach her. She was already slipping, and her grip was precarious enough.

I glanced around and went to a tree nearby and broke off a limb. I raced back to the rim and guided the branch down to her. I said, Jill, you have to grab the branch, and I will pull you up. You can do it. Just grab the branch and hang on.

She yelled, I can't; I'm slipping.

I said if you want to live you have to do it.

She knew it was true; this time, she had to save herself.

It was as if she was having a life review. All the times she had let others come to her defense or to guide her life the way they thought it should be. An awakening within herself to finally take charge and be accountable for her own actions and destiny. I thought this was a pretty good time for her to finally get her act together.

She looked at the branch and up at me. Okay, she said, okay.

With that said, she concentrated on the motions she would have to do, and indecision vanished from her mind. She let go of her grip on the ledge with one hand and grabbed the branch. Once she had one hand on each, she let go of the shelf with her other hand and was now gripping the branch with both hands.

I said, "good girl." I started pulling her up.

It seemed to take forever, but eventually she came over the rim onto solid ground. Once she was on flat ground again, I let go of the branch and went to her, pulling her farther from the edge before I stopped and let her go.

I reached out and brought her into an embrace. She clung to me hard. I knew that would help settle her down. Maybe I needed a hug also, though I don't know why, I like being alone, right?

She broke down then as all the horror of the last few minutes came fully to her mind. After a long cry, she finally loosened her hold on me. I let go of her, and we both sat there looking at each other.

I knew she had a million things she wanted to say to me but was too ashamed to say it. You could read it on her face.

I saved her the trouble or humiliation; however, you want to think of it.

"Now you're free, I said. Jack tripped as he was trying to push me over the cliff; he could not stop himself from going over the edge."

That pretty much said all that was necessary. Jill could never be sure it happened just that way but accepted it as the truth.

I had a while to contemplate the last few days as we silently continued into town and was surprised at myself that I was looking at life a little differently than previous self-evaluations.

I was starting to care about what happened to the lady, to Jill. And not only her but the whole town. I was finally getting it.

A society needs membership to function. One could not solely be responsible for only oneself. It takes a group cooperative effort to make everything work together.

Maybe next year, when I take my vacation and seek the solitude nature provides, I might alter my policy of oneness and bring along a couple of people that have tried to be my friends and see how that works out. Who knows?

I guess Jill might not be the only one who can look inward and see a different light shining. A change in perspective.

Finally, in town, we went to the police station because we needed to inform the authorities of all that had happened.

As we went into the building, everyone said good morning, sir.

Jill looked at me but didn't say anything.

We continued forward until we came to the desk Sergeant.

He was busy doing some paperwork, and without looking up, he said, "how may I help you?"

I said, "you can show the lady more respect, Sergeant."

He looked up.

He saw who I was and said, "Sheriff, your back. We were getting worried about you. You're over a week overdue. How was your trip? Did you bring us some deer meat?"

I said, "that could wait, and no, I didn't. This lady has to make a statement about an incident that happened up on the ridge.

"You need to send a recovery team to the valley floor to recover the body of her husband. He fell off the cliff there."

That got the Sergeant's attention.

"Yes sir, and I am sorry for your loss Mam," the desk Sergeant added.

The Sergeant left to get things rolling.

Jill looked at me in total disbelief and said, "You're the Sheriff?"

I said, "guilty as charged." Then I added, it seems that is what everyone says, maybe I need to work on that.

CHAPTER 5 •

I AM

A RUNNER

Yes, running gets in the blood, doesn't it? There is nothing more exhilarating than coming in first place in a race, or for most, just finally finishing a 5k, 10k, or even 15k and up, marathon.

Getting to the magical inner sweet spot where you seem to get an entirely newfound energy boost and just go and go while passing up many other runners as you glide along the designated route is always a special time.

With so many running options it is hard at times to choose which one to pick. First, you have to decide what type of runner you are, short or long distance, track or relay, open road or wilderness runner, competition, or charity, the possibilities seem endless.

Next, you have to choose the proper equipment which will best suit the chosen style of runner you wish to be. An off-road wilderness style runner has different foot gear than say a track or field or street runner would use. Trail runners encounter trees, plants, insects, rivers, streams, rocks, mud, hills, mountains, ruts, and any number of misfortunes such as sprained ankles, cuts, and abrasions from falling or scraping up against something, etc.

The street runner can mostly rely on a flat hard surface, and find shoes that best suit the distance runner for comfort and endurance.

Another gear to consider is clothing. One must always think of the weather conditions. Most runners pick fair days to run and use a wicking shirt. That is a shirt that pulls sweat away from the body.

Women absolutely need a sports bra.

A very important product to always carry along is something to prevent chafing, Body glide, Vaseline, or powder.

Most important of all is when running long distances, runners need to have water. It is always better to have too much than not enough. A plain water bottle fits most beginners. But avid runners usually buy their own personalized bottles.

Next to water one of the most important pieces of gear to a long-distance and trail runner is the watch or smartphone. They can be very useful in helping the runner set their pace and to use the GPS function apps when needing to know the location or even listen to music with the earbuds. Or just to keep in contact with others it can be a great security device.

Think of the many times runners fall or get lost on trails and need to get help and find themselves without communication. Not too bright. A few ounces of extra weight are well worth it.

Now you have a feel for the things you need to be a prepared runner, like clothing and equipment, but the next very important thing a runner has to be aware of is the safety factor.

Let me explain. You go out on your daily run, just like you do every day. No big deal, right. But how many times have you been lucky in getting back home safely?

When you ran down the street, did anyone just miss you while backing out of their driveway? Did the loose dog chase you, what if it had been one that could attack you? What about at the corner, did the car stop for you at the crosswalk?

And you wearing earphones and can't hear anything around you. Anybody coming up on you? And how many times did you forget to look both ways at a street light before running out into traffic?

I could think of a hundred ways not to make it home again. And that is just before lunch. Yes, safety is not given the attention it should have. You hear daily of someone getting mugged, murdered, kidnapped, raped, or a combination of all the above.

Let's not forget being hit by vehicles of all sorts; cars, buses, bicycles, skateboarders. Need I go on.

Runners have a full plate and don't even realize it. I wonder what the numbers would be of deaths of runners as compared to mountain cliff climbers. They, I believe, rank better than runners because they know how to prepare for their journey.

Complacency is probably the biggest mistake runners make. I run this way every day, and nothing ever happens. This is a safe path. Blah, blah, blah. I am not saying you are the next target of some mishap or criminal attack. But you never know. The ones you read about daily in the news thought the same thing. Not me I'm careful. I won't even go into the multitude of horror stories, we have all heard them, and it is tragic enough without dwelling on them.

Just be aware of your surroundings at all times. Running is wonderful. It's just not worth dying or getting seriously hurt over, ok?

Now on to other more fun topics on running.

Did you know there are running contests of all kinds in every state in every county and practically in every town? You can't sneeze without someone yelling let's have a race. There are races for prizes, trophies, and fun. They come in all sizes from sack races to 50k races. That's a lot of in-betweens!

There are many kinds of races. Some to raise money for charitable causes. Name something, anything, and I will bet you that someone will race or earn money running by the mile to help out the cause.

They have endurance races that make you do miles and miles in horrific conditions. {Unless you like that sort of stuff}. Mud races, mountain races, and city street races.

Mom's running and post-pregnancy races, who does that? Now those are some hard-core women runners.

One race I always watch when I can be there is the running of the bulls. Now those folks have real incentives to keep moving.

They have runners dressed in any number of costumes for any occasion that comes to mind. If you need to run, I guess you might as well enjoy yourself, right?

They have children of all ages competing. Kids, teenagers, young adults, middle-aged, and seniors. I say children because aren't we all kids at heart when we run.

If you yell race, a runner will come.

I recall, years back now, how a runner had witnessed a thief grab a woman's purse. He didn't want to get hurt himself but neither did he want the thief to get away with the purse. It really was comical.

The thief took off and the jogger ran after him. Just staying far enough away so as not to be in any harms-way. The thief soon caught on and tried to dissuade the jogger from following. But eventually realized the jogger was not going to get close enough or let the thief get close to him, so as to get caught by the thief, nor, was he going to let the thief get away.

So, both just ran and ran. The thief stopping periodically to rest and the jogger did likewise. They had a conversation of sorts. The jogger telling the thief to just drop the purse and leave. The thief not thinking that was such a good idea explained in detail how he felt about the jogger and kept trying to run away.

After a few times stopping and talking the jogger tells the thief he can do this all day long as he is a long-distance runner and so far, hasn't even broken a sweat.

Finally seeing the folly of his misadventure, the thief concedes and drops the purse and leaves. The jogger gets the purse back to the woman and all is well again. I love those kinds of stories.

This brings me to the health aspects of running. Did you ever hear of an obese long-distance runner? If you had, I'll bet you he didn't stay that way for long.

A 97-year-old man is running as best as he can across America right now. He is, like so many others, trying to get attention for his own special cause. Everyone that does this kind of running believes they need attention from everyone who will listen. You have to give him credit. That is one endurance run. Good luck.

There seems to be no consensus, on whether running would be bad for your joints. Some say it causes joint deterioration from impacting your bones so much. Others say it is because you run in the wrong way. Who knows for sure? In the long run, {no pun intended} it is about now. Not the future. I see a lot of elderly people running still, and I see a lot of people who never ran farther than to catch a bus sitting in wheelchairs.

The point is if you like doing something and no one can figure out if it's bad or not, why worry about it.

One nice part about running is that after a while your body releases endorphins, that produce a calming effect that gives runners a euphoric state or a runners-high, as sort of a reward by the body. Now, who doesn't like a good high once in a while, eh? You just have to run your rear off to get it.

Now that we have done our homework and shown all the different things runners must deal with, let's change course for a minute and follow a runner in motion and look into a moment in time of a running woman's thoughts. The scene is: she is running down a countryside dirt road with flowers in the fields and mountains in the distance. A great place to run.

Her mind is speaking.

The day is so wonderful. I have finally finished college and have said yes to my boyfriend's proposal of marriage. That will get me out from under my parent's roof, and rules. It is time I started my own family and he is the perfect man in every way. And yes, I honestly love him to the depths of my heart and soul.

Running is my favorite thing to do, it seems to clear my head and allows me time to think out here in the wide-open space of the country. Just me and nature, embracing and absorbing the beautiful majestic landscape, smelling the crisp clean air, and all under a magnificent morning sky.

I love running for so many reasons. Not only for the health aspects it brings, but also the freedom to move about, to speed your way to another point, to compete with others of like mind, and to challenge myself to greater heights of endurance. I find I gain more confidence and am more self-assured in life. It is hard to pin down just exactly what it is. I just simply love it.

This, time of year, is especially my favorite. The flowers are all in full bloom. The snow on the mountain has mostly all melted away and the grasses have covered it all in such wonderful shades of green.

All the birds and small animals doing their thing all around and happily sharing it all with me. It truly is a wonderful life.

Wow, running sure is good for her. I think we should all get on that road to run. What a positive attitude. Those endorphins are certainly kicking in for her.

If she is a sample of the people who are runners then it is no wonder it is as popular as it is.

So, is running a sport, a hobby, a way of life? Or is it just something one does to stay fit and healthy? Maybe one or all of these. One shoe doesn't fit all feet. One trail or route doesn't fit all runners. Running encompasses the most inclusive and diverse interests people have than most anything else I can imagine. If you don't like to run uphill, find a place that is all downhill, it's just that simple. Actually, all that downhill running sounds easy. I just might go up to the top of a mountain road and see what downhill running feels like. But if you like a challenge take to the stairs. I bet there are a lot of those around.

The ways to run are as numerous as the stars. Just start walking, then speed up more and more until you find yourself running, and the world is yours. Pack a snack and plenty of water and see how far you can go.

CHAPTER 6 •

CHRISTMAS
IS MORE THAN A DAY

Preface

Unlike all the rest of the year, Christmas has a special place in people's hearts. It is a time to celebrate Christ, a time to be of good cheer, a time to reflect on life and the world, a time to be with family and friends.

A special time to give and receive with love in your hearts, and especially a time to make your children the happiest they can be. To happily watch their eyes bug out, and their faces light up, as they tear into the presents that Santa has brought them.

It is a time to share with the community and the world the unique feelings that only the ethereal Christmas message radiates and conveys to all.

Most anyone you ask could not tell you why they feel this way at this time of year. It is merely a favorite holiday to celebrate, but also, for some reason, it is the most anticipated and observed of any other day of the year.

It is a magical thing, which somehow exudes excitement, pleasure, and joy in its celebration.

This is a different Christmas story, a real-world Christmas. It is a story of an older man who has lost his belief in how Christmas is supposed to be. A man who has lost that spark that everyone else has for this time of year. A man who just wishes to be left alone in his misery and sorrow.

Introduction

Not everyone can say they had a visit from a spirit. Not everyone would want a visit from a ghost. But some such as Andy would welcome such an appointment if it was from his wife who passed just one year ago. He has never gotten over that loss, and it affects every waking moment.

He lives as if the world had played a cruel joke on him when his wife was taken in death and left him to go on living. The very last thing he would have wanted to do. And to top it all off was the salt on the wound of when it happened; Christmas Eve. How ironic is that? The one time of year that his wife most loved to celebrate. The one time of year, he actually felt like doing for others.

Well, that all changed when Anne passed away. Now he just wallows in self-pity and sorrow. He is determined to grieve himself to death so that he could once again be with the love of his life.

There was nothing anyone could do to break that stubbornness, not even his children who worried over him.

It was a done deal in his mind, and nothing could shake him out of it. Or so he thought.

This is, after all, Christmas time.

CHRISTMAS
IS MORE THAN A DAY

Opening my eyes, I remember what day it is. I start crying again. I had heard time heals all wounds, but this hurt is beyond repair. Missing Anne is too powerful. This day last year, I awoke to find her lying next to me, cold. I knew she had left me sometime in the night.

The love of my life had departed, and we could never say our goodbyes.

I had such a hard time getting through the following days. Christmas just passed me by, unnoticed. I had no reason to celebrate much less be of good cheer.

I know Anne loved this time of year. She would do all kinds of things, getting ready for the big day, setting up the tree, buying gifts for the children and later the grandchildren, all her friends, and family galore.

It put us in the poorhouse till May when we finally paid off the credit cards.

But I have to say, making her happy was worth it all. I loved seeing the twinkle in her eyes come alive when that time of year came around. It must have rubbed a little off on me too because I liked helping her do all the things she loved.

She made me lug in a big evergreen tree and help her decorate it just right; then, we would sit and take all day wrapping the presents she bought.

It was an unspoken tradition, I suppose, that all the kids and grandkids would come over and unwrap the presents we had so carefully wrapped just before with complete abandon. Ripping and tearing until every last one was seen had been the only objective.

The happy screams of delight coming from the grandkids as the very thing they had asked Santa for magically would be there, and all of them

running around in the torn-up paper playing with their toys.

Then, after a while, we would all gather around the table and eat of the food Anne, and the ladies had cooked with love and gaiety. Then we would contentedly sit around and catch up on what we had all been doing that year.

It all seems so distant now; I just don't have the pleasure or joy I used to feel during this time inside me any longer.

A big part of me is missing, and I don't know how to fix it.

I was always good at fixing things. No matter what it was, just let me at it, and before long, it was working again. But not this. Something inside me is broken beyond repair. I am unable to fix myself; too much of me is missing.

I opened the drawer by my bed and re-read the last poem I wrote after Anne's funeral. I used to write her poems all the time, but this one was the last I had left in me. I never touched a pen to write ever again.

It reads

***

Yesterday was the hardest day I have ever had to go through.
To pretend I was strong and not lose my sanity.
And now I have to go on and finish this life without you.
With nothing of you to hold on to but our many memories.

Tonight, as I sit in our swing and stare up at the beautiful night sky,
I reminisce of all the times we tried counting the uncountable stars.
I remember how comforting and peaceful it always was and why.
Because in our field of dreams, you were eternally my brightest star.

How do you pick up the pieces of your life and keep on going?
When your world is torn apart because your one love has gone.
To wake up each morning to a home as empty as your soul.
And facing each day with the knowledge, you're all alone.

Darling, I'll miss you as the days begin to lose their light.
And the night commands the hours to slow my thoughts of you.
But someday my time will come and once again we'll be together.
For life has its seasons, but our love endures through it all.

***

I knew the poem by heart, but it feels better to read it.

I finally got out of bed; it does no good just to lay there. I found it is a lot easier, cooking for myself, to just make a bowl of cereal. Anne would make me all kinds of things. She loved to cook, and I loved to eat. It was a perfect match.

***

On the other side of town, Andy's son was having a crisis of his own.

"Linda, I don't know what to do. Dad is so down all the time now, overpowered by grief. Since Mom passed away, he doesn't have that spark of life. I am afraid he is just wasting away; he is grieving himself to death."

Linda said, "Mark, I know this is a trying time. You feel like you need to do something to help your father carry on with life, but this appears to be something he has to work out within himself.

"The best we can do is support him and show that he is not alone. We probably should visit him more often than we have, but to be honest, it is hard on all of us.

"We all cared a great deal for your mother, and it hurts us also not having her around any longer.

"I suppose that is why we don't go over as often as we used to. It reminds us of our losing her. Does that make us culpable in your fathers' anguish? I think so to some extent! But it doesn't change the reality of our feelings.

"Even the kids miss her. She was the anchor that bound all of us together. Without her, we all simply drifted apart. I feel ashamed at even saying it, but without your mother, we have lost the connection as a family unit."

Mark said, "I think I should step up somehow and give assistance and support in helping dad come to grips with his, or I should say, our loss of mother. Life can be very painful at times.

"It is compounded by the season, I am sure. This is the worst time of year to lose a loved one. It always comes to haunt you and spoil the festivities."

"I have been thinking, just mull it over for a while, and we can discuss it later, but as an idea, do you think we could ask Dad to move in with us?"

Linda gasped; "Mark, are you serious? In his condition around the children? Do you think that would be wise?"

Mark said, "please hear me out!

"We bought a home way too big for our needs, and there is ample room for him. I think living alone like he is, is not working out. Here, we could keep an eye on him, and I think all of us together could help everyone in the healing process.

"Besides, he could help with the kids, and he is good at fixing things. We have a lot of things that need attention around here, and we both are pretty busy. Just think about it, will you?

"Not to change the subject but I can't find one person who qualifies for the job of manager for our company. It is strange that in a city this large, not one candidate I have interviewed has passed my necessary requirements. I may have to settle for a person of lesser qualifications, though I am sure that would be a disaster."

***

Christmas Eve is a time to be happy and thankful, a time to celebrate all your blessings.

***

Well, that works for most people, but the man next door to Andy does not have much for which to cheer. His company has just decided to downsize due to the economy, and he has been laid off.

This is just great; John was thinking.

The day before Christmas and I get the boot. All those years of dedicated service to the company, and this is what I get? How do I tell my family? What am I going to do now?

As he enters his home, he is greeted by his three children and his wife. They do not know yet of his layoff. He sees no reason to spoil their happiness. There would be plenty of time later for that. He hugs them all and kisses his wife.

She sees in his face, something that should not be there. Yes, something that is there, but should not be a frown. There should be a smile. He is not smiling.

She asks him, "honey, what's wrong?"

John looks at his wife and not wanting or able to say what happened just yet, said, "let's talk later."

And with that said, he grabbed up his youngest and swung her around all the way to the family room, where he pretended to play with them all happily. He was not going to ruin Christmas for any reason.

As the day waned, everyone was preoccupied and obsessed with their own personal struggles. Each was dealing with their problems as they felt was the only way left to them.

But this is Christmas!

After putting all the kids to bed and having retired to the bedroom, John was finally confronted by his wife, Lisa.

"Ok, John," she demanded. "You have put it off long enough. What is going on?"

Gathering his strength and love for his wife and swallowing his pride, he told her.

He said, "I have been laid off from my job."

Caught off guard with that statement, she said, "oh, John."

Anything else she might have had to say caught in her throat. She didn't know what to say. It was devastating news. All she could think to do was to go to John and hold him in complete silence. Not just to comfort John but also for herself. This could change their whole world.

***

It was almost midnight, and Andy had finally drifted off to sleep. He never got a lot of sleep anymore. He slept as he could, and that would have to do.

He began a dream, as he often did. Since he obsessed over his wife all the time, is it any wonder he would also dream of her?

She came to him a bit differently this time. It was like she was talking to him not as a memory but from one person to another. Like she was right there with him.

Is this what they call a lucid dream, he wondered. Where it feels so real, and you actually get to interact with it, to control it in some small way. He was pleased about that. To converse with Anne again as if she were still alive.

It started with him waking from his sleep, hearing his name being called.

"Andrew, Andrew, wake up, Andrew; I need to talk to you," said the voice.

Andy knew that voice but was afraid to open his eyes and spoil the dream said, "is that you, Anne? I have missed you so."

Anne said, "Andrew, I need to talk with you and have but a short time."

That got Andy's attention. He sat up in bed and opening his eyes, saw his wife at the foot of the bed. She was translucent and sort of floating in the air. His night light gave off just enough light to make her out.

"Anne, it is you, I am not dreaming, you're really here." He was in ecstasy.

Anne said, "Andrew, I have felt and heard every thought you had toward me. I know I left suddenly, but these things do happen. You don't choose when or how.

"I have come to give your mind rest and peace. To balance your life with reality in this world and to share the knowledge of what is to come. The world, as you know it, is not the end. Life was and will be before and after birth and death.

"So be content in the now of your existence. We will again be together at a later time. This sorrow you have needs to stop. It serves no one and keeps you from living your life to the fullest. There are many who still need you. Don't be selfish in your love.

"Our children have suffered because of your constant grieving. You are tearing their world apart. You need to let me go. Remember me as I remember you, but don't be obsessed with me. Live your life and rejoice in it. Our time will come again."

Andy said, "But Anne, how can I let you go? You were my life, my world."

Anne said, "love your children Andrew, they need you now. I am happy where I am; you need to be content also.

"My time is finished, and I must go. But before I do. There is one thing I must tell you. Find it in your heart to help others less fortunate and in great need. It will reap numerous rewards. I love you. Goodbye, for now, my love."

Anne faded away, leaving Andy alone once again. He stared at the area she had been, frozen in place hoping Anne would return, but eventually, he knew she would not.

He felt such love come over him as he had never felt before. Was she sent back from heaven to give him relief from his despair, to give him closure to his suffering?

His mind was full of thoughts, but then a small light flickering in the window drew his attention. It was faint, but it was growing brighter. He got up and went to the window to see what was causing the light. He saw in an instant.

The neighbors' house was on fire. It was where they had put up the Christmas tree. Somehow, the lights must have started a fire.

He ran to the phone and dialed 911.

"Hello, 911; how may I help you," said the person who answered.

Andy said quickly, "there is a house on fire at 1313 Amar Road. You need to hurry; there are kids in that house." He hung up.

He knew the dispatcher would take too much time, asking a bunch of questions that could wait till later to answer. He needed to make sure everyone was out of the house quickly.

He ran down the stairs dressed only in his pajamas, robe, and moccasins, which he always used as slippers.

Not a minute to waste, he was thinking.

Running out, he saw no one outside the home next door; there was no activity inside the house either.

He started yelling, "hello in there. Wake up. Your house is on fire."

No response.

He ran to the back, where he knew there to be a sliding door into the living room.

He yelled again, "hello in there; your house is on fire, get out."

Still, nothing was coming from inside.

"Ok, he said, I got to get in there quickly."

He looked around and saw a few concrete blocks used to build walls with and grabbed one and threw it into the glass sliding door. That did it. He reached in and unlocked the door. Then moving quickly, he slid it open and ran into the house. It was filled with smoke, and he ducked lower to avoid the heaviest of the smoke. He went into the kitchen and grabbed a towel from the hanger on the oven, and wet it down. He then put that over his nose and mouth so he could better breathe with such choking smoke.

Andy yelled again as he went toward the bedrooms. He finally heard the father yell back through the door. " What is going on? Who are you? What are you doing in my house?"

Andy yelled, "Your house is on fire. You need to get everyone out, now."

John opened his door and seeing the smoke, yelled to his wife, "Lisa, get up, the house is on fire. We need to get the kids out now."

Andy went to the first door and opening it; he saw a little girl in the bed. He ran over and grabbed her, and the covers, and ran outside.

Andy put her down and said, "stay right there little one." He ran back toward the house as John and Lisa were bringing out the other two children.

He stopped and asked, "where is the main electric box?"

John said, "on the side of the house around the corner going to the back."

Andy ran to it and turned off the electricity.

Coming back, he saw the fire department was arriving. They quickly put out the fire. It was not too bad. They had caught it early. The house would need a lot of repairs, but it was just the area around the tree that did most of the damage.

He stood next to the family, who were devastated. They were out and safe but now had no place to sleep until repairs could be done.

He suddenly remembered Anne's last comment. Help others in need. Did she know this was going to happen? Was this what she was talking about?

He looked at the family. The mother was crying on the husband's shoulder as all the kids were hugging the parents and also crying. It was an unfortunate accident and a terrible thing to witness, and on Christmas eve at that. Tragedy around here is beginning to have a scorecard, Andy thought.

The firemen placed a do not cross tape across the front door and rear broken sliding door. No one could enter the home until the city inspector deemed it safe. That was that.

Ok, Andy-boy, what are you going to do. Let them stand there all night. Where is your humanity, man? He felt like a good angel was on one shoulder, and a devil was on the other one fighting it out.

Finally, after arguing with himself for a few minutes, then remembering his wife, and it being Christmas, he spoke softly to the father.

"Look, I have a big house, and it is empty at the moment. I wish that you would share it with me for a while. It is late and tomorrow is Christmas. There is no need for you to stand here all night and freeze. Please come, be my guests, and we can figure all this out tomorrow."

John was a proud man who would never accept charity for himself, but this was different. He had a family to look after.

He looked at his wife, who he could tell was all for accepting the invitation, and then he looked at his children who were staring at their home. Not a time to be stupid, he said to himself.

He had been standing there and wondering what it was that he did that was so bad as to cause this much trouble to befall him in so short a time. It was devastating and left him a broken man. The only thing that saved him was the thought of his family. He had to carry on for them.

John looked at Andy and said, "I haven't even thanked you for saving us from the fire as yet, and here you are inviting me into your home. I am beyond words, but words must be said.

"First, I wish to thank you for saving my family and myself from the fire. What you did was truly heroic. I can never repay you enough for that alone.

"Now, I must thank you again for caring enough to open your home to us in our time of need.

"Yes, I will take you up on your most generous offer to let us stay with you."

Christmas is a time of heightened emotions, Good and bad. Those having a wonderful time are ecstatic. On the chart of one to ten, they feel eleven. But it also goes that those having troubles during this time have elevated senses of woes that would not reach such a pinnacle during other times of the year. It affects everyone the same way.

***

When morning finally came, Andy called his son and daughter. He explained what had transpired the night before and asked his children to see if they could get some presents and a small tree for the young children of John and Lisa. He would pay them back.

Now, this was totally shocking to Andy's kids. That was the last thing they had expected from their father on Christmas morning. They were surprised and delighted. Not about the situation with the family next door, which was terrible, but how different their father was. He seemed like a changed man, and for the better.

Mark called his friend who happened to own a toy store and told him of the tragedy of Christmas eve, and his friend asked John to meet him at the store. He came back with the trunk filled with toys for children of the age group Andy had mentioned. Mark and Linda's children had already ripped into their presents, so there was no reason not to go on over and give the children at Dad's house their gifts.

Everyone was still asleep as it had been a long hard night for all of them. Mark and Linda and Andy's daughter and husband, Vicky and Sam, and of course, Andy himself all put up the tree and placed the presents under it just in time for the arrival of the kids and John and Lisa.

John looked at everyone standing around and asked, "what's going on?"

Andy said, "Santa asked me what happened to the children next door, and I told him they were staying here with me.

"Well, he told me, please give the children the presents he had for them, and here they are.

The kids all looked at Andy with big bright eyes, and the oldest one said, "did you say those presents are for us from Santa Claus?"

Andy said, "that's what he told me. They are all yours. Better hurry up and open them before he decides to come back and get them."

That did it. They ran to the pile and like all children, ripped and tore, all while giggling and laughing.

John said, "there you go again. I am never going to be able to pay you back."

John turned away with tears in his eyes and walked into the kitchen, too ashamed to face them any longer.

Andy said, "what did I say, I am sorry. I was just trying to help."

Lisa said, "it is not you; we are so grateful for your kindness. John lost his job yesterday. He had been a manager for years in a big chain of stores, and they just laid him off due to a downsizing in the company.

" He spent years working for them, and they just let him go. So, he is feeling pretty down right now. It has nothing to do with anything you have done.

"He is a proud man and has always been a good provider for us. I guess this being Christmas has made it all the harder to accept."

Mark said, "excuse me for a minute." He went into the kitchen where John had gone.

Linda went to Andy and said, "Mark and I have been discussing your living here all alone, and we think you should come live with us.

"We have a house that just screams of needing someone to take care of it. We are useless in that regard. Also, you could be closer to all of the grandkids and us, of course. It would be a win, win for everyone.

"We also think it would be a good way to get the family all back together again. This would be a perfect time for all of us to regain the bond we once had. We all miss that more than you could know."

Andy looked thoughtfully at Linda. She didn't believe, not even for a moment, that he would accept the offer, but she had to try. If today being Christmas didn't get him to change his mind, then it would never happen.

Just then, Mark and John reemerged from the kitchen.

"We have an announcement, John declared. Linda, meet the new Manager for our store.

"I am not giving it to him for any other reason than he is exactly who I have been looking for. Talk about fate intervening. It is a Christmas miracle." John went to Lisa and hugged her.

"Yes, it must be a miracle," John said.

Andy, seeing how well all of the problems worked themselves out, made his own decision.

He began to speak, "Mark, Linda. I accept your invitation to come and live with you, on a let's see if it works out contingency. You might live to regret it.

"But then there is always Vicky and Sam over there trying to hide. I might split the time and give everyone some space once in a while.

"As for this house. John, you and Lisa, and your kids are welcome to it for as long as it takes to get your own home repaired. No rush.

"I had someone very special come to me recently and told me I needed to be more outgoing and friendly. I plan on doing just that with the time I have left. No more sulking. Life is to be lived."

Andy stopped for just a moment, and looking up to the heavens said, "Merry Christmas Anne." And then, gazing at his family and new friends, he said, "and a Merry Christmas to all.

Chapter 7

WEIGHT ON ME

SUB-CHAPTERS

Introduction

Second chances, or a do-over. How often do people wish for that? How many times does it happen? And, when it happens, how does it change one's life. Do the people learn and benefit from the do-over? Or, do they simply make the same mistakes again and again; stuck in the never-ending cycle of repetitive behaviors.

How hard is it really to actually change the way people approach their problems, and resolve for the last time the reoccurring underlying reasons for their failures?

Life is complicated for sure and compounded by multitudes of distractions. Each one straining a persons' power of will to reject those temptations and to finally succumb and seek an escape from it all.

Some who find it hard to stand up to such intrusions of their personal space find temptations and weakness will bow to the desire to escape. And so, allow themselves to be comforted by such things as drugs, alcohol, food. Anything that lets them hide from or mask reality; anything that comforts and satisfies their denials.

Any distraction from dealing with their problem will suffice. We all have them. But most learn to deal with them before they get too much control over our lives. Interventions hardly ever work. People usually have to reach a point of total desperation before seeking any interference in their situations.

This story is, in the beginning, about such people. Those seeking to change or alter a behavior out of control. A behavior that has taken over their lives and has prevented them from enjoying all that life has to offer.

Their food addiction is all that matters, or so they have convinced themselves. Many have come to seek help in their desperation to eradicate the behavior by any means possible. Some were drawn for the sheer appeal of another fad diet.

The main character promises this help. It will not be easy. It will take absolute dedication to complete. But the reward is deliverance from the stranglehold now gripping them. A way of rescuing their lives and remaking their bodies into their former selves, and recovering their self-respect and pride.

But only one of this latest group to seek help had the absolute desire to take on the challenge. A yearning need so strong as to risk everything to gain back all that had once been.

Someone who just might make it this time, with the help of a dedicated man.

But as in all stories, one theme is not always consistent with the narrative. Plots have a way of changing. Scenarios and settings change and develop. Actions have consequences. Enjoy.

Sub Chapter: 1

Don't Take It Personally

Joe stood looking, or, more like peeking out, at the crowd from the side of the stage, thinking maybe, he should have double-checked the weight limit of the floor.

Another group looking just like the last. He was not impressed. But, he surmised, that if he had been, then chances just might be they would not need him to fix their problem.

He sighed and went to the podium in the center of the stage. Tapping the microphone to see if it was in working order, he heard the squeal from the feedback and tap he had given it and began to speak.

"Hello and welcome. My name is Joe Manning.

"I suppose you're all wondering why I asked you here today?" Joe started smiling.

An old saying but it still gets a laugh, a tried-and-true ice breaker.

"Well, as you can see from all the people around you, all are on the rather large hard-to-fit clothing size."

Might as well hit them hard and separate the wheat from the chaff, Joe thought. There was simply no easy way to introduce and begin with the subject matter politely, just say the truth, be direct, and to the point.

"No, I am not a clothing salesperson. Rather, I am here to offer my services as a weight loss specialist.

"Yes, I can see from your expressions that you think this is an insulting way to visit upon you such a tender subject. Well so be it. I am not here to coddle and try to appease your overly-stuffed denial of the obvious. This is surely not the first time you have been accused of being overweight. But hopefully, you will take this opportunity to make it the last.

"I am here only as an arbiter of the truth and facts. And, if you accept my challenge, I will arrange and guide you through a guaranteed way to gain back the figure you once had before life took you down the isolating and lonely road of obesity.

"I am here to give you a chance, an opportunity, to be who you think you are inside. I want to remove all that holds you captive, to dissolve and finally be rid of that second, and for some, that third person you have been carrying around for so long.

"The weight loss program I am proposing, as all methods try to do, involves a proven method of exercise and restriction of calories, but with a unique twist. It will not be easy, and as a matter of fact, it will be very hard. But it will work, and you will see the results in a very timely manner.

"All it takes is your commitment to the program and up to three months of complete dedication on your part. From that moment you will be able to look in a mirror and see the best-looking person you can be.

"In this program, you will share in a truly unforgettable adventure into the wilds of nature. You could call it a roaming camp excursion.

"Here is the plan so everyone can see for themselves what the undertaking will entail. All of the participants will be taken to a very remote location, and as a group, aiding and encouraging each other, you will find your way from that location to other locations and so on

until you reach the finishing point. How long that takes is entirely up to you, your motivation, and your ambition in completing your preset goals.

"At that time, you all will be at your desired fitness level. There will be no need to spread out the chairs as they are now for you to sit comfortably and accept the coveted completion award you will have genuinely earned because you will not be the person you are now.

"You will be a new person. Confident in your actions, afraid of nothing, and ready to start your life anew as the one finally released from the prison of obesity and constantly being demeaned by all around you for how you look. I dare say the world will be your oyster, and you, the beautiful pearl inside.

"But be forewarned, this excursion is not for the faint of heart, it is for those daring and ready for a truly challenging life change. You will be tested to see if you can stand the rigors of what is to come. I would wish no harm to any of you. If there should be cause for medical attention, those people will be airlifted out. "But I warn you, it is only for the near-death injuries I speak of, not the weak who will seek to quit because it is harder than they thought it would be.

"If being able to quit at any time along the trail were the case, I dare say most, if not all, would fit into that category at some point along this Trek. Your journey is designed to reconstruct you from the inside out.

"This program will endeavor to re-create and produce a new you, one who you would be proud to be, not the one everyone thinks you to be.

"So, I will leave you now to contemplate and decide if this is an avenue you wish to explore. Those who are left when I return will be assumed ready for the next step of passing the physical.

"Many of you are already past the point of attempting this trip. You have been too long at the table for even me to help you. Your heart may be too weak at this point to endure the pace I will set.

"From those few who stay, and also pass the physical, will be questioned by me as to their mental state. This is crucial. Not everyone is capable of withstanding the hardships you will confront, so, why bother continuing past this point, A desire to change and willpower must be strong within you.

"Look deep into yourself and answer these questions, could I go through such an ordeal? Am I strong and dedicated enough to take on this challenge? And lastly, is my desire to finally make the change powerful enough?

"I thank you all for coming and I appreciate the time you have allowed me to speak to you. For those who will be gone when I return, I say to you now, goodnight."

With that all said, Joe left the stage and waited in the dressing room he had been provided for one hour. This would give everyone time to talk and discuss among themselves and to contemplate inwardly if they truly could accept and complete such an undertaking.

He wondered how many would leave. There had been around fifty people there. He knew from prior trips he would only get a few at best. Once he went out and found all had gone, but that only happened the one time.

He sometimes wondered why he had chosen to do this kind of job. It certainly did not pay all that well for all the time and effort he had to commit. But he did not have anyone waiting for him anywhere so the time away was of no importance.

He did kind of like the comradery that eventually developed among all the people as they went along the trail, maybe that was what drew him to this work. The nearer they all got to the end, the closer it seemed they became. But, once they all finished the course, it was like a spell had been lifted, and they all went back to their previous lives and disappeared from his.

Sure, they all said they would keep in touch, write, drop in and chat, but it never happened.

Joe didn't hold it against them. After all, they had just gotten a new lease on life with their new bodies and confidence in themselves.

There were many new things to try, new people and friends to seek out and experience, maybe find someone to love. They probably got caught up in all of that, and just forgot about the promises.

Out of sight, out of mind, as someone had once said.

Finally, Joe walked back to the podium and stared out at the sea of empty seats. Well, he thought, I guess it happened for a second time.

Wait, there was one left. She was sitting in the front row, center. He had been looking over her because she was up so close and he had been focusing on all the seats out farther. They both stared silently at each other for a long minute.

Because of his job, Joe had unconsciously evaluated the lady as a prospective client. Young, about his age, without all the weight he guessed she could be a beautiful woman. She would do well after taking his program. There were about three months of hard work wrapped around her waist. Just the kind of clients he was looking for; get the right results in the right amount of time.

Joe had never had just one client before. It caused him to wonder, after all he had promised the crowd, if he could tell her, it would not be possible or profitable to take just one person on such a trip.

He hadn't stated during the speech that a minimum number had to go. Also, besides the obvious financial barrier this would entail, he wasn't comfortable taking just one female on the trip.

It just wouldn't look right, and if she squawked for any reason, he could be in big trouble even if he did nothing to her. These days the man is always guilty, never innocent until proven.

She finally said, "well? I guess you're wondering why I stayed here tonight?"

She had used her own personalized opener line back at him. That impressed him and showed she had a sense of humor. He could not help but smile. It also broke the spell of silence he had been under and he spoke.

"I am sorry I just froze up here, Joe began. It is just that, I have never had only one person to stay before. I set a minimum number in my head of the people I would need to make such a journey and never considered having just one to accept my offer.

"It would simply be financially impossible to even consider just one applicant even if you were to pass my physical and mental tests, not to mention the inappropriateness of just one female client going.

"So, I hope you can understand my impossible to resolve dilemma. I thank you for your consideration and interest in the program but the situation would be entirely untenable."

She just sat there looking at him.

Finally, after another awkward moment of silence, She, said, "I have tried every way I could to lose this weight alone. I have found nothing that worked. I am at the point of despair. I cannot continue to carry this burden any longer. If I have to do something drastic to fix myself, so be it. If you refuse to help me so be it.

"I now know your secret and will undertake this journey alone if need be. I am done with the multitude of torments I endure constantly from others.

"If it is money you need, I will give you a blank check. I am a very wealthy woman.

"If you are worried about me yelling you did things to me, I will sign any waiver from prosecution you wish.

"I think your plan is the best thing I have ever heard to motivate me and force me to finally make this weight disappear. It may be the only way I can make it
happen. I am willing to take on your challenge with complete acceptance of the rules.

"Are you willing to honor your commitment to do your job?"

The lady looked him straight in the eye, even though she had obviously started tearing up, she was a proud strong woman.

Joe was stunned. Here for the first time, he had heard in a client's own words the desperation they all must have felt in coming to his seminars. From her plea for help, he realized how utterly serious most felt about their situation.

He felt a pang of guilt as he recalled the callous words he had uttered to the crowd. How completely devoid of empathy they must have labeled him. He would never use such hurtful language again in future seminars.

That just might be why many of the potential clients did not stay. They had already endured all the snide remarks from people they could handle. They were not going to pay some offensive jack-ass to give them more. Some life lessons come harder to learn than others.

Most he knew, did not have the determination this lady had articulated in her testimonial, but her desperation allowed him a glimpse into their inner pain.

Her declaration was proof enough for Joe that here was an honest and authentic desire to succeed, and failure was not an option.

He wanted to help this lady and he also knew she would hurt herself or worse if she tried to go it alone. He had offered the service and was, for better or worse, now obligated to provide the assistance.

Next time he would stipulate the minimum number of participants needed to start the trek. That initial mistake was on him.

Joe simply said, "be here at seven in the morning. We will outfit you with your gear for the trip at that time. And just to cover the bases I will take you up on the check and the liability issue, but I promise, you have nothing to fear from me. Also, I will not charge more than what is appropriate."

The lady, getting her composure back together said thank you, turned, and began walking from the theater. Halfway up the aisle, she stopped and slightly turning said, by the way, my name is Ms. Barbara Hall. She then continued to exit the building not turning back again.

She didn't want Mr. Joe Manning to see the most-happiest ear-to-ear grin she could ever remember having on her face.

Sub Chapter: 2

Getting To The Trail

It was not hard at all getting Ms. Hall's pack together. It took very little time at all. Joe was used to working with several team members at the same time and working out each personalized kit.

The outfitters' store had everything one could need for hiking long trails under any conditions. From one end of the country to the other from top to bottom, the store could supply any situational need.

This was just one pack and one person, so, the time used was minimal in adequately finding everything she needed for the initial portion of the trek. Everything else needed for the next portion of the trip, and the next, and so on, would be supplied at those preplanned and pre-stocked locations.

After a three-hour ride, escorted and dropped off by his planning and logistics partner, they were soon standing on the starting line. Well, it wasn't a real starting line, just an imaginary semblance of a beginning.

The trees were full of green leaves, the brush was almost nonexistent on the trail, which would make the first leg much easier. The weatherman said no foreseeable bad weather for a long time, that was great. People not accustomed to hiking would not like to trudge through a rainstorm, especially on the first day or so.

Joe looked at Barbara and said, "This is where the journey begins. At this point is where your whole life changes. A new beginning. A new you. From this moment forward, you will be challenged like no other time in your life.

"Just keep reminding yourself when you need someone to lean on or keep you from quitting, you are the only one this is all for, no one else. I am simply here to see that you are safe in your quest. I will not carry or pamper you. You will succeed on your own or not at all.

"Are you ready, Ms. Hall?"

She looked at Joe and said, "are you going to talk all day or are we going to start this thing?"

Joe smiled.

He said, "all right then, the adventure begins."

He started walking at a constant pace, one he thought would be the right speed for her initial jaunt. He wanted to test her capabilities for the trail ahead; to see how much she could tolerate at a time before she needed a breather.

She didn't realize he was keeping track of her as much as he was. She thought he was just walking and she was to keep up, period. But he was constantly analyzing her condition.

He was used to keeping track of several clients at the same time so just one was a piece of cake. This gave him more time to enjoy the wonders and beauty of the land. Something he hadn't done as much before due to his need to herd and manage his whining clients and their constantly recurring needs.

So far Ms. Hall had shown more stamina and spirit than anyone before.

He could see how out of shape she was, but that came with the territory at first. She would get in better condition as the days progressed. The thing he admired most about her was that she had yet to call for a break or water or anything. She was proving to be a force of nature, one tough lady inside.

He had deliberately pushed her farther than usual just to get a reading of her character and see whether she would be a sniveler or show some backbone. She passed the backbone test.

He called for her to stop and take a rest. She spotted a nice big rock and just fell back against it as she sat down and let the pack shoulder harness fall away.

She said, "now that is the best backrest I have ever had."

After a few minutes, she grabbed for the water and drank large and satisfying gulps of water.

Joe said better slow down a bit on that. You have to make it last until we get to the next location. Everything you are carrying to eat and drink has to get you to the next camp. You can eat a snack bar right now that will give you more energy for the climb

coming up. She looked at him, "climb," she asked questioningly?

"Sure, Joe said casually, you didn't think this was just a long winding trail, did you? We are just getting into the woods here, but later, the terrain will get more rugged and steeper. This is nature in all its majesty. There are no elevators out here. We take the old-fashioned proverbial stairs here, one foot at a time up to Heaven, though some would say it is Hell getting there. Breaks over, let's go."

Barbara groaned as she slowly got up. Then putting on her backpack she started after Joe who had already begun to walk.

This was going to be a long hard venture and she was already privately wondering if she was really as dedicated in her attempt as she thought herself to be.

She had to set her mind to accept that hunger was going to be her most devoted companion and constant enemy, and that she must overcome the need to want food. She had to stop fantasizing about large meals, heaping piles of fries, cakes, cookies, pies, ice cream. Yes, two seconds and I already went through ten thousand calories in my head. She thought, this was going just great. The day wore on. Ms. Hall was showing signs of exhaustion. Since she was his only client, he could show a little more leniency.

He said, "okay it is going to be sundown shortly and we need to set up a campsite. I don't know if you have any experience in that department so we will end the day a little early to get you educated on the proper method of campsite building. There isn't much to it other than the basics. Firepit, tent, food preparation, and toilet facilities."

Joe guided Ms. Hall through all the things that make up a campsite. Finally settling in, they heated the evening meal. Ms. Hall had looked at the cooking food as if it were the most important thing in her life. To her at that moment, it probably was. But after it was ready and all had been consumed, she still felt the need for more.

In her prior life, as she calls the time before the trek started, this meal was just the appetizer, the soup before the meal. Now it was the whole meal.

Barbara was bone tired and it had only been a short day. Maybe, even just half a day, as they had just started on the trail at noon. She was dreading the coming morning and a whole day of hiking.

But there was also the underlying thrill of finally taking charge of her life, and committing herself to change the vicious cycle of self-destruction she had been on. Food had been her crutch, her safe place, her excuse to hide from the world. But it was also the cause of her sorrow, her health problems, and her loneliness. It was that loneliness that eventually drove her to this point. The lack of any companionship in a meaningful way by someone she could love.

Her weight was always a big problem in that regard. No one wanted to be stuck with, much less be around, an overweight woman unless they did it to get close to her money. So many phony men, all seeking her affection only to get close to her simply for her money.

She finally stopped trying to find the love she so desperately needed in her life and so reinforced the problem with more eating and getting even more overweight. A vicious cycle.

Just before going to her tent to sleep, something she needed badly, she had a request of Joe.

"Mr. Manning, if we are to be together for three long months could you possibly call me by my first name? It is just the two of us here and the formality seems a bit silly in this situation."

Joe had wondered if she would get around to asking him that. Being outdoors, roaming through nature was not very harmonious with proper protocols. This was as relaxed an environment as one could imagine.

Joe said, "only if you call me Joe. I have never been able to appreciate a formal atmosphere, I am more of a kickback, and drink a beer, kind of person."

Barbara said, "I would like that."

They both looked into each-others-eyes for a little too long. It became uncomfortable, and Barbara broke the spell by looking away and said "goodnight, Joe."

Morning came as if by magic. Barbara had no sooner closed her eyes and she began faintly hearing somewhere in the distance Joe calling her name.

She was having a lucid dream with her running through a field of beautiful flowers toward Joe who had his big strong arms outstretched waiting for her to close the space, and be engulfed by him in a passionate embrace and long deep kiss.

Jerking awake now as Joe beat the tent with a stick she yelled out, "okay already I'm awake, give me a minute."

She lay there for a few seconds and wondered why she had dreamed such a wild and crazy dream.

Getting dressed was unusually hard this morning; she was really feeling yesterday's activities now. She could smell the food cooking and that spurred her into action. She came crawling out of the tent and saw Joe squatting at the campfire holding a frying pan.

"Well, well, he said as he looked over at Barbara. Look who finally decided to get up."

Joe had let her sleep in an extra hour. He decided last night that as she was the only client, he could take a softer approach to the intense body-building and weight-loss regimen he usually followed. Focusing more on the quality of the trip than the quantity of the march. He didn't want to drive her to quit right from the start. So, it took a couple of days longer to finish, that was no big deal.

This softer approach would give her more time to get in better shape without the pure misery and venomous behaviors he usually received from his prior clients. This is not to say it will be easy, far from it, but it will be more in line with making it a doable and enjoyable experience for both of them.

Barbara came over to the fire and looked greedily at the meager meal Joe had put into the pan.

Barbara asked him upon seeing such a small portion of food, "is that all we both are going to eat. That looks very small."

He laughed. "No, Joe said, this is all for you. I have already eaten my breakfast. Remember, this is your trek. I am just the guide and as such, must maintain my caloric intake in a normal fashion. You're the one on the diet, not me. So, I thought it would be better if you did not watch me eat.

"As a group, which I usually have had, you all would be sharing the same meals so it would not be a problem. But watching me eat would be a psychological nightmare. You would feel I am deliberately starving you. That is far from the truth. I am furnishing you with strictly the right number of calories for you to keep going and still lose the weight that you signed up for. It comes from a long-used tried and proven formula. So just get used to it. This is your life for three months."

He handed her the pan and she began to eat, even though it was still a little too hot.

Soon after a short lesson from Joe on how to break camp and secure the packs for the day's travel, the two set off once again. A routine that would soon become second nature to Barbara as it was already for Joe.

As the first week on the trail was winding down, Barbara was still struggling but yet determined. That was a good sign she was not a quitter. He knew the resupply was at the next campsite for the following week and also a tent shower. Something they both needed very badly. They could finally wash away a week of sweat and dirt.

But the shower was more than that. It was a way to refresh yourself. Nothing out here was more invigorating than to feel the cool water, soap and shampoo wash away all the grit, grime, and smell. It also refreshed your soul. You feel like a new person, in a new skin. And then to sleep that night with a filling once a week treat, a meal of actual real food in your stomach was heaven.

Joe also had a new set of clothes that would better fit Barbara. This helped her feel like progress was being made and she didn't have to waste precious sleep time washing clothes in the river and streams they came upon. She learned to use water purification tablets when she drank more than she needed and had to find other sources of water.

Joe already knew she would need to do that. It was all part of his teaching the client to be self-aware and independent, as well as self-sufficient. If something should happen out here, she needed to be able to survive on her own.

So, along the way, he taught her how to fish, which when caught were used for evening meals, also what plants and what parts of the plants were edible.

Just as expected when they arrived at the campsite her whole outlook brightened. She was finally through her first week. An impossible task if not for Joe. He seemed to know just when to slack off and when to push harder. He made her trek more into a vacation than a forced march. He made it fun and exciting.

She looked at all the new gear, food, and clothes. Then spied the shower tent. Barbara looked at Joe and asked, "What is that?"

He grinned and said, "that is a shower. It is a once-a-week treat along with a great meal as a reward for good behavior and accomplishment.

"You stuck to the program without so much as a little whining. That is a first to see for me. Most everyone complains about something sooner or later. You sucked it up and were a real trooper, as hardcore as they come."

Joe knew he was spreading it pretty thick, but she was soaking up the praise, and it made her feel good about herself even more. She did find moments she wanted to scream "enough already," but she had kept it to herself. So yes, she did feel better about herself for that achievement. And, since this was the reward, that seemed to help make it all easier to suffer through.

Joe knew how important giving encouragement was to people or they would lose the motivation to continue.

***

Joe let Barbara use the shower first. He had gone to the stream and collected the water, filling the tank twice. She must have been a really dirty girl or was just enjoying the shower a lot.

He had to do with just one fill of the tank because he was not about to ask her for a refill for himself, even though the water was so nice and refreshing.

The meal consisted of a bowl of vegetable soup, followed by salmon and a fresh salad served with vinegar and garlic chunks in oil. Desert was a sugar-free apple pie with cinnamon sprinkled on top.

Barbara was in heaven. It was the first time in a week she could partake of the luxuries of her home life again.

The pair were starting to get to know each other better as the days progressed. They had little in common because of the differences between the worlds in which they dwelled, but they still found interests between them.

Joe was fascinated at how many places around the world Barbara had been and the wonders she had seen and experienced. He would listen to her describe the many events and functions and tours she had enjoyed. He had always wanted to see the world, that was half the reason he joined the service. They promised exotic locations, get to see the world for free. Well, all he ever saw were war zones and death, so, hearing her describe all the things he only dreamed of was exciting.

Barbara was learning about a world she had never considered before as she went along the trail. She had traveled the world and yet had never thought about the land around her, just the attractions. How was that even possible to miss? There was so much to learn between them.

As they walked through the woods Joe would tell Barbara about all the wonders nature provided. The animals all living harmoniously, though sometimes cruelly for the victims of predators like bears and wolves and such.

But it was all part of the bigger plan of nature controlling resources and coexisting. Trees and plants supplying food, shelter, and nourishment for birds, squirrels, rabbits, and insects. Everything working and sharing in a natural state of harmony.

Aside from political views, most people are pretty much alike. They all want to find happiness, to enjoy life in some small way, however, they can. Maybe leave some legacy from which others could remember them. But most people want to find love. It is the most sought after, the most obsessive force of the human endeavor.

Even when people are not actively seeking love, sometimes nature takes a hand and with ever so subtle hints, lends a push and pull to get people closer, even when they are unaware. Like Joe helping get Barbara's pack on and properly adjusted. Or when she slips on wet ground and Joe catches her just in time. Simple little things, but they add up over time, and these two had a lot of time remaining together.

It seems this pair is falling into that situation. Without knowing it, they are getting to like each other more than the situation requires. No outside promises are needed to be kept; no other people are contesting for their affections. It is a clear field for both, so why should it be a surprise to think love could not happen.

Sub Chapter: 3

Watch Where You Step

It had been nearly two months and two weeks since Barbara and Joe had started the trek. They had enjoyed almost every moment of the journey.

Almost, because there had been a couple of times it was pretty scary. The bear is one that comes to mind. Oh, sure there had been more than one bear but most of the time they ran off with a little coxing from Joe and his banging pans. Not very musical but effective to scare off bears.

But this one bear had come into camp in the middle of the night. He was not bashful at all, he was hungry. Usually, these bears were products of campers and hikers feeding them, and so the bears would lose their natural fear of people.

Well, this one was just loving how cozy Barbara's tent was, nice and roomy inside. Always room for one more, right? Imagine how surprised Barbara was when she awoke and felt something rubbing up against her. She panicked, thinking it was Joe not being able to control himself any longer.

She did not know what to do. Was she going to allow him to do it? She was still in the process of figuring that quandary out when the bear grunted then growled. In an instant, her uncertainty of Joe and his manliness was replaced with the fear of being eaten by a bear. She screamed.

That scared the bear. That also freaked out Joe who instantly jumped out of the tent and stumbled around looking for the bear spray. He had let his guard down. He usually kept the spray close at hand just in case something like this happened. Now he could not remember where he had left the spray. He started to yell and hoped between the two of them yelling the bear would take the hint and leave. It worked, but not before the bear tore up Barbara's tent in his attempt to retreat. It is amazing how fragile a tent is to a bear. He had tried to run through the back wall and only succeeded in pulling the tent and Barbara along with him until the tent finally split and the bear disappeared into the night, leaving Barbara in a blind panic and hysterical mood.

Joe had no choice now but to hold her for the rest of the night, or no one was going to get a wink of sleep.

Barbara woke first and felt Joe's arm over her snuggling his body up close and personal. She didn't seem to have a problem with it. It was pleasing and comforting to be held by him. She lay there wondering about how he felt about her. She knew she was starting to look at him more closely in a new personal and affectionate way. He was a very handsome well-built man. He turned her on from the moment they first met, but back then she knew he was not interested in her, the way she looked, and she was just a client.

But the weeks they had been together changed how she hoped he looked at her. He seemed to show her every kindness he could. Was that him just doing his job or was he starting to like her also. He had always been the perfect gentleman. She never once had a fear of him, nor did he give her any cause to be. He was true to his word about leaving her alone in that way. In a way, she was sad about that and yet happy too. She was so mixed up right now.

In a way, she was glad the bear came into the camp. It had scared her to death but it brought about this moment. She would savor this memory for a long time.

She felt when Joe finally awoke and finding his arm over Barbara left it there. She now knew he was thinking along the same lines she was. He was enjoying her closeness.

"Good morning," he whispered softly into her ear.

Barbara feeling unusually brave turned around and said, "thank you for saving me last night," and kissed Joe softly on the lips. He kissed her back. She felt a surge of passion well up inside her and she immediately sat up and said, "come on, it's getting late and we need to hit the trail."

Joe just laughed and left the tent to prepare breakfast. Both knew what had just happened. Everything was changed; it was the beginning of romance 101.

Another hard knock with bad luck on the trail was when the two had come up on a high cliff. The trail was skinnier than Joe had remembered it being. Then he saw it had collapsed at some time earlier. He did not like the way it looked and decided to go another longer way for safety. Barbara asked how much time that would take and Joe said a couple of days. Barbara said, "why don't we just try it. It looks safe enough."

Joe said, "Looks can be deceiving on something like this."

But Barbara was impatient in her naivety of such things and goading and hounding Joe into a big mistake. He knew the ground was dangerous but was swayed by her charms. He finally relented.

He first tossed the backpacks over to the other side to help with less weight across the edge.

Then he decided to tie a rope harness around each other just in case and he lassoed a huge rock on the other side of the fallen path. Barbara went first and Joe followed.

It was starting to look like Barbara was right, but as they had gotten only about half the distance across, the ground just gave way. That left Barbara and Joe falling and swinging over to the rock holding them, and preventing them from falling any farther.

They were now dangling from a rope a good fifteen feet below the rock. Barbara was screaming and freaking out. She was in front of Joe on the rope. Joe yelled for her to stop thrashing around and calm down. She was tied to the rope and was not going to fall. That seemed to help her panic.

She asked in a gasp, "what are we going to do?"

He thought for a minute and said, "I am going to climb up to you and as I pass, you climb on my back and wrap your arms around my neck. I will pull us both up."

She asked incredulously, "you can do that?"

He didn't know for sure but they had no choice at the moment.

He just said, "Sure I do this all the time," trying to reassure her and get her on board with what must be done.

One thing was for sure, the longer he hung there the more tired he would become. He was glad he worked out a lot, it would sure come in handy right about now.

He was also glad it was near the end of Barbara's trek and she had lost most of her weight now. That meant they had a chance. He started pulling himself up hand over hand locking his feet onto the rope below him. That way he could kind of jack-knife his way up. He had a bit of trouble climbing over Barbara Now came the hard part. She grabbed his neck for dear life so now he only had his arms to pull them up.

It seemed to take forever but he finally got over the edge and Barbara grabbing the rope, pulled herself up onto the safer ground. As soon as he got himself up and safely on solid ground, he collapsed. He didn't think he could have made another foot. Never again, he promised himself, will I bypass safety rules or common sense.

When they both decided it was time to continue Joe noticed he had somehow lost his satellite phone, probably when they fell and getting Barbara on his back. She might have knocked it from his back pocket then.

He only needed it for emergencies but since the trip had been fine for the most part, he hadn't used it except to call his coordinator once in a great while to keep him up to date on their progress and to set up the next rendezvous points. Joe didn't have too much worry over losing the phone. He figured they were pretty close to the end anyway.

And if things got too worrisome, he was sure his buddy and business partner would send out a search party.

Wouldn't that be embarrassing, Joe thought.

The pair had made it to just under three weeks of the end and thought the rest of the way was a piece of cake to hike. Barbara was in great physical condition now. She was even keeping up with Joe at his faster pace. He would try and get her blood flowing faster by speeding up and she was matching him every step of the way, and not even breathing hard.

Joe had impressed upon her to never let your guard down, ever. He had learned that rule the hard way overseas in the service. You never know what you might step on. He knew the trail and all its mishaps. What he saw now was no trail mishap. This was a big problem.

This was a booby trap.

He threw his arm out and stopped Barbara from stepping in it. She looked at his face and asked, "what is the problem?"

He said, "do you see that pile of leaves right in front of you?"

She looked down and said, "yes, what about them?"

He said, "stand back a few steps please."

He grabbed a big branch and stuck it into the center of the leaves.

Suddenly the ground erupted and the branch went flying toward a tree close by.

Joe said, "if you had stepped into that bunch of leaves that would be you hanging upside down from the tree right now."

Barbara said, "what is going on here? Why would someone set up something like that? Is that supposed to catch an animal for some hunter? Is this some kind of sick joke?"

Joe was looking hard all around while she was talking.

"No, on all counts, Joe stated flatly. That trap is designed for only one animal, a human. We are not alone out here. Someone wants to capture us and he or they could be watching us right now.

"So, let's get going before they decide to move in. We might be able to see or hear them coming if we're moving. Keep your head on a swivel, always moving around. Look everywhere all the time.

"Don't forget to watch where you're stepping. If you see or feel anything is out of place stop and let me know, let's go."

Joe was instantly transformed into his old mindset. It was like he had never left his special forces unit. All the instincts and life-saving training just reappeared into his memories, his whole being.

He was now point man on patrol and he had always been damn good at war and survival. He had left many enemies dead in his past that had tried to end his life. He was still standing. His platoon called him a natural. Everyone wanted to be next to him. The chances of surviving went way up when close to Joe.

This was not going to work, Joe thought, just trudging along with no security, no gun for defense, open to any attack. I need to take it to the enemy on my terms. Joe decided to set up camp early and recon the area. He tried to make it look like they were just doing the usual things they always did. He did not let Barbara in on anything. He wanted to get her to act naturally, and to do that, she had to be kept in the dark so all would seem routine in nature.

Barbara and Joe ate their meal while talking and joking as if nothing had occurred. But just before nightfall Joe told her his plan of action.

"We can't just wait around for this guy or guys to come at us again. They tried the easy way already, that did not work, so, the next try will be a much greater assault. I need you to hold on to your knife inside your tent and wait. I am taking it to them. We stand a better chance by doing that.

I think they did not simply come for us because they were unsure if I was armed or not, but they will definitely come tonight.

Thinking about his next course of action, Joe decided on a plan and informed Barbara.

"First, I am climbing that tree to see if I can spot any movement, maybe get a location of the campsite. Then go from there. I will have to figure it out as I go."

Barbara said, "this is so crazy, why is someone doing this?"

Joe said, " On my last phone call, my partner had told me about the police warning everyone of a possible gang robbing Hikers, that may be all there is to it. But I am beginning to wonder about that. I didn't tell you because "I didn't want to upset you. There was nothing we could do about it out here anyway.

"Have you ever heard of a false flag operation?"

Barbara said, "no."

Joe continued. "Well, it is a fake mission designed to draw attention away from the real mission, whatever that may be. Like, if you want one group to get the blame for something someone else is doing. You make it look like the ones doing it, are actually a whole other group, so they get the blame, not you."

Barbara said, "okay I get the concept. But why this situation? How could that possibly be relatable to our dilemma."

Joe asked Barbara. "Is there anyone that stands to gain from your death?"

That threw Barbara a curveball she was not expecting.

"Wait a minute, you're thinking this might all be about me, she asked?"

"Right now, it is all just a feeling I am getting. I have heard of thieves robbing hikers before but they don't usually stick around to rob over and over, and that trap was not set by any robber. They would just pop out on you and at gunpoint take your goodies. That was set by a professional. He knew our exact route and probable path in order to get the trap in just the right spot. It would have worked too, except for my past experience."

Barbara looked at him in a different light now. Here was someone she thought she knew and now she finds there is a whole side of him of which she was completely unaware.

"So, are you telling me the man I thought I knew is more than he pretends, Barbara asked?"

Joe calmly replied, "I was not trying to hide anything from you. It is just I don't like to talk about my time in the service. It is not something that makes for good dinner conversation. It is not a thing you want to remember.

"It is one of the main reasons I chose this job. It gets me out into nature where peace and tranquility abound; a place where the bad memories become fewer, a place to calm and recover my soul."

Barbara was seeing a completely different man now. He was not only a guide, he was a soldier, a patriot. And, he had, no doubt, been through more horrors than Barbara could imagine.

Now he was her hero, ready to risk his life to keep her safe from harm. She was the probable cause of forcing him back into the fight. And, he looked ready and willing, which meant a lot to her.

She didn't say anything, what was there to say. She simply came over, sat down next to him, and hugged him closely, they both embraced each other for a long time.

Joe, finally seeing it was near dark, started to climb the tree. He went as far up as he could go and began scanning the area. He saw a faint glow from a fire about a half-mile away downwind. These guys knew their stuff. The light from the fire had been masked by a barrier of rock but the glow from it could be seen as it brightened the surrounding area. Now he knew their location, it was time for action.

He went back down and decided on a different course of action for Barbara. He had her pack a smaller carry backpack with food and water items and her sleeping bag. She had her knife for protection and other needs she could use it for.

He decided that she should not stay in the tent. That would be game over if they came and she was alone. He had her go to a rise about fifty yards away from where she could watch the camp. If they came, she was to use the compass and map to get to the next drop point where she could wait with the supplies for Joe.

If after a day and he was not back, find your way out. Joe told her she had all the skills she needed now to make it on her own if necessary. Don't wait on him, he stressed that point.

Joe gripped Barbara by the arms and said," don't worry, we will make it out of this, just do your part if needed, I will handle the rest." Maybe I am completely wrong about this, that would be great.

"Just one thing Joe asked, you never said who would gain from your passing?"

Jill said, "I only have one relative with the ability to inherit from me, my cousin William Hall, he manages my affairs. Dad left me everything and his brother never did make it very big so my cousin did not inherit much. I gave him a job as my business manager to help him out. I can't see him as the one behind all this."

"I will say though, as Barbara was now remembering more past encounters, he has been very disagreeable lately. I think he might be a little jealous of me getting everything. He wanted me to give him a share of the businesses so it would be fair.

"I told him that was not going to happen. He had no claim to my fathers' fortune in the slightest. I told him If he wants money, earn it, as my father did. He was so mad.

"Now that you made me think about it, he just might be capable of such a thing. He is a rather mean man. He has been divorced twice for abusing his wives. I only helped him because he was family. I can see now that might have been a big mistake."

Joe said, "I see red flags all over what you just said. This journey for self-help, with you being gone for so long, must have allowed him time to think and decide a course of action. I think I know what that action will be. Maybe, now that we know the why, let's see if we can stop the how."

Sub Chapter: 4

The Chase Is On

Joe made his way through the woods as silent as a cat. Never making even a twig break. As he neared the camp he slowed to a stop and watched and listened for any sounds. He could hear a few voices and decided he could pick out at least four.

Did they have any guards posted around the area? He moved on his stomach while circling the camp and found no guards. He assumed they were not worried about him or Barbara.

They figured they could catch up and do what needed to be done with no problems. They must have known Joe was not armed by now, and the girl was no threat in the least.

As he came closer, he could finally hear the conversation going on.

"I'm telling you, one guy blurted out, we should get more money for doing all of this. What he is paying is chicken feed. This is some serious stuff we're planning." Another guy seconded the motion.

The obvious ring leader said, "I know he thinks he is only paying us that small amount but I have an idea. We do the kidnapping as he wants. But instead of killing them after the ransom is paid as we agreed, I think we should then keep the woman alive until he pays us to do her, that way we get a lot more. After all, this is two jobs, right? The kidnapping and then the hit." All of them agreed that was a better plan.

Joe had it all now except the who. He pretty much knew who that was, but his name had not been spoken yet.

The leader spoke again. "Okay, morning comes early so let's get some sleep. We will take them before they get up in the morning while they are still asleep."

Joe had heard enough and was starting to turn and head back to give Barbara a heads up on what was happening. All of a sudden, he was getting this horrible shock in his back. He started convulsing and jerking uncontrollably.

He was making audible noises that alerted the group in the camp and they came running, guns were drawn. After what seemed like an eternity the shocking stopped and he lay still. The group had him covered and he couldn't have fought back even if he wanted to. They tied him up with plastic ties and carried him back to camp where they tossed him unceremoniously near the fire.

One guy was holding a police stun gun. He said, "that was easier than I thought it would be. I got lucky. Joe here just crawled right under me in the tree I was in, he couldn't have made it any easier without shooting himself."

They all laughed.

Joe was furious with himself. He was out of practice. He didn't even think to look up. It was just too obvious. He had to give this guy the winning round, he just didn't think these guys were that expert out here in the forest. He had a suspicion that this guy was no ordinary thug like the others.

"So, let's kill him and go collect the broad one guy piped in. We can get the first part of the plan done and sleep in."

"That is not such a bad idea the guy from the tree offered. But keep him alive, pointing at Joe, until we get back just in case.

"I have a feeling this is not going to be as easy as you might think. This guy Joe here is no slouch. I don't have all night to ask him what we are going to find when we get to his camp so let him alone until we return. If we have the girl no big deal. But, he emphasized, if we come back empty-handed, I want him around to explain things."

Joe looked at him and said, "you seem to know my name, what is yours?"

The guy looked at Joe with a very sinister stare and said, "if I told you I would have to kill you, maybe I'll tell you later," and laughed.

Joe not wanting to seem scared said, "okay, Tree Hugger, it is."

That made a couple of the others giggle until Tree Hugger stared at them with his piercing eyes. They dropped their gaze and went to get the equipment they might need to round up Barbara.

Soon they were ready and Joe had been securely tied with plastic police ties, hands, and feet. They left one guy there to guard Joe.

Tree Hugger walked over and said, "for your sake, we better come back with her, or I promise your last night on this earth will very, very, painful."

"Well, good luck then," Joe said.

Tree Hugger grinned and said, "under better circumstances, I think I could like you, but alas all is not well." He moved down the trail into the dark woods and was gone, followed by the three other men.

Now it was time to make his move. They had made a fatal mistake. They had put his hands in front instead of behind his back.

Ordinarily, he could break that with a downward thrust by forcing the plastic to stretch and snap but they had put three plastic ties on him. So, he had to rely on his belt.

They had checked him for weapons but left his belt. He had a nylon belt but the buckle had a built-in knife blade. It was a cool device. All you had to do was pull the blade from the buckle and you had a knife.

The only problem was the dingleberry across the fire pit was watching him like a hawk. He needed to get him to look away for a few seconds so he could loosen the belt and extract the knife.

"Hey fella, I need to pee," Joe said.

"Life is tough all over," the goon said.

"Ah come on, I need to go really bad," Joe said as he continued his ruse.

"Piss yourself for all I care," the hoodlum responded.

Joe saw this was not going well so he changed tactics.

"Look, I don't think Tree Hugger is going to like me all pissed on and stinking if he is going to torture me for a while, do you?"

That hit a nerve. He thought about it and how he would look for not taking care of such a simple thing. He wanted no trouble from that guy, that is for sure.

He said, "okay you can stand up and pee against that tree over there. But if you so much as sneeze I will drop you right then and there, got it?" Joe said, "sure, I get it. I just need to pee, and thanks. It would be just too embarrassing to pee myself in front of someone."

"Shut up and get going, just remember what I said," the thug said.

Joe picked himself up and hopped over to the tree and leaned into it with his forehead. He took his belt loose and got the knife out of the buckle. He unzipped his fly and pissed. He really did need to go after all. All the while he was peeing, he was cutting through the plastic ties. Since his back was to the guard, he was not seen doing the cutting. The guard was standing behind him and right in line with the fire right behind him.

Joe said, "oh man, that felt good."

And as he zipped up, he quickly threw himself backward and down to the ground. The guy shot at the air where Joe was supposed to be a split second before and Joe continued through the backward rolling motion with a two-footed kick into the guys' crotch which did lots of painful things as well as forcing the man backward as he fell into the fire.

He started screaming and thrashing around as he rolled himself out of the fire. Joe kept following up his rolling motion and was at hand to beat the guy in the head with a campfire rock. It was quick and done.

Not wasting a second Joe cut his feet ties. He wanted to be free just in case any other surprises were around, none happened. He got the guy's pistol and checked for more ammo. He found a couple of clips, free is always a good deal. He was glad to see it was a forty-five, lots of stopping power. He also looked through the tent for any more goodies and found a pair of night-vision goggles. Very nice he thought. He also found a Bowie knife which he put on his belt.

These guys were very accommodating he thought. He also grabbed a canteen and some food supplies and put them in a sleeping bag which he secured with a small backpack. This was just in case he had a longer trek than he planned.

"Boy scout motto, be prepared," he said, that was Joe's favorite saying.

He checked the gangster and found he was dead.

"Oh well, play with fire and get burned, he whispered. This one had it coming and it was self-defense after all. He did try to kill me," Joe confessed to himself. He started back to his camp as fast as he could. He figured the goons would have just gotten there and would be searching for Barbara. He could only hope she would stick to the plan and run upon seeing the men in camp.

***

Back at camp, Barbara was getting anxious. She was worried about how long Joe had been gone. She almost broke the agreement she had made to sit tight and wait until Joe came back when she saw the movement below. Jumping up, she was ready to run back to camp thinking it was Joe when she saw there was more than one person, maybe a lot more.

The light was not the best but she could see moving shadows, then she heard voices and yells. Flashlights were turned on and they scanned all around. She ducked as some of the light came up to where she was. Had they seen her? She was scared to death now.

What had happened to Joe? Did these men hurt him, or worse? She knew that she should quietly leave as Joe had instructed her to do but she didn't want to abandon him.

What if he needed her and she just left him to die? Could she live with herself after that? But, what could she do alone, and against all those men? Her mind was in turmoil. Then she heard a sound coming from the side. Had they found her already? Was this to be her end?

She took out the knife she had and braced herself to do what must be done to at least take one of them with her if possible. She heard a low whisper, "Barbara are you there? It's Joe."

She said, "Joe, is that truly you?"

She heard him say, "yes it's me, I'm coming in, please don't stab me."

Then he was there. She dropped the knife and hugged him with all her might. He said, "okay, okay. Let me breathe a little will you! Man, you're getting strong."

She was so happy and relieved to see him and find he was no worse off than when he left.

She asked, "what happened out there?" Are they really, bad guys? Are they kidnappers? Tell me something!

Joe said, "whoa, there. Give me a second, will you?" "First yes they are kidnappers but I can only assume it was your cousin as they never said the name of their boss." Barbara exclaimed, "you talked to them and they told you they were kidnappers? How did that happen?"

Joe said, "hold on and let me finish, will you?

"I snuck into their camp and listened in on their conversation."

She said," oh my, wasn't that dangerous?"

Joe said, "well yes, as it turned out, it was dangerous. "I got captured."

Barbara freaked out asking, "you did? How did you get loose?"

Joe said, "all this is a long story and we don't have the time right now to talk about it. We have to move now. We have been here too long as it is, come on."

Joe handed her the knife she had dropped and both slipped into the night.

Joe had looked at the camp and saw the men were still looking around so now was a good time to beat feet out of there before they expanded the search. He knew Tree Hugger was going to be very disappointed when he got back to camp. He was the type to take this very personally, and Joe knew this was not going to be over until it was settled between them. This was not Joe's first rodeo.

***

From below, the man known as Tree Hugger was standing and looking at the ridge. Yes, that would be where I would go, he thought. A clear view of the camp from a long distance. It would be a nice head start when she found out they were there. Joe obviously had a well-planned escape for her.

Well, she could wait, tracking her should be no problem in the morning. I have unfinished business with Joe back at camp. I almost wish he would escape so I could see which of us is the best. I could envision a good competition between us. I love the challenge of battle, and I have never lost. Could he be the one to finally beat me, I wonder!

It was the first time the man had ever doubted himself and his abilities. This Joe character somehow had gotten under his skin. Maybe it would be better to just kill him after he had his little chat.

Sub Chapter: 5

Who Will Make It?

Yes, the race was on. Though the competitors were not evenly matched in numbers and equipment. But then again, Joe was not your ordinary scared rabbit running from the wolves. He was a highly trained soldier who had seen and participated in many battles. He had come face to face with many enemies, infiltrated into and through their ranks, unseen, and walked away alive. One more point; this was Joe's home turf, he knew it well, the forest and land are his friends.

So, if the men now tracking Joe knew what Tree Hugger had guessed, they might quit now and accept their losses.

Back at the campsite Tree Hugger stood grinning as all the other men cursed and promised retaliation and revenge, in a more colorful language of course. They had seen what Joe had left them. A dead guard and no Joe to interrogate. Tree Hugger saw the evidence from the fight. Yes, this guy was good. Securely tied up with an armed guard watching him like a hawk and he still gets away.

He also saw that Joe was now armed and a night vision binocular and knife were missing. So, his adversary was as well-equipped as himself.

He could only assume Joe had no phone, which surprised him being out here in the wilderness and all. Maybe something had happened to it. That would explain why Joe hadn't called for help yet. He certainly had plenty of time to do so.

That meant Tree Hugger was the only one with a satellite phone so he had one advantage. He could call in reinforcements if he had a need, just in case he could not catch them before they reached civilization. He could not allow them to do that.

Being honest with himself, he was not at all comfortable knowing Joe had an equal advantage, but fair is fair. "You claim you're the best, well now it is time to prove it," he uttered to himself.

Joe had called a halt for the night to get at least a couple of hours of sleep. He knew Barbara could not keep up the same pace as he could. And, being too tired reduces the mind and body to less than 100 percent. This situation is critical and requires focus and heightened senses, this is no time for mistakes.

He had taught himself to sleep anywhere and anytime because in a wartime situation you get to sleep when you can, not when you want. So, he could continue the mission day and night with just a couple of hours of sleep every five or six hours.

Joe knew he had to keep moving as fast as possible because the bad guys were hot on their heels and very pissed off. There were too many men at one time for Joe to handle together, especially with Tree Hugger along. Joe was sure he was probably as good as himself. He was utterly outgunned and outmanned. That meant he had to even the odds a bit more.

He had a trick or two of his own to play.

He reached a cliff edge and saw just what he was looking for. He told Barbara to continue on and he would catch up in a little while. She asked him why he was staying back and Joe just said, "I got a surprise for the guys."

She looked at him but did as he asked and kept going on the trail.

Joe got to work.

***

The guys coming had set a quick march pace to try and catch up with Joe and Barbara. They weren't expecting anything to happen to them. They figured it was a race to get to civilization and the sooner they caught up the better. They knew Barbara was the weak link and she would slow Joe down. That was true, but Joe had plans to also slow the bad guys down.

As the goons were rounding a corner at the cliff edge of a deep canyon, the lead man tripped a vine trap. The vine had been connected to a tree branch that had been pulled far back and latched to the trip vine to prevent it from swinging to its original natural position. When the man released the latch pin, the branch swung violently out toward the cliff edge which just happened to have the men walking by.

The branch hit two of the men hard and knocked them off the trail and into the valley below. Their screams could be heard all the way down.

Tree Hugger was impressed. As he listened to the last man besides himself yelling obscenities, and further promises of retaliation and revenge he was looking at the trap. It was a basic and simple trap, well placed, and deliberate. Joe knew his craft.

For the first time in his life, he felt a little fear. He knew he was in Joe's home court. Joe had every advantage of surprise now, and Tree Hugger only had one more man between him and Joe, and Joe was armed. The odds had just flipped.

Tree Hugger decided he did not like how this was going. He pulled out his phone and called a number. After a short conversation, he hung up. Help would be coming and the odds just flipped again, in Tree Huggers' favor.

So, he was clearly cheating he thought, with no guilt about it and accepting his decision easily, in this game, he reassured himself, the winner makes his own rules.

***

Joe did not wait to see the ending to his little surprise. He already knew he would probably get at least one and if they bunched up on the corner as he hoped, he might have gotten more.

That was wishful thinking he said to himself. He knew Tree Hugger was too smart to lead them from the front and take a chance of getting himself caught in one of Joe's inevitable traps. He would hang back and let the chips, or in this case, men, fall as they might.

Most men who fight have a code of honor in battle. It is vicious while in combat but honorable, there was respect between them. Joe did not see Tree Hugger as holding to any code but his own. That made him very dangerous, but predictable. You can expect those kinds of men to play dirty and without mercy at all times.

So, Joe simply thought about what he would do if he was without any honor and the only thing that mattered was winning and he could see into the mind of Tree Hugger.

Joe knew the men had to stop them from getting home. The game would be over then if that happened. So as of now, he figured they had only one alternative, put another group in front of Joe and Barbara to intercept and block them.

Joe figured that up ahead somewhere they would run into another larger group, a final show of force.

***

The helicopter hovered as four men loaded with equipment slid down the rope. Once on the ground the helicopter took off and circled the area looking for Joe and Barbara. Barbara and Joe watched from a quarter mile away as the men disembarked from the helicopter.

Joe said, "Dammit, we were so close to being on the other side of them. We could have made it easily but not now. We are boxed in. Four in front, I don't know how many behind, and a chopper in the air."

Joe heard the helicopter coming and told Barbara, "get behind that fallen tree and lay low."

The chopper went by slowly and Joe said, "it's okay for now. But if you hear it again, find something to hide behind. I have got to take that thing down somehow or we're toast." Then he devised an idea, a perfectly crazy idea.

He told Barbara the plan and she said, "you're crazy, that is the stupidest thing I have ever heard. It's suicide. Only a moron would try such a thing."

Joe said, "thanks for the confidence-building pep-talk.

"It is all we have. This has to work or it's over. I have no choices here, just trust me."

Finally, Barbara agreed with the plan. She knew Joe was a super soldier and had a lot of experience in doing crazy things. So, she had to trust in him and help with whatever was needed. It was her life on the line as well.

He told her to go a half-mile to the east and when she heard all the noise she was to run as fast and far as safely possible to the north. The noise will make all the men in front and behind come running to investigate so that should give her the chance to slip by the men in front of them.

Barbara said, "and what about you? Do you think I am going to just run away and leave you to fight all those men alone?"

Joe said, "after I take down the chopper, I will do the same as you and will catch up as fast as I can, I promise."

Joe was not at all that sure he could take the chopper down much less get by a group of men coming for him, but he had to show a good face for Barbara. If she made it out that was all that mattered.

She looked at him and knew he was lying. He was going to sacrifice himself to let her get away.

She reached up and took his face into her hands and kissed him. "You, big lug, come back to me alive," she said pleadingly. Then she hugged him tightly, probably for the last time she believed, as tears welled up in her eyes.

Joe said, "show some faith will you, I am not that easy to kill. Now let go of me, time is running out, you need to get going now," he said, as he pulled her away from him and pushed her toward the direction she needed to go.

Barbara turned once more to face him, smiled, and started off. She knew she had zero abilities to help Joe. She didn't even have a gun.

Joe went to the spot he thought the chopper would pass on the next trip through the area. He had tried to keep track of the grid the chopper was following to cover the area in the search for Joe and Barbara. He set his trap, or diversion as he thought of it, and then climbed the tree he hoped would best fit all the calculations, conditions, and outcomes of his plan.

He heard the chopper coming, he had made it just in time, and apparently, luck was with him, this time. The helicopter was right on course for his plan.

The chopper was flying low for better sight of ground activity, just above the tree line. Joe waited until the chopper was close by. Then he pulled on a string attached to a silver mylar food bag he had rigged on top of the next tree over. It didn't fly but the flash of brightness from the sun glinting from it as it moved around caught the eye of the plot and he immediately turned and came right for it to investigate the anomaly it created in his search.

That put the pilot very close to Joe. Since the pilot was focusing on the mylar bag he did not notice Joe in the next tree over pointing his pistol at him. Taking careful aim, Joe shot at the pilot through the glass. He kept shooting until he saw blood splatters all over the windows and the pilot. He had got him.

There was a problem though, the chopper had started turning around and around as it lost control and dived in the direction of the ground. It was hacking through the trees around Joe as it tore itself apart. Blades were flying away from the chopper, one just missed Joe as it went sailing past his head. That was too close for comfort, he thought.

Then when the chopper hit the ground, it was spinning wildly as it crashed into his tree and shook him loose from his perch by the force of the jolt. He tumbled down through a couple of branches and barely grabbed the third one which stopped his fall.

The chopper had not caught fire as yet so Joe climbed down the rest of the way as fast as he could just in case it did start burning. He did not want to be above it should the wreckage burst into flames.

"No barbecue for Joe please," He muttered. He let himself fall the last ten feet, landing on a pile of soft pine needles, and collapsed on the ground.

He kissed the earth and said, "thank you, thank you, thank you." With no time to rest, Joe ran to the chopper and grabbed a rifle that was lying in the rear compartment. He crawled to the front through the mangled frame and tested the radio, it still worked. He tuned it to the station the rangers used and quickly gave an SOS message.

"Help needed badly at the mountain peak pass. Robbers have us cornered. Come with the calvary."

Joe didn't know if anyone had heard but he couldn't wait around for a response. The helicopter was catching on fire. He quickly got out and grabbed a couple of clips he saw lying around and ran.

He heard yelling from far behind him but he just kept going as fast as he could go. Then he heard the boom of the chopper blowing up. He ran for half a mile and then cut north following the same path Barbara was supposed to go. He just kept running. He wasn't sure anyone was following him but he was taking no chances. He had to catch up to Barbara.

Then just ahead he saw her. She had popped her head up as soon as she recognized him. She ran to him.

"Oh, Joe My sweet darling. You're alive," she cried, as she wrapped her arms around him squeezing the life out of him. I heard the explosion and saw the smoke; I was so worried about you"

Joe, gasping for breath, said, "let go of me, I can't breathe with you hugging so tightly."

She quickly let go and backed away saying, "oh, I'm sorry, that was stupid of me. Here, sit down for a few minutes and rest, you must be exhausted."

Joe said, "keep a watch for anything that moves," and he collapsed on the ground trying to get his breathing back under control.

While he was doing that, he was also evaluating how far they had gone north. Had it been enough to pass the new patrol? He thought he had, but he could not be sure of their location any longer. And so, he reluctantly got up and said, "we have to keep moving."

Tree Hugger had finally reached the burning helicopter. He was amazed at such a feat. And Joe only had a pistol. All the team was there now and waiting for orders.

It spooked them to know their adversary was skilled enough to pull this kind of thing off. Maybe they had watched too many movies but this guy fit the stereotype of the super-soldier on the big screen. They were not keen on finishing this mission. Especially after finding out from that other guy how he had gotten himself free from an armed guard, tied up and all no less, plus how he had got two more of them with the booby trap. It was just uncanny, unnerving, and demoralizing. Tree Hugger had to admit this Joe guy was either crazy, just damned lucky, or very, very good, maybe a combination of all of the above. In any case, he was long gone now, and he had no clue as to which way to start tracking except to continue toward civilization and hope they could catch up.

He figured they must have swung around the side while he and the others were coming to the crash site. That makes the most sense. It would also mean they would have wasted time and distance Tree Hugger was not going to do.

He was heading straight as an arrow to the exit as it were. The last mountain peak trail that must be crossed to get back to civilization. It was a slim trail through a gorge and the only way out. He must get there first or all is lost. And he just hates to lose.

He told everyone. "We are double-timing it to the mountain peak trail. We will get him there. Anyone up for a little payback?"

Every man yelled, "hell yeah," but it just didn't sound like their hearts were in it.

Sub Chapter: 6

Only One Way Out

Joe had tried to beat Tree Hugger to the pass but he saw once again he had just missed getting there in time. Luck was a fickle thing at best.

He watched as he hid just back of the tree line before the pass narrowed into the slim trail through the gorge. He saw men spreading out to find places to hide and wait. Barbara and he were not getting through this way. The only alternative was to climb the sheer face of the mountain. That was not a very enticing option. Not to mention he would have to do it in plain sight of the men hiding. If just once anyone turned to look up, he would be toast, a sitting duck, target practice. That is if he could even get to the cliff.

He studied the face of the cliff for a possible route up. He thought to himself, I can't believe I am even considering this.

Barbara saw him looking at the cliff and said, "I know you're not thinking of doing what I think you're thinking of doing, are you?"

He looked at her and said, "I think I was," and smiled.

Getting serious Joe said, "we have no better alternatives. We can't go back, there's not enough food and water. We can't stay here, they have forever to wait us out, and they can get more supplies. It would be just a matter of time before they found us anyway.

"See that crack going up and across over there? It looks like I could get a good grip and with the jagged rock formation itself, and I think there would be plenty of places to place my feet while I rest my hands."

Barbara said, "and what about all those men. They can see you clearly enough."

Joe said, "I would have to do it after dark."

Barbara gasped, "are you insane?"

Joe said, "well, there have been rumors to that uncertainty lately. The only hope we have is to get behind them. I would have the advantage of surprise when I attack."

Barbara was shocked now, "are you thinking of taking on all these men alone? Even if you could get up the cliff wall, how could you possibly do that?"

Joe said honestly, "with a lot of luck and years of experience in doing just that."

Barbara didn't say anything else. She heard in that one last statement all she needed to know. This was a real man. A real honest to God, Hero. If he thought he was capable of doing the impossible, well maybe he just might be.

He obviously had a lot of experience in doing just this kind of crazy stuff. Didn't he just tell her that very thing? Who was she to beat him down at this point with doubts? He needed to be at the top of his game and he very much needed her support.

"Okay, Barbara said, as if accepting the inevitable, what can I do to help?"

***

Just about ten o'clock and as the moon was high, casting its faint glow upon the cliff, Joe set off toward the cliff. He would have to take out a couple of the guards along the way to get there.

As he crawled along the ground using the high grass and bushes for cover, he finally made it to the first man. He had come up on him from the side. He tossed a small rock over his head so it landed on the other side just a few feet away. The man turned to look toward the sound and Joe quickly closed the distance and grabbing his head in his hands twisted it around to an unnatural position, breaking the man's neck. He dropped without a sound.

Dropping low again Joe crawled to the second man. He would not be sneaking up on this one, he was leaning against the cliff wall. Joe took out his bowie knife and threw it. The man gagged and choked on his own blood as the knife went into his throat. He fell and thrashed around for a few seconds and then died.

Joe had always kept in practice throwing his knife. He did it mainly because, like the game of darts, some guys just liked throwing knives more. It was fun, it took skill, and now it was paying off.

Joe walked over and retrieved his knife, wiping the blood off on the man's jacket. He had a clear path to the cliff now and half crouching he went to the crack in the wall. He wiped his hands on his pants to get any oils off so there would be less slipping. As he got higher, he could see the other men. They had been guarding in place all day and were tired and bored, and best of all they were focusing on the woods. They knew that was where Joe was.

He had come to a gap on the wall where the crack just disappeared. He hadn't seen it from below, but now he saw it was gone. This spot must have broken off at some time in the past. The crack started up and over just a little farther on, but he would have to chance a leap to get there. If he missed or slipped or failed to get a good hand-hold he would be dead. He wasn't getting any rest where he was so he had to just go for it before he got too tired to do it anyway.

He crunched down as far as he could hoping the rock under his feet was solidly placed and leaped. He barely got one hand into the crack on the other side of the gap and he was dangling one-handed until he could stop his swinging and get another hand into the crack. He moved along quickly until he found a foothold on a rock abutment. He was only seconds away from losing his grip because his hands were starting to cramp.

He finally made the top after resting a good five minutes. Before he pulled himself over the edge, he peered around. Sure enough, there was a guy with a scoped rifle laying down and watching the edge of the woods.

Joe knew that he would have been cut down immediately if he had tried coming up the trail. He was a good twenty yards away and the guy was focusing on the front, so Joe slowly climbed up and snaked his way behind the guy. He got up on his feet and crept close enough to jump on him, which he did. As he fell on top of the guy, he slammed his face into the ground as hard as he could. Then before the guy could get his senses working again and yell out, he took his head by the hair and jaw as he had done with the other guy down below and quickly twisted it until the neck snapped.

"Sorry fella, but you backed the wrong team," Joe muttered.

Tree Hugger was getting impatient and bored, so for something to do he decided to leave the campfire and check on the men stationed around the cliff.

He wandered over to one side and saw two guys talking about what they were going to buy with their shares of the ransom money.

He went up to them and said, "Hey, your jobs are to watch for the two people out there, not talk about how you're going to spend the money you haven't gotten or earned yet."

They grumbled but did as he said. One guy said, "I'm going to get a cup of coffee, I need it, and walked off the get himself some."

Tree Hugger walked over to where the other two were supposed to be and saw one had been killed. He immediately lowered his stance and looked quickly around. Seeing nothing he bent over and moved quickly to the other man. He was dead also.

Tree Hugger started thinking. He knew Joe was here somewhere nearby. He wondered why Joe had not fired upon him yet. He was a sitting duck out here.

Then he started thinking why Joe had done this and he looked back at the cliff. Of course, that was just what he would have done, climb the cliff, and get us from behind.

He knew Joe had already made the top because he could not see him on the face of the cliff, and there was no telling how much damage he had done so far. Tree Hugger did not like the idea of trying to chase down Joe in the dark.

But then he had a revelation. Wait a minute, if Joe was here, then the woman was out there in the woods waiting for a signal. He knew what he needed to do now. It would be suicide to take on Joe here and now. It would be much easier to find the woman now, and with no harm to him. Yes, that was a much better plan.

It seems funny how luck just keeps flipping back and forth with him and Joe. It was like destiny was on a collision and only one of them would emerge as the victor.

"They say the bad guy never wins, but I am still here to prove that old adage is false," Tree Hugger boasted to himself.

***

At just that time, back up on the cliff edge, Joe took the night vision binoculars he had strapped to his backside to keep them out of the way during the climb and checked the area on top where he was for other men. Finding none he went along the edge of the cliff until he found a way down to the trail.

Now he was behind them. They were not looking in his direction so he could use that extra advantage. He started coming down the trail and as he reached the lighted area ahead, he saw a guard at the campfire. He was getting a cup of coffee, Joe assumed. He saw no one else around. Where was Tree Hugger? That worried Joe a lot.

As the guard turned and started back to his post, probably out in the opening somewhere, Joe quickly caught up to him before he could make it to the canyon gap opening and reached around to grab his mouth and prevent him from crying out as he shoved his bowie knife into the guys back and into his heart, killing him instantly.

Joe slowly dropped him onto his face and pulled his knife out. Wiping the blade once again as he had done before on the guy's clothes. Joe grabbed the rifle the guy had and checked to see if it was ready to fire and had a full clip.

"Thanks, he said. You fellas sure do know how to make a guy feel welcome. Giving me everything I need, when I need it."

It was time to finish this.

Joe went to the opening to the valley and saw one guy. He could not be crept up on. and Joe did not need to anyway. He was going to shoot him and Barbara was to fire the rifle she had, just to draw any others Joe could not see out so he could take them down as well. It was a good plan, but it did not work as Joe had planned.

Joe, being as fair and honorable a soldier as he could under the circumstances, called to the guy, and when the guy saw who it was, tried to shoot Joe. Well, that was fair, wasn't it? Joe shot him three times. He heard Barbara shoot then.

He waited for others to pop up but none did. Oh, crap, he thought was that all of them?

No, Tree Hugger is still missing. Then he heard more firing. Wait a minute, Joe reflected, Barbara was supposed to fire only one time, what was that all about. As he waited to see if anything else happened, he heard Barbara yelling, and then he could see two figures coming into the light.

"Oh, hell no, Joe exclaimed, you have got to be kidding me."

Tree Hugger was holding and pushing Barbara in front of him so that Joe could not shoot him.

"Okay, Cowboy, Tree Hugger said, as he stopped a few feet away. He was holding a pistol to Barbara's head. This game is over. Drop your rifle, now." He emphasized the comment by pulling back the hammer on his pistol and touching it to Barbara's neck.

Barbara said, "don't do it, Joe, he will kill us anyway. At least I will know you took him down, please." She meant it and Tree Hugger knew she meant it and Joe knew she meant it.

So, tree Hugger did the only logical thing he knew of to make sure he would come out of this alive, he started pointing the pistol at Joe and was just getting ready to fire when Barbara pushed his arm up and the bullet went high. Joe was not waiting for a second shot. He jumped onto both Barbara and Tree Hugger. As he did his main concern was to get control of the pistol.

Barbara crawled away from the battling men. They were in a life and death struggle now. This was the battle they both knew would inevitably have to happen.

Finally, Joe beat the hand Tree Hugger was holding the gun in against a rock a few times until Tree Hugger let go. The gun went sailing off and the two went to fists. Fast and furious as it was, neither seemed to gain on the other. They were equally matched in skill, prowess, and stamina.

Barbara was looking for the gun. She did not want this to end with Tree Hugger winning. Not after all she and Joe had endured. She finally found it and held it up for a good shot.

She yelled, "stop it, stop it right now or I am going to shoot you as dead as I would a snake." The two had knocked themselves apart for the moment and Tree Hugger stopped. He knew he was toast if he continued.

"Okay, he said, you win. You got me."

Joe was thinking that was too easy, He was not quitting that fast. This matter was still between them.

Joe walked over to Barbara to get the pistol and as soon as they started to transfer the gun between them, Tree Hugger grabbed behind his back and brought out a hidden knife which he rapidly threw at Joe. He was lightening, fast.

Knowing to watch for any trick, Joe was ready and ducked to avoid the knife but was, even then, too slow. It hit him in the shoulder just as he fired at Tree Hugger. The bullet hit Tree Hugger in the chest, but he was still trying. Coughing and choking on his own blood filling his lung, he got up somehow and came for Joe again.

"It's not over till it's over," Tree Hugger said as he pulled another knife out of his boot and advanced on Joe.

Leaving him no alternative, Joe said, "you want it, you got it." He shot Tree Hugger twice more, ending the battle to get home.

Joe went to Tree Hugger's body, and with the knife still in his shoulder turned Tree Hugger over and got out his wallet.

He pulled out his driver's license and an old military ID. He read both. The driver's license read Jim Holder but the old military ID read, John Hicks. He thought about that name for a minute, there was something familiar about it. Then it hit him.

"I knew this man, Joe said astonished. He was the deserter from my company years ago now. He left his post and his platoon to be slaughtered just to save his own skin.

"Well, it has caught up with you, hasn't it, John Hicks, Joe said in disgust. I am just glad I was the one to give it to you."

Barbara said pleadingly and very concerned, "come on Joe let's try and fix that wound. You're bleeding something awful and there is nothing left to be done here." Joe, leaning on Barbara, went back to the tent the bad guys had put up and found a medical kit.

They came prepared just in case someone in their group got shot or hurt. Joe regretfully had to teach Barbara how to treat a knife wound and suture up the cut. The hardest part was pulling out the knife. Man, that hurt more than when it went in.

Barbara and Joe spent the rest of the night sleeping. In the morning Joe heard a helicopter. "Oh, crap he said, are there more coming?"

Joe forced himself up trying to ignore the pain from his shoulder wound and grabbed a rifle as he left the tent. He went to the clearing and there, getting off a marked police chopper, were several men all dressed in police tactical gear.

He remembered the SOS he tried to send from the downed helicopter. He knew these were the good guys, or at least he hoped they were. If not, he was done anyway. He could not take on these guys the way they were outfitted.

Joe suddenly felt very weak, I lost too much blood he thought. He dropped the rifle and waited for the men to come up. When they stood in front of him, he said, "what took you so long?" Then he passed out.

Sub Chapter:7

One more thing To Do

It took a long time to finish the investigation. After all, there had been a lot of bodies, and it looked like most had been killed without a fight. So, self-defense was a problem to explain. Barbara gave her statement to the police and she was soon cleared of any of the killings. There was zero evidence she had participated in any of the wrongdoings. Joe on the other hand was not pleading innocent at all. He told them he had done all of it, which was true.

The officers and the District Attorney had a hard time believing he could have done all of this alone. But all the evidence showed he was a solo act. All the excuses given by the pair for why they had to do what was done fell on deaf ears. It was election time and somebody had to take the fall.

Barbara told them it had to be her cousin that set it all up but there was no proof of that, just her word was not sufficient. There was not even anyone left alive to say otherwise.

The only saving possibility was all the men killed had criminal records a mile long. So, there was no illusion these men had been going to do something nefarious. But you can't convict without a crime. And, so far there had been no provable crime.

It was a bad situation for Joe. Unless he could prove with verifiable evidence those men were actually gunning for the two of them and were professionally paid assassins, and who it was that paid them, he was toast. It would go down as Joe simply went on a killing spree, what fun, eh?

It all looked like, from the District Attorney's point of view, as if the bad guys were just trying to defend themselves from a nut-job.

The only thing Joe and Barbara could do now to clear Joe is somehow getting her cousin to confess.

Yea, good luck with that, right?

But Barbara knew she had to try.

She talked the cops into letting her wear a wire as she confronted her cousin. No harm no foul if it didn't work, right?

She went to his office alone late one night and began telling him how horrible the whole ordeal had been.

"William, I just don't get it. Why would someone want to kidnap me? I never hurt a fly. Mr. Manning said he thought it was you. But we are family, I told him he was wrong. I can't think of anyone else that would want to do this to me.

"I think I need to get back into the business, and maybe by once again engrossing myself in work, I can put all of this horror behind me.

"But I am sorry to say, that would mean you would have to leave. We can't have two managers; now, can we?"

William was suddenly furious. He had been casually sitting back listening to Barbara prattle on about her nearly successful kidnapping. He was gloating to himself how he had almost gotten the kidnapping and murder done, and also that he had gotten away with it, free and clear.

The police were charging this Manning character with the crimes. What a joke. What a twist of justice.

Now, this BITCH, thought she was going to take everything he had worked for from him. Not only that but do it so casually, so flippantly, so damned cold-heartedly, it infuriated him.

And being a hot-headed fool, he jumped from his chair and leaning over his desk yelled, "what, do you mean, you're firing me, ME?

"I built this business while you were out stuffing your face and spending your inheritance. You don't deserve any of this. Your father was a tyrant and he treated my dad like a piece of crap. Always telling him he was stupid and reckless in business. He tried to make it big but luck was just not with him. He died broke and left me nothing.

"Then, you come along, acting all high and mighty, and give me a job to manage and find a way to fix the company which was on the brink of insolvency. I worked my butt off to make it profitable again. And now you tell ME, I am FIRED!

William was working himself into an emotional rage. He could not contain himself any longer. He was done pretending; it was time for long-overdue action.

"Well, let me tell you something BITCH, about my little secret. I was the one who tried to have you kidnapped. I was going to get my just reward for all the years I slaved over this business.

Now William could not stop himself. He was certain no one would be able to repeat what he was about to say. He had to gloat.

"I hired and made the deal with those men who came after you. They were to keep the ransom as payment for kidnapping and then killing you afterward. I would inherit the business and my dad and I would finally get what should have belonged to us all along. I was going to let things calm down before I got someone else to do it right the next time but you have pushed me to act right now."

William opened a drawer and pulled out a handgun.

He pointed it at Barbara and said, "get up we're going for a little walk."

Barbara said, "a gun, what are you planning to do?"

She sounded scared as hell. Of course, she was, he was planning on killing her right here and now.

He said," I should have done this myself from the first and none of this would have even been a problem."

William was looking at her with such hate in his eyes, it radiated over his facial muscles causing them to tighten in a diabolical grin. It frightened her to her core. Such hate, such evil. She could not understand how he could have kept such raw hatred from showing for so long. The man must be insane.

Then he started voicing his intentions and the repercussions of what he was about to make her do. He was relishing this final moment and torturing her with knowing how she would meet her end.

"You just got too close to the edge and fell off of the balcony, he began. Maybe you committed suicide or became despondent over Joe taking the blame for your troubles. Maybe life was just not worth it any longer, or you just got careless and slipped, who can or will say for sure. "One thing is sure, I will finally be rid of you, now move it." William motioned Barbara over to the glass sliding window with his pistol.

Barbara began to beg," no, please, I am sorry. You can have it all, just spare my life, PLEASE!"

William was loving her groveling pleas; he had her begging for mercy. It was a dream come true. He would remember this moment for a long time, and he would drink a toast to it as he did.

No one was in the building, no one knew she was even here. He went to the glass door, slid it open, and pulled Barbara through. As he was getting ready to throw her over the balcony rail the door to the office opened and the police came in. They ran to the balcony and told William to freeze.

He looked stunned, "what, he gasped, the police?

How?" The words were stuck in his throat.

Then, a little light bulb flickered in his brain, it grew brighter and brighter as the truth of all of this finally dawned on him. It was all a setup. The bitch had set him up.

He stopped thinking, and he lost his reasoning power. His only thought was to get revenge against his cousin at any cost. He knew it was over for him but he was sure going to take someone to hell with him.

William steeled himself for the finale' yet to come. He grabbed Barbara's arm and with a bone-chilling voice said, let's take a walk, shall we?

He quickly started climbing over the rail while pulling Barbara along with him.

The police were having none of that nonsense and all of them fired into William. He was peppered with bullets that were actually helping by pushing him over faster, taking Barbara with him over the rail. He never let go of Barbara until he finally was starting to fall.

He wanted to keep his grip on her but for some reason, his strength had left him. An unexplainable numbness had set in and he could only feel himself falling, falling all the way down to the street, far below.

As he saw the ground coming toward him and with just seconds from impact, his last thought was, I always hated the name William.

Meanwhile high above, Barbara was still holding on to the railing with one hand as she dangled from the outside of the building screaming.

A policeman grabbed her arm and held it until another officer could get a hold of the other. They pulled her up and onto the safety of the balcony. After she regained her composure, she looked at the policemen and said, just as Joe did, "what took you so long?"

It was over. The police had their irrefutable, incontrovertible, indisputable, incontestable, undeniable, unarguable, and unquestionable evidence. Joe was exonerated, cleared, absolved, vindicated, and freed of all charges. He was a liberated man. His release took a while though, paperwork was always slow in a bureaucracy.

But eventually, he was able to walk out and let Barbara treat him to the best meal he could think of, at a restaurant of his own choosing.

He chose to go to a place that had a great salad bar.

Before going in, he stopped, turned to Barbara, and said, "we have to watch our caloric intake you know. We still have two more weeks on the trail to finish. You can't get the completion award until you do."

Barbara laughed, pulled him into a close and personal full-body embrace, and whispered, "complete this." And for the first, but certainly not the last time, Barbara gave Joe a long and passionate kiss.

Chapter 8

SUICIDE

THE LAST MOMENT TO REFLECT

The hardest part of killing yourself is not doing it, the hardest part is figuring out the way you want to do it. Do you wish to leave a big mess and a letter of Boo-Hoos'? That would make everyone finally take notice, wouldn't it? Maybe then, you could get the overdue support and concern you needed before your demise. But it would be too late then, wouldn't it?

Or maybe, just use some drug of choice that will take you to the next life with no fan-fair, slowly and quietly drifting off to sleep leaving everyone wondering what happened or why you did it.

Perhaps you never even told anyone you were feeling despondent and they would be perplexed in your actions. They might assume it was just an unfortunate accidental overdose.

So, as you can see, the act of taking your own life is not as simple a thing to do as one might imagine if you bother to overthink it.

Not just taking your own life, but maybe, as is so often done, you decide not to leave without taking someone else with you.

Yes, conceivably, someone who has made you contemplate such a drastic course of action in the first place. Why should they be allowed to go on living? What makes them so special? Why should they be allowed to continue enjoying all that the world has to offer while you lay rotting, buried in some cold isolated plot of ground? Cut off forever from contact or feeling; disconnected in every way from humanity.

So many ways, and so many choices, when nothing matters any longer. When there is nothing or no one to stop you and no way to prevent it.

There would be no repercussions, no jail time, no worry of punishment of any kind. But there would be a kind of satisfaction in not leaving alone.

Then, if you do go that route, you must consider how to end their life as well. Now it is starting to get complicated. It makes your brain reel from all the possibilities. This was not your intention at first; murder was not your primary goal. Is it necessary to have so much complication in such a simple act?

Upon reflection, do you start to wonder if maybe you have any right to force someone to join you on the path you have chosen for yourself? Just because you can't deal with the world and all the problems it sends your way doesn't mean others should share in the end of your misery, does it?

Now you're starting to sound a little crazy. You only started out wanting to do a simple little thing like killing yourself, and now it has manifested itself into a discussion with yourself on the subject of morality and fairness.

Be careful, if you keep thinking too long you might try to talk yourself out of it. You wouldn't want that, now, would you?

Maybe you should consider making it more spectacular, give everyone a good show. Many people decide to climb up on a building and let a big crowd gather. This method would give you more attention than you could ever have hoped for in your own troubled life.

Yes, people would be talking about the jumper for a long time. And, of course, the memory of you falling all the way down and leaving such a bloody mess on the pavement would certainly leave an indelible mark on many. They would long remember that.

It might even give some contemplating doing what you did a moment to pause at the sight of you there all bloody, broken, and grotesque, and rethink their own course. You might think of it as a public service.

Maybe you could postpone your unique inevitable departure from life and start a club for suicidal people. Give guidance, and help them find the way most appealing to themselves. It would be, at best, a revolving door for members though, as most would not be members for long, for obvious reasons. But being members could be beneficial. Not all that contemplate ending it all really want nor intend to. They are simply feeling sorry for themselves at that moment. And, given time to ponder their situations, might have a change of heart. Better to wonder sooner than say, as they are plunging toward the ground after jumping from some high elevation, or after consuming a deadly concoction.

Most people simply need a friendly ear to listen and help rationalize their predicaments. Generally, they are just silly misunderstandings and could be worked out if given enough time to focus on the problems.

What percentage change their minds after it is too late? Such a statistic would probably be hard to verify, again, for obvious reasons.

There are a few people who contemplate the deed in their daily regimen. They wake up each morning and then at some point they have a difficult and troublesome moment during the span of their day and just think, " I could end it all now and be done with all this nonsense once and for all."

Or, others wish it on someone else, which is more popular; "I wish that person would just kill themselves and I would not have to tolerate them any longer."

These people are not serious contenders, but are non-the-less troubled and need guidance or intervention.

So, perhaps joining a club would be helpful if doctors were not an option. These people would be around for a long time and could help to keep the club going. It would be cheaper than prying professionals who would only want to stop you from completing your chosen path. And there would be plenty of people at the club to listen to you tell your tales of woe.

An added bonus could be that most of the listeners would eventually take their own lives so the chances of your secret confessions getting out would be lessened by attrition. And the comradery of like interest also adds to the sincerity and honesty of direct and candid discussions. A win-win for all.

It would alleviate the possibility of a straight-jacket and or forced psychotic drugs the practitioners would no doubt require of you.

If you think this is a silly idea, just remember the statistics on suicides each year and if these individuals had known of such a club, how many do you wonder would have sought it out? Just the curiosity factor alone would perhaps bring in many.

And joining could be anonymous. Just choose a moniker, an alias. No one needs to know who you are if you are so inclined.

There are some who can't do themselves in for whatever reason, and decide to make others do it for them.

One such tale was of a guy who had succeeded in charming a husbands' wife away from him and the husband decided to end it by forcing the wife stealer to kill him. It was a win-win for him. He would be dead, the wife stealer would be in jail, and the wife, hopefully, would live with the guilt she had caused all that transpired.

The husband confronted the wife stealer at his home and put a knife and a gun on the table in front of both of them in easy reach. The husband told the wife stealer to reach for any one of the weapons he wanted and the fight to the death would commence.

The husband started counting down and was almost at the end of the time to reach for weapons when the wife stealer ran screaming out of the house to never return.

That was not part of the plan but it did solve the husbands' problem. His wife decided he was a much better man than she had thought by risking his life to get her back and they reunited. The husband didn't tell her he was just trying to die and it didn't work. But he was happy with the outcome so he canceled his death wish plans.

Sometimes just the attempt is sufficient to alter the desire for self-destruction. After all, conflict resolution was the main goal anyway, was it not, however it might have been accomplished?

Another story that has played out on many occasions is the suicide-by-cop scenario. Anyone who has a death wish can simply approach an officer with the obvious gestures signaling their desire to kill the officer and he will get his wish.

The officer is not usually the suicidal type and wishes to go home unharmed to his family. So, a knife or gun-wielding individual seeking a way out of this world will most certainly get his wish fulfilled.

There is a sad element to the suicide pandemic going on lately. The military has a lot of disturbed individuals who have made it through long periods of war. They come home and just can't get over all that they went through. It haunts them day and night. The experts call it Post-Traumatic-Stress-Disorder. A fancy name for "I can't deal with this alone."

It is perplexing how one can justify putting all that effort into staying alive while fighting, just to return home and finish doing what the enemy could not. It goes against rational thinking. But then, this is suicide we're talking about, isn't it? An easy answer to a difficult problem.

It is obvious the government has no problem with it. The suicide rate is higher than the casualty rate, and still, they do nothing to stop it.

Oh, that's right, they do give them psychotic pills, which has worked out well, for the drug companies.

Instead of a suicide club, these soldiers should start a survivors' club. They could get together to talk over their problems with like-minded individuals and possibly work through the depressions and flashbacks they are dealing with.

It makes no sense to let the enemy win after you have defeated them, does it?

Here, in the above example, is why some have yet to take the proverbial plunge. Why after all that has happened in their lives they still cling to hope, a way to save themselves, a reason to stick around.

Sometimes the suicidal still care about what goes on in the world. There is yet a connection; a concern and interest for favorable helpful outcomes. Or, maybe they are merely grasping at something tangible to cling to.

Those who are determined and have set their course are unchangeable and the act will be done. But those who care about others find it hard to commit to self-destruction. If for no other reason than a need to find a solution for the needs of those who depend upon them. Putting ones-self last for the greater good.

Many depressed people have used the excuse that they are indispensable, and others would be lost without them to help.

Fathers see the necessity to continue to provide for the family. Mothers feel they are essential in family bonding to love and nourish her husband and children. And what a devastating blow it would be if either of them was to disappear.

The list of reasons to end it all is only limited by a persons' imagination. You could sit all day and write down numerous reasons why life was not worth living. Then you could write just as long a list as to why you should not. If you compare the lists, you might be surprised at the number swinging one way or another. This might give you pause to address your life in general.

Maybe self-evaluation would be a good thing. To investigate the possibility if you have a propensity toward suicide, and you may not have even been aware of it.

You might think at this moment you could never do such a thing and the next moment find yourself actually considering it. Circumstances change all the time. People are always changing their situations, their lives. One minute your riding high and making a fortune and the next your flat broke and on the street.

People generally have a certain tolerance to change. But extremes can cause chaos and depression which could lead to suicidal thoughts.

Many change their convictions when they hear bad news from a medical prognosis. Many do not wish to die a slow and painful death and would prefer to choose a quick and painless one as the alternative. Who can blame them?

Some may even want to help stop the suffering of a loved one if not for the ramifications of such a deed by the laws, legal and moral, imposed on us by government and religion.

Many have opened the door to suicide through self-inflicted means by changing the laws governing such acts.

Most all other locales have stood strong against it and refuse to allow the suffering and dying to end their pain.

You better make sure you do it right if you plan on it or you will be punished with jail time jail for the attempt.

A paradox emerges in the fact you can murder your unborn babies all day long with no problem.

Let's see now, you can't kill yourself if you're already born but it is ok to let someone else kill you if you're not born yet.

Does the ironic contradiction of this not prove and expose the hypocrisy throughout? Are murder and suicide just a difference of opinion on how you look at it?

Those who can't fight back get killed with no say-so about it and those who can fight back aren't allowed to and must suffer until the end.

The subject gets really confusing, doesn't it?

Mothers are allowed to murder their unborn with impunity but not a live person. It simply boggles the mind.

So, now we come to a point where we must consider if the subject of suicide is a debatable legal and moral question. Or is murder sometimes acceptable, but only on the government, terms.

It is not left to the individual to decide freely and with no consequence unless you plan on killing a baby. One must certainly, if so desirous, complete the act of suicide in secret or before anyone can stop them.

Maybe there is an answer here after all, by using the legal abortion laws. Possibilities abound when one opens the mind to alternatives.

Suicides are so numerous in society that maybe we should legalize centers that accommodate them. This way you won't have the necessity of cleaning up the mess they would sometimes leave, or have to run around collecting the bodies. They would be all conveniently assigned to a room made for the suicidal person to finish the deed, just like an abortion clinic.

And taking this to its obvious progression even further, what If we could bring in those we don't want around any longer and let the clinic handle the nasty job of disposing of them for us. It would be a booming business. You could start clinics all across the world to be rid of any who prevent you from living the life you want.

Get rid of all the old people who are forcing you to take care of them.

Tired of your husband or wife, just drop them off at the clinic and your troubles are over.

There are endless scenarios to contemplate, and the upside is we could finally get the population explosion under control.

Murder, suicide, life, death. It all blurs into the same thing after all. It is simply one's desire at the moment, whether it be a mother wanting her freedom, or a person wishing to move on for whatever reason, or an individual wanting someone else to die merely to satisfy the convenience of the moment. It all comes down to the same thing. Dead is dead, and people will make laws to reinforce their beliefs of the moment. So basically, society can change the rules anytime it wants, and fit them to the wishes of its peoples.

The message of this story is, make sure you watch what laws the government and the people are passing, you just might be next on their list of possibilities.

Put another way, be careful who you elect, for the next decree could be coming for you if you do not fit into their mold.

Chapter 9

IT STARTED WITH ONE SONG

Have you ever had a song that just would not go away and continually played in your head? No amount of distraction could shake it loose and allow you to go about your business. It would not be so bad if it were a good tune but it was one that you heard simply passing by or was stuck listening to in an elevator. Now there are some real catchy tunes, right?

Well, I decided if I could not get the medley out of my head then perhaps, I could substitute it for one of my own. It was worth a try.

So, in desperation, I set down and began writing my own song. I was surprised that in a short while I had actually written a song. Now I can't say it was a good song but a song it was nonetheless. I was proud of it because it was something I had produced. I began to sing it aloud and with a few changes it began to sound even better. Maybe I was just getting used to it, I thought to myself.

I decided to sing it to others to see if they agreed with me. I, of course, picked a good and loyal friend to test it on first. I didn't want to be embarrassed if it was a dud. And also, I could hopefully elicit silence from my friend if it was not up to par.

I was rewarded with a resounding "way to go" from my friend. I was asked if I was going to write more and I had to think about that. I had not even contemplated that far as yet.

I had, after all, just written the song as a way of replacing and thus alleviating my agony from the song I previously had stuck in my head.

Now I was facing a new challenge of whether or not I could complete another song of equal or better quality.

I had learned a few chords on the guitar years ago and decided to see if I could learn to play better. I would need to have some instrument to aid me in my musical journey.

I have since discovered, looking back, that I would have been better off learning how to write music.

I had to change and diminish what I heard in my head to fit what chords I could play. I had lost much of the beautiful and flowing sound content in the translation to basic chord progressions.

I have come a long way from those humble beginnings. I now have many songs in my portfolio.

I have decided I would like to try my hand at writing a story that includes some of these same songs in a musical love story variation of sorts.

It would please me if not anyone else. But of course, I would be happy if others felt like I do when they hear it. Such is always an author's wish.

Who Needs Wings?

Flying down the highway, going as usual, way too fast for such a winding downhill course. I was distracted by the thoughts overpowering me from the verbal fight we just had minutes before when up ahead I could make out a dog crossing the road. I jerked the wheel a little too hard trying to avoid hitting the animal and only succeeded in losing control of the car.

It started sliding sideways as I headed straight for the turn in the road I was obviously not going to make.

I thought, well, this is it; my luck has finally run out.

I hit the edge of the road and the car started flipping as it went airborne over the embankment.

I watched in fascination, which was in a combination of my panic and fear, as the cliffside came into view just to be replaced with open-air and water. It repeated this scene over and over until at last, I could see the water coming up to meet me from below. Man, that was a long drop. I had no delusions as to my fate when I hit the water. I would either die on impact or drown when I went under.

It is funny how things slow down to a snail's pace when you go through a catastrophic encounter. Your mind speeds up substantially and you can think about all that is happening somehow in a super-fast way, I supposed.

As I hit the water, I could feel the rush of it coming in. The car is immediately engulfed and begins to sink to the bottom of the ocean. I am just a little way from the shore where I had seen very fleetingly, people enjoying the beachfront.

I thought, well, this would make their day; seeing a car come out of nowhere and crash into the water right in front of them.

I had inexplicitly landed with the tires down and so I was spared the head-first certain death. But that was quickly over-ridden by the water coming in and displacing all the air. I would soon drown as what little air I had left would be displaced if I did not do something soon. I tried opening the door. That was stupid.

The pressure was too great and I decided that would just let me drown that much faster.

I looked out the window as the water was coming up to my neck by then and to my surprise, I saw a couple of young men swimming up to the car. They looked at me and gestured for me to roll down my window.

I thought that was stupid. That would take all the rest of my air away.

Then it dawned on me that I was going to drown anyway and if I had any chance at all of surviving, I would have to get out of the car.

As the door would not open then obviously the window was my only option.

I signaled to the men, ok, and taking one last deep breath, began to roll the window down.

Water poured in with a rush and before I could even finish rolling down the window the car was completely filled with water and I tried to pull myself out of the window. I couldn't do it. I forgot to release the seat belt. Dumb, dumb, dumb.

I quickly released it and pulled myself out and began swimming to the surface.

The men had already started up, probably because they needed air more than me.

I wasn't sure I would even make it but desperation is a powerful thing. I could feel myself starting to black out from lack of oxygen but broke the surface just in time.

Gulping large quantities of air, I soon was able to get myself under control and swam to shore.

The two men accompanied me to shore, swimming on either side of me so that I was assured I would make it.

There were several people there now. All very curious to see the idiot that thought driving into the ocean was a good idea. Sure, the weather was great and the sun was shining brightly; all making for a magnificent day for a drive. But really, weren't there better ways to get to the beach?

Suddenly, once I saw I was safely on shore, I became dizzy and weak. I collapsed onto the sand and was vaguely aware of the people gathering around me.

I could hear, as if in the distance, someone yelling, get back, get back, give him some space. Then I passed out.

I dreamed then. Or, what, at the moment, I thought was a dream.

I was standing in a bright light. There was nothing else around that I could see, just the intense light surrounding me. It didn't hurt my eyes but I did feel an overpowering love emanating from it. I knew I was dead. I could see my family off in the distance and wanted to go to them. All those I could see had already passed away so I knew I had to be dead as well. But something kept me from moving toward them. I wanted to go so badly. I also noted that my loved ones had younger and perfected bodies from before their demise. So, I knew you could change your appearance and be seen as you would like to be on the other side.

Then from somewhere, I heard a voice. It declared; my time was not now. I had to return. I wanted to stay. It was so peaceful here.

Then the light began to fade and I woke once again in my body in the hospital. They had been working on me. I heard someone say we got him back. I was sad.

As soon as I could, I wrote down this song.

WHEN WE MEET AGAIN

AT NIGHT GRANDPA WOULD READ FROM THE BIBLE.
SOMETIMES NOT EVEN LOOKING AT THE WORDS.
AND GRANDMA WOULD PLAY SOME OLD GOSPEL TUNES.
THE LOVE OF OUR FAMILY, THROUGH THE NEIGHBORHOOD, WAS HEARD.

WHAT TIMES WE WOULD HAVE WHEN WE ALL GATHERED.
BRINGING OLD MEMORIES FROM THE PAST FEELS GOOD.
WHAT A JOY IT WAS TO SHARE OUR FAMILY TIME.
BUT EVEN BETTER WILL BE THE DAY, WE GATHER AGAIN FOR GOOD.

Sing CHORUS:

MOM AND DAD HAD NURTURED AND WATCHED US GROW TALL.
THEY GAVE TO US A BOND CARRIED WITH US FROM BIRTH.
AND DAILY THEY WOULD SHOW THEIR LOVE FOR US ALL.
IT WAS LIKE A PICTURE, OF HEAVEN HERE ON EARTH.

THERE WERE TIMES WHEN LIFE WOULD MAKE US STUMBLE.
BUT FAMILY WAS ALWAYS THERE TO HELP YOU THROUGH.
AS OUR TIME GROWS SHORT IT IS LEFT TO THE YOUNG.
TO CARRY ON TRADITION, AND THE LOVE FROM ME AND YOU.

CHORUS:
WHEN WE MEET AGAIN, WHAT A DAY IT WILL BE.
THE SOUND OF THEIR VOICES, RINGING IN THE AIR.
THE JOY AND THE LAUGHTER, THE MOMENT OF EMBRACE.
AS WE STAND IN GODS LIGHT, AND FIND THEM WAITING THERE.

I was told I had bumped my head somehow and caused swelling of the brain. They had gone in and released the pressure built up but I had died for a short while.

I didn't need them to tell me that. But I understood then why I was able to see into the next life. I am no longer afraid to die. I now know what is waiting there.

I finally was able to go home and my wife and I had some deep discussions about our relationship problems. I was seeing things from an entirely new and drastic viewpoint, to say the least. She on the other hand would take some intense convincing. I had not been the most ardent of companions to her in the past. Dare I say I was a big jerk.

So, I wrote this song for her.

THIS TIME

EACH TIME, I LEAVE YOU, IT'S FOR THE LAST TIME.
AND EACH TIME, I WALK OUT, IT'S OVER FOR GOOD.
AND EACH TIME, GETS HARDER, THAN THE LAST TIME.
SO, FOR, THE FIRST TIME, I'M STAYING WHERE I SHOULD.

CHORUS:

DARLING, I LOVE YOU, I CAN'T FIGHT IT ANYMORE.
I CAN'T KEEP MY MIND STRAIGHT, WHEN I WALK OUT THE DOOR.
SO PLEASE TAKE ME BACK, FOR THIS ONE FINAL TIME.
AND I'LL PROVE I CAN CHANGE, IF AGAIN YOU'LL BE MINE.

CHORUS:
THIS TIME, IS THE LAST TIME, I'LL COME HOME TO YOU.
BECAUSE THIS TIME, IS THE LAST TIME, I'LL EVER LEAVE YOU.
THERE'S NO PLACE IN THIS WORLD, ANY BETTER THAN WITH YOU.
AND NOTHING ANY HARDER, THAN SAYING WE ARE THROUGH.

I knew I would have to show her I meant to change and be the man she wanted, and also, I wanted to be the man I knew I could be. That was not necessarily easy. I thought I could just be that man. And at first, I was giving it a good try. But old habits are hard to break and I found myself beginning to slide back into my old ways. I would stay out late at night and come home drunk.

I couldn't even tell you why I did it. I just loved having a good time and my wife was a homebody. She liked to do things around the house, like entertain friends with dinners and barbeques and living for the kids.

I was too wild still and sought out bars and drunken buddies to spend my time with.

I found myself sitting at a table in one of the many bars I frequented and while contemplating my surroundings and of course feeling no pain a new song idea came to me. This is that song.

I HAD TO THINK OF YOU

I WALKED INTO THE BAR ROOM AND ORDERED UP A DOUBLE.
AND SAT DOWN AT MY FAVORITE PARKING PLACE.
AS I WAITED FOR MY ORDER, I STARTED THINKING UP A LINE.
TO USE ON EVERY WOMAN IN THE PLACE.

Sing CHORUS:

THEN I SAW A PRETTY LADY, WHO LOOKED LIKE A MAYBE.
AND DOE-SEE-DOED HER ALL AROUND THE BAR.
SHE SAID THAT I WAS FUNNY, AND THINGS WERE LOOKING SUNNY.
 CAUSE I TOLD HER I WAS A BIG SINGING STAR.

Sing CHORUS:

YOU SURE DO KNOW HOW TO SPOIL A GOOD TIME.
CAN'T HELP THINKING OF YOU HOME AND ALL ALONE.
THAT LOVING FEELING YOU GIVE ME, KEEPS ME COMING BACK.
SO, I BETTER GET ON HOME BEFORE YOU'RE GONE.

                    CHORUS:
AND FOR A WHILE THE LAUGHTER RULES THE AIR.
AND FUN IS FLOWING FROM EVERY CHAIR.
AND THE TIMES I HAD ARE JUST WHAT I LIKE.
BUT LIKE ALL THE OTHER TIMES, I ALWAYS THINK OF YOU.

FINALE': BECAUSE THERE'S NO ONE ELSE THAT LOVES ME LIKE YOU DO.

Of course, the song didn't change anything. It was just a fun addition to my list of songs. Even though there was a lot of truth in it, it mattered little to my conscience. I carried on with my wild ways.

I got a letter from a good friend of mine in the service and he was despondent over a letter he received from his wife. She has been sending him letters and her words just kept getting less affectionate with time. He was sure she was losing her love for him and it was tearing him apart inside. Here he was overseas fighting for our way of life and his wife, alone most of the time was finding other means of entertainment and so losing the love she once had for him. I saw a lot of this situation in my own predicament.

I had also gotten one of those same letters when I was in the service and could sympathize wholeheartedly with his anguish over the whole thing.

It brought back a lot of painful memories and I began to wonder if maybe that had something to do with why I was fighting myself to keep my own relationship at arms-length. Could it be I was sabotaging my marriage subconsciously?

I wrote this song while thinking about my friends' dilemma.

ANOTHER DEAR JOHN LETTER

WHEN I GET THIS FEELING, DEEP WITHIN MY HEART.
IT TELLS ME THE MEANING, OF LOVE GROWING COLD.
WHEN I SEE YOUR PICTURE, IT TEARS ME APART.
I'M WONDERING, IF YOUR LOVE FOR ME, GROWS OLD.

Sing CHORUS:

I'VE HEARD OF GUYS WHO GET, THOSE DEAR JOHN LETTERS.
BUT I NEVER THOUGHT, I WOULD GET ONE FROM YOU.
BUT I FIND MYSELF, WAITING FOR THE LETTER.
THAT WILL END OUR LIVES TOGETHER, ME AND YOU.

        CHORUS:
I WRITE YOU, AND TELL YOU, HOW MUCH I LOVE YOU.
AND HOW IT HURTS, TO BE SO FAR FROM HOME.
THE LETTERS I GET FROM YOU, GROW SMALL AND FEW.
AND THE WORDS TELL ME, WHAT I SHOULD HAVE KNOWN.

After writing that song I was so moved emotionally I had to stop everything and do a lot of internal reflection. It seems I was doing a lot of that lately. Maybe I was getting close to finally accepting the fact I needed to get my act together or bad things were going to happen.

I had gone to the bar to ponder these questions over a drink, which I needed like another hole in my head. I came home a little less drunk than usual and when I went to the bedroom and saw my wife asleep. I sat down in the chair next to the bed and watched her sleeping. While doing so I wrote this song.

MIDNIGHT FIGHT

WILL YOU WAKE UP WANTING TO BE MY WIFE?
WHEN VERBAL WORDS SEEM TO FADE AWAY?
WHEN SLEEP TAKES YOU FROM YOUR TROUBLED RAGE?
AND PEACE IS WITHIN YOUR HEART?

OR WILL YOU AWAKE TO ANEW THE SPAT WE'D HAD?
THROUGH TEAR WETTED EYES, AND THOSE HEARTFELT CRIES?
THROUGH BITTER WORDS, WE DO NOT MEAN TO SAY?
OR WILL YOU AWAKE TO LOVE ME AGAIN?

AND THOUGH YOU SLEEP WITH DREAMS YOUR OWN.
AND SHARE THIS BED AS WE ALWAYS HAVE.
WILL YOU LOVE ME ANY LESS THIS DAY;
WHEN YOU AWAKE TO FIND ME STILL AROUND?

I was near the bottom now as far as hoping to get my life back in order. I knew something would have to give.

I decided to take some time off and go on a sabbatical of sorts to try and get my head on straight. I knew going on this trip with my wife would probably not be a good idea, as I was not doing well with her at this point in time. I needed time alone to do some soul searching and self-reflection. I opted for a road trip; ergo a cross-country excursion to try and make crucial adjustments to my attitude and lifestyle.

I figured my wife would wholeheartedly agree to that decision. I knew she was at her limit of tolerating me and my shenanigans. It turns out, she was more than agreeable, she helped me pack.

So, after securing the few things I thought I would need for a short trip in the camper I jumped into the pickup.

Once I hit the interstate and realized this was really happening, that I was actually heading down the road on my, "get yourself together tour," as I called it, I immediately began to loosen up.

I turned on the radio and put on some music. I caught myself smiling several times that first day. I even began singing along with the music on the radio.

After driving for two weeks, I had traveled across the country. Simply observing and taking in everything I witnessed along the way; just letting my mind relax and encourage a sense of inner peace.

I soon realized a whole lot was going on all the time out in the world. I had been so preoccupied with myself and my own situation that I had lost contact with the people.

I had reveled in its vices: cruelty, inhumanity, drunkenness, self-absorption. But I had not even contemplated its kindness, charity, compassion, goodwill, and mercy.

People were living their daily lives while going and coming in mass randomness.

Everyone had their own individual stories to tell and yet, had a cohesiveness to everyone else at the same time. The whole of the country was working, living, and loving each other in complete harmony.

What a revelation. We were all interconnected in unison to the country at large and also co-existing in its integral separate individualism. It is what makes everything work as a whole. I knew it all worked this way, but I just never thought about it in that sense before.

I had settled in for the night at a campsite and as I was practicing on the guitar, all of this came rushing back to me, and I wrote this song to commemorate the idea.

THIS COUNTRY I'M IN

SUNNY DAYS, AND MOON FILLED NIGHTS.
MAKES THIS LONESOME HIGHWAY, PURE DELIGHT.
FIVE HUNDRED MILES, OF CONCRETE AND TAR.
DODGING EVERY COP, WHO HAS ON HIS RADAR.

DRIVING THROUGH DESERTS, ALL SANDY, AND BARE.
PULLING UP MOUNTAINS, TO FRESH CLEAN AIR.
WHERE IN AMERICA, HAVE I NOT BEEN?
AND EVERYWHERE A WONDER, THIS COUNTRY I'M IN.

Sing CHORUS:

MEETING FRIENDLY PEOPLE, FROM ALL ACROSS THE LAND.
READY AND WILLING, TO GIVE A HELPING HAND.
FREEDOM STILL REIGNS, AND PASSIONS RISE HIGH.
AS A SCOUT TROOP RAISES, OLD GLORY AS I PASS BY.

THIS COUNTRY'S SO BIG, THIS COUNTRY'S SO WIDE.
AND THERE'S SO MUCH TO DO, THAT I HAVE NOT TRIED.
BUT HEADING DOWN THE ROAD, I'M GONNA SEE IT ALL.
BECAUSE AMERICA, IS STILL THE BEST OF ALL.

CHORUS:
TAKE ME FOR A RIDE, AMERICA.
SHOW ME YOUR GLORIES, AMERICA.
I TRAVEL YOUR LANDS, FROM SEA TO SHINING SEA.
AMERICA, YOUR STILL A WONDER TO ME.

FINALE': AMERICA, YOUR STILL THE ONE FOR ME.

I decided it was time to head home and show my wife the new me. I had transformed myself from the drunken fool to a stable sober lover of life. I could see the good in everything around me now. I wasn't hung up on all the negativity that seemed to be chained to me in the past. When I got home, I found a note on the kitchen table from my wife. It read, well, I think you know what it said.

I was too late in my decision to change; the harm had already been done. I was going to have to live with it now. I dropped to my knees; I couldn't hold myself up. I just wept for hours it seemed. I had lost the only real thing I had in my self-made sorry life.

This was a dark and lonely time in my life. I barely remember half of it. I do remember writing a lot of songs dealing with a lost love. It was all I seemed to be able to write at that time in my life. Here are just a couple.

IM STILL WISHING YOU WERE HERE

I'M STILL WISHING YOU WERE HERE.
HOLDING ME CLOSE IN YOUR ARMS.
BRINGING ALL THE HAPPINESS AND CHEER,
YOU GAVE ME WITH YOUR MAGIC CHARM.

SOMEDAY I HOPE TO GET ALONG.
AND FACE THE WORLD AS I USED TO DO.
OR, FIND JUST WHAT I DID THAT WAS WRONG,
AND TAKE THE ROAD THAT LEADS ME BACK TO YOU.

Sing CHORUS:

THE DAY YOU LEFT I COULD HAVE DIED.
HOW COULD HEAVEN EVER END.
ONE BROKEN MAN JUST SAT AND CRIED.
ONE BROKEN HEART WOULD NEVER MEND.

I GUESS THAT I SHOULD SOMEDAY CALL YOU,
JUST TO FIND IF YOU'VE CHANGED YOUR MIND.
BUT I'LL KEEP HOLDING ON TO DREAMS OF YOU,
FOR I KNOW THAT I'M JUST NOT YOUR KIND.

       CHORUS:
YOUR MEMORY IS LIKE AN ECHO.
IT JUST KEEPS COMING BACK TO ME.
BRINGING THE FEELINGS THAT WON'T LET GO,
THAT MY LOVE WILL ALWAYS BE.

    Another song of that same time shows I was obviously and truly in a bad place emotionally. I had after all just come back from getting my act together and to have this hit me square in the face was more than I could handle.

I loved my wife. I had just screwed up for way too long for her to accept my excuses any longer and just because I came back a new man wasn't going to change any of that. She had heard that story way too many times before to take another chance. She was over me for good.

YOU SAY IT'S ALL OVER

YOU SAY IT'S ALL OVER, ALL OVER NOW.
AND THAT I WILL, FORGET YOU SOMEHOW
DARLING THAT'S NOT SO, I'LL DIE LOVING YOU
I JUST CAN'T LET GO; OF THE LOVE WE ONCE KNEW.

I GUESS THAT SOMEDAY I, MIGHT WAKE IN MY BED.
AND FIND NO MORE TEAR STAINS, FROM THINGS YOU HAD SAID.
BUT LIFE IS SO USELESS, EACH DAY I'M ALONE.
FOR HEARTACHES AND TEARDROPS, ARE ALL I HAVE KNOWN.

Sing CHORUS:

HEARTBROKEN TEARDROPS, I CRIED ALL IN VAIN.
DREAMING YOU'D COME BACK, AGAIN AND AGAIN.
SOMEDAY I MIGHT FIND PEACE, AND NOT FEEL SO BLUE.
BUT NOT FOR NOW DARLING, I'M STILL MISSING YOU.

IF LOVE WERE A MOUNTAIN, AND I WAS A CLOUD.
MY THUNDER WOULD ECHO, THROUGH CANYONS SO LOUD.
MY TEARS WOULD WASH THAT MOUNTAIN, RIGHT TO THE SEA.
AND CLEANSE ALL MY MEMORIES, AND SET MY HEART FREE.

CHORUS:
IF HEAVEN WOULD OPEN, AND SAY WON'T YOU COME.
I'D SAY I HAVE BEEN THERE, DOWN HERE WITH SOMEONE.
IF THERE WERE SOME WAY THAT, I COULD HOLD YOU.
YOU KNOW I'D DO WHATEVER, YOU WANTED ME TOO.

I'll give you one more to show the state I was in. Any more and it would bring you down as well, I would think.

WHEN YOU ONCE WERE MINE

HOW LONG MUST I WAIT, FOR THIS PAIN TO GO AWAY?
HOW LONG TILL THE MEMORY, OF YOU, STARTS TO FADE?
HOW LONG MUST I WAIT, AND KEEP PRETENDING THAT I'M FINE?
HOW LONG HAS IT BEEN, SINCE YOU ONCE WERE MINE?

EACH DAY I AWAKE, TO FIND YOU STILL GONE.
EACH NIGHT I LIE AND WONDER, JUST WHAT I DID WRONG.
EACH MOMENT WE'RE APART, SEEMS LIKE AN ETERNITY.
EACH DREAM ALWAYS ENDS, WITH YOU BACK WITH ME.

MEMORIES ARE LIKE PICTURES, OF THE DAYS I HAD WITH YOU.
MEMORIES DON'T JUST FADE, JUST BECAUSE WE ARE THROUGH.
EVERYONE KEEPS WONDERING, WHY I DON'T MOVE ON.
IT'S BECAUSE, IN MY MIND, YOU HAVE NEVER REALLY GONE.

COULD YOU TAKE JUST A MOMENT, FROM YOUR BUSY LIFE?
COULD YOU TAKE JUST A MOMENT, AND REMEMBER YOUR, MY WIFE?
LOOK IN YOUR HEART, AND YOU'LL SEE AT A GLANCE.
WE WERE MEANT TO BE TOGETHER, AND GIVE IT ONE MORE CHANCE.

HOW LONG MUST I WAIT, FOR THIS PAIN TO GO AWAY?
HOW LONG TILL THE MEMORIES, OF YOU, STARTS TO FADE?
HOW LONG MUST I WAIT, AND KEEP PRETENDING THAT I'M FINE?
HOW LONG HAS IT BEEN, SINCE YOU ONCE WERE MINE?

      You would think in a love story that eventually the two lovers would get back together, but that didn't happen, I am sorry to say. I had gone too far and the love that had once been died from too much abuse of affection.

      It took a long time for me to come to terms with the reality of my situation. I knew I had to move on and start again. That door had closed for good and it was irreconcilable.

      So, I spent a long time getting my act together. I had quit drinking and going out to bars because I had finally conceded to the fact that was my most detrimental flaw.

      I would never be able to find another, "love of my life," as long as I continued down that path of self-destruction.

Eventually, since I had once again joined the real world and became a sensible and likable man again, I was blessed in finding another lady who was leaning toward a relationship with me. I also was getting to the point where I was having strong feelings for her as well. Once again love was in the air.

I had cultivated the friendship until it bloomed into a girlfriend, boyfriend situation. That would soon hopefully, bloom into a more serious relationship.

I had tread very carefully since I was still damaged goods and would have been devastated if I had been rejected again so soon after my last.

During this process known as falling in love, I wrote another song. This would be the first song in a long time that didn't have a sorrow-based lost love theme. It made me feel encouraged that I was finally getting back to living again.

IT WAS IN A FLEETING MOMENT

IT WAS IN A FLEETING MOMENT.
I SAW A TWINKLE IN YOUR EYE.
TELLING ME I WON'T BE AS LONESOME
AS I HAVE IN YEARS GONE BY.
SO, TAKE ME IN YOUR LOVING ARMS
AND STAY WITH ME TONIGHT
AND LET'S FIND OUT IF IN THE MORNING
OUR LOVE IS STRENGTHENED TONIGHT.

LET'S FIND OUT IF WE WERE MEANT
TO BUILD A CASTLE OF OUR OWN.
AND SHARE A DREAM OF CHERISHED LOVE
INSTEAD OF BEING ALONE.
IT WOULD TAKE ME JUST A MOMENT
TO GIVE MY ONE REPLY.
THERE'S NOT MUCH DOUBT ABOUT IT
YOU'RE THE REASON WHY.

YOU WOULD NOT BE SORRY IF
YOU TOOK THAT MAGIC FLIGHT.
FOR I KNOW WHAT WE HAVE IS LOVE
AND THAT'S WHAT MAKES IT ALL RIGHT.
SO, STAY WITH ME AND TALK AWHILE
AND FIND OUT IF IT'S TRUE
THAT YOU MIGHT LOVE ME HALF AS MUCH
AS YOU KNOW I DO YOU.

I was so ecstatic that I finally wrote an upbeat song I tried again with another. But this time it was just a simple poem. One that I wanted to end this story with. One that tells, if she says yes, that my story will have a happy ending.

I will leave you with your own guess as to her answer and conclusion because my story is but one of many that have been played

out all across the world in a myriad of situations, possibilities, and
endings.

THE GIFT

I here and now give this gift.
It has been long overdue.
I should have given it long ago
But, finally, it's here for you.

So, take it now and pull the bow
and see as you behold,
If what I give is fine enough
All the sparkle set in gold.

I want to watch your face light up
and to see that magic grin.
To see how much joy, I've given you
by the tears upon your chin.

I know this doesn't start to make up
for a long and stressful life.
I only wanted to love and please you
My one and only, Will You Be My Wife

Chapter 10

FUN

TIMES

A Life Revisited

Sub-Chapters

INTRODUCTION

I have found that not every moment of one's life is memorable, especially to others. *I know, shocker, right?*

As an example of this, I think of people's reaction to someone starting to drag out old pictures to show, and how the reaction of everyone universally is the same. Just shoot me now and be done with it all.

I can't think of a faster way to kill a party than trying to show family vacation films. Or flop down a huge album of long-dead relatives. You can watch as people's eyes glaze over from immediate boredom.

That is unless your sole reason was to get everyone to go home in the first place. Now that would be a stroke of genius. You can actually watch how fast people will try to engage their brains to find excuses to leave. It is amazing how, suddenly at that very moment, they just realized they had forgotten about any number of things they neglected to do and needed to go immediately to rectify it.

I am not going to try and bore you in that way. This is why I selected only what I considered the most entertaining parts of my life to write about.

I admit I did try to embellish the stories, though all true factually, with a bit of witticism and candor to make the reading more enjoyable. After all, even the most bizarre of stories could use a little flair to liven it up.

I left out the daily routines we all do that make up the majority of our lives. I focused only on the parts that made an impression upon me as being interesting and noteworthy.

I hope you agree.

Sub Chapter 1   •

Bumblebee

I sat watching the tiny hole in the wall of the old abandoned wood-framed two-story building. I probably would never have seen it or paid it much mind if not for my obsession with hitting things that were challenging. It's not that I ever saw a future in it or anything like that. I never saw a future in baseball, or golf, or tennis. I didn't even know they existed. I just like to swing and hit things. Batting is my passion.

In my neighborhood, there are few things to do for entertainment. You have to get very creative to find things of interest that might help pass the excruciatingly boring hours of the day.

This day I had been abandoned by my neighborhood friend who, usually always together had, most of the time, seemed to come up with something to challenge our equally uneventful schedules with more and more dubious behaviors as almost all young boys tend to do.

We were no different or special in our attempts to satisfy our need for doing something, anything, to keep our curiosity and the continual need for action satisfied. We were simply two average kids persuading each other to do whatever came to mind.

It usually worked pretty well most of the time. Other times it turned out to be a really stupid idea.

One such time I remember was when we both got bee-bee guns for Christmas. Well, maybe it was my older brother that got it, but I borrowed it for a while let's say. What could go wrong with that scenario, right?

Anyway, to make a long story short, we had made the obvious decision to play war. They were just bee-bee guns after all.

After we both received a few welts from the enemy fire I figured it was time to seek some cover and sneak a shot from ambush.

We had a carport built from stacked railroad crossties. For those not familiar with what that is I will explain. Crossties are the long wooden squares railroads lay down and mount the train tracks to them.

It was, I thought, perfect cover with just enough room to see through the gap between the crossties to spy on my prey. Well, I wasn't as stealthy as I had imagined. My best friend had seen me go into the carport and saw me peeking out at him. I watched him as he quickly pulled up his bee-bee gun and fire at me. I had no clue the bee-bee could be so accurate. It was as if time had slowed down to a crawl as I watched it come straight at me. I thought it would not be able to go between the crossties, but sure as rain is wet, it came through the slit I was looking through and hit me right between the eyes.

While I was dealing with the shock of how such a thing could happen and pain from the direct hit between my eyes, I was also thanking any and all my Guardian Angels for the overtime they obviously had been putting in to keep that bee-bee from putting my eye out. Needless to say, that stopped my participation in the war games.

I think my friend was getting me back for winning the fight we had over a broomstick we found. A much-coveted prize, to dirt poor kids.

I remember we both reached and grabbed it at the same time. We pulled and tugged for a long time until I started swinging him around in circles. He finally let go and went flying. I had won and got to keep the broomstick as the prize.

It would have been better if he had won as that broomstick would bring me much grief later. But at the time I was king and I finally had my trophy bat.

It was at that time I began exploring ways to practice swinging and hitting anything flying or standing still. Things like bugs and bees. The plants gave me plenty of things to hit standing still so that my aim was soon very accurate.

I noticed the bees were of special interest to me. They challenged my prowess as a good aim with the broomstick, and as I had been stung a few times, payback on them only seemed appropriate.

I found that bumblebees were especially good for practicing. I felt that if I could hit those flying by then I would soon be a great batter and if I was ever challenged, I would be a natural to win any contest.

The bees gave me the incentive to be great because if I missed, I would have a mad bee to deal with. I soon learned through my training that a mad bee was a terror to deal with. So, I strived to be the best bee batter I could be.

I finally got to be so good I could pop off a bee with very few misses. And, I learned how to fight off the ones I did miss the first time.

You see I learned that a bee can't sting you if, while he is flying at you, you hit him with your hand on top of his back. He just falls to the ground where I take no chances of him getting back up and stomp on him. That ends the battle.

As a side note, I want to explain that I was not a bad child, I was a feral child, and as long as we made it home in time for supper, all was good. Mom had run off and dad was always working, so we all were left on our own with no guidance. And at that time insects were plentiful and no one said they were of any importance in the larger scheme of things.

Getting back to my story, I soon became obsessed with bumblebees. They gave me the thrill of danger and skill. I guess that is how big game hunters see themselves as they hunt a dangerous wild game animal.

I soon started wondering where bumblebees lived as I had never found a nest as other bees had. I made it my mission to find out where the elusive hive was.

I would sit for days watching the bees coming and going, morning and evening, and I soon saw a pattern of flight. I followed them in the evening going one direction, and in the morning, coming from that direction. I soon tracked them to a small hole in the wall I mentioned earlier.

I had no idea the bees lived inside the walls of buildings. That was why I had never located a bumblebee hive before. I was elated. I had finally found out their secret. I also thought I figured out a good strategy for getting a rapid batting round going. What could go wrong, you might ask at this point?

The hole was so small that only one bee could come out at a time, and they didn't seem to come out all that fast behind one another. So, I deduced, as one steeped in ignorance, that I could handle the flow coming out, as it was perceived at the time by a rational thinking observant brain not yet fully developed. Some might call it a dumb as a rock move. Anyway, the plan was set. In my mind, it was a piece of cake. I had practiced and was as ready as I would ever be. The day of the big hunt was at hand.

It was a fine sunny day and the wind was still, so all the conditions were excellent for my crusade. Sneaking up to the wall I hit it with my broomstick lightly and waited. Nothing happened so I hit it harder. Nothing once again. I decided it would take a lot more aggressive action to bring them out so I whacked the wall several times hard and waited. I got a reaction at that time. A bumblebee came out and began to fly. I watched it go around in a circle and then come at me. Bumblebees are easy to spot and fairly easy to dodge as they are slow at maneuvering so it was easy to duck out of its way. I waited for the bee to come around again and this time I hit it. One goner bee.

Pleased with the outcome I looked at the hole and saw no more bees coming out. I thought that was encouraging. That bee had probably just come out to investigate what all the racket was about.

So once again I went to the wall and banged on the building. I got a little cocky and said, come out, come out, it's time to play.

Well, this time I saw back-to-back bees coming out and I knew I was in trouble. I took off running. Live to fight another day was my thinking.

The bees had other plans though. I had kicked the bear and now must pay the price.

As I ran, I looked back and saw fewer and fewer bees following me as I ducked and weaved. I was thinking if I just keep going, they would all give up as the perceived threat was gone.

I finally had only one bee I could see that just refused to let me go away peacefully. Maybe he was a friend of the one I had killed and was out for revenge.

Well, it was on my terms now. A one-on-one duel. Just the way I liked it.

I slid to a stop and jumped sideways and it went sailing by. I had it set up as I raised my trusty batting stick for the final strike.

It did as anticipated, and I swung on it. But I had been running a long while and was tired and breathing hard so my aim was off just a little on the swing. It just grazed the bee enough to knock it to the ground but not hurt it much. They were a very tough bee after all. I saw it immediately get airborne before I could reach it and head straight up toward the sun. I had never seen that maneuver before but guessed it was to attack me in such a way as I could not see him coming.

That was one smart bee. I had no choice but to look at the sun and wait for the inevitable impending strike coming my way.

Sure enough, I had guessed right. I saw the bumblebee coming straight at my face and I ducked just in time to make it miss.

That made me realize this was no ordinary foe. This was a bee far advanced above the normal intelligence of its fellow bee brothers and sisters. This was a super bee and I had just volunteered to become its most ardent enemy.

Now I was in panic mode. I took off running again and soon heard the bumblebee right behind my head. Its buzzing wings giving me even more reason to go faster than I thought possible. But luckily, I had gained the speed I needed to keep pace with the bee buzzing behind me. We were both evidently going at the same speed as it could not catch me and I could not outrun it. It became a contest to see who could outlast the other and score the contender's final victory.

For me it meant the freedom from being stung; and for the bumblebee, it would mean bragging rights to its hive as the one who got to sting me. I was, of course, rooting for myself.

I suddenly realized I was near my home and without thinking I decided to try getting indoors and end the chase. I was getting tired and knew the bumblebee could go for much longer than myself.

I had to open the screen door to get in which would take a precious second or so to slow down and initiate the maneuver so as I came up to the door I quickly ducked and dug my feet in to stop suddenly. The bee had not anticipated this and went flying past me.

I knew I had but a scant second to get through the door before my nemesis would be back.

I grabbed the door handle and flung it open all the while not hardly stopping at all. My one mistake was not closing the screen door behind me.

I realized my mistake as I once again heard the buzzing of wings behind me. I ran through the house, my fear was palpable now, as I started screaming and running. The bumblebee had broken me. I was reduced to a spineless jellyfish of cowardness. My only thought was blind fear and the utter desire, at all costs, to get away from the bumblebees' stinger.

The moment came as I reasoned it inevitably would when, while I was running through the living room, I passed by my sister sitting on the couch. She had heard me screaming as I ran and yelled at me, "what's wrong?"

My final and most stupid mistake was turning to tell her. That act alone was just the opening my antagonist needed. That split second of slowing down just enough allowed my arch enemy the momentum needed to catch me. And, oh man, did he catch me!

The bumblebee stung me in the area of my eye. I could never be sure if it was directly in the eye or somewhere near it because it felt like someone had swung a bat right at my eye. I had never felt such horrible pain before in my life.

I instantly knew of my mistake as the pain engulfed me and all I could do in my panic and pain was grab at my eye and keep screaming at an even higher pitch as I turned and continued running through the front door and all the way to my friends' house, across the tracks and down the road. By the time I got there, my eye had swollen to a baseball size lump.

My friend was sincerely sympathetic. He laughed until tears came to his eyes. Well, at least he cried for me, right?

I never did find out if the bee had made it home or was killed when I grabbed and slapped at my stung eye.

I can only hope it made it because the bee deserved the honor of my defeat. He had truly proven himself as a worthy opponent, and his heroic efforts to satisfy his desire to have me never harm the humble bumblebee again was set in stone.

As a peace offering to my friend for taking the broomstick, I gave it to him and told him where to find the bumblebee hole. I figured he could use a lesson in manners also. What are best friends for, right?

Sub Chapter2

Fire in the Weeds

It was only one little match; I was only having a little fun. That was what I told myself. Now I was waiting for my dad to come home and give me the worst licking I ever had in my life. I figured that would be the way it would happen because that seemed to be a regular occurrence for me. This time I knew I deserved it, in spades. I completely crossed the line on this bonehead escapade. I would probably get the moron of the year award with a special commendation for being a crazy fool.

You wonder what I did that would warrant such self-conviction?

Well, I should start at the beginning because I need to take my mind off of the present situation for as long as possible. My end would come soon enough.

It all started, as incidents, I get into always seem to do, when my friend and I would run out of normal things to do. Boredom sets in and our overly active minds take over. I often come up with some real doozies that my, on-again, off-again, sense of right and wrong usually work to temper to a draw and soon dismiss as going too far.

I say usually because in my case that is not nearly as often as I would have hoped it would. So, my sitting down comfortably all the time was hampered by the frequent spankings I inevitably received for inappropriate behavioral remedies from my actions.

My middle name should have been chaos. I seemed to lack the filter that most people have to see the problem some things could cause. Well let me take that back, I saw the same problems I just thought I could control them. I was after all, seven years old now.

I had outgrown things like burying cigar boxes with my treasure under the house. That pirate phase was short and beneath me now. I was capable of much greater things. My mind was awash with new and exciting possibilities. Options were plentiful.

I would go down to the general store on the corner and dance and sing for the grownups and they would laugh and give me pennies that soon earned me enough to buy a candy bar. I thought I genuinely knew how to manipulate the people to get what I wanted. I didn't realize that they were just laughing at the fool kid dancing, and giving me money let them laugh a little longer. They had nothing better to do anyway. They were good people and truthfully meant no malice toward me. I loved the attention so I would have done it anyway.

As I look back at my younger days from my waning years I remember with fondness as that being a special time for me growing up. I remember the old dilapidated wood building general store in the rundown neighborhood with great fondness. It was where all the local men would gather to hang out and tell their tall tales; competing with one another for who could tell the best cock and bull stories.

I loved to play with the huge parrot in a big wire cage that talked or at least said words it had heard. There was also a big barrel of dill pickles. I loved those pickles. They seemed to have a more robust flavor and crunch than any I have had since.

Outside, it had a gas pump connected to a huge tank that was suspended in the air about ten feet by a sturdy metal stand.

The whole area was inhabited mostly by dirt-poor cotton farmers, but being poor never entered my mind. It was just the way life was. The whole family would go out and pick cotton, dragging those long sacks behind us, trying to fill them up.

I was too young to make much difference but we all had to pitch in to help the family eat another day. I didn't like picking cotton as it was back-breaking hard labor. Your fingers would bleed from the constant gripping and pulling of the cotton from the plant bulbs. But in retrospect, somehow, I think it made a better man of me by working hard, and it taught me to better appreciate and respect what I had because I had earned it.

I remember wearing clothes handed down from my two older brothers. Each wearing their clothes until they outgrew them and subsequently handed down to each succeeding younger person. As the third in line to receive, I had to wear clothes that were ragged and by then too short even for me. My shirt was way up my arms and my pants were way too high also. I would have to go to school in those clothes. The shoes were too tight and I would carry them more than wearing them. I liked going barefoot anyway.

It was strange looking back that no one made fun of me. Kids always love to pick on and make fun of the different ones. I suppose it was because we all were dirt poor and shared in the same difficulties. So that way of life was simply normal for us.

We had a man-made wash (a waterway) running behind our house that gave us many hours of fun. We would take the big washtub and a bunch of us would get in and float around. My big brother would scare us all by rocking the tub from side to side and once I fell in. I was especially scared because I just knew a water moccasin was going to bite me in the water. I swam as fast as I could to shore.

I can't remember when or how I learned to swim. It just made sense to do what it took to move forward and so also stay afloat. Especially if you wanted to get away from snakes in the water, a real incentive to learn quickly. I had always been a quick learner. I never said I was a smart learner, just a fast learner when it came to life in general.

We would sail downstream and once I found a cave on the shoreline. I crawled into it and saw the wall was covered in blue crystals. I didn't think anything about it then but I wonder now as an adult what that had been. It looked like the inside of a geode when you cut it in half. It wasn't a solid wall but more like a section here and there.

In the spring, as the farmers were plowing their fields and getting them ready to plant more cotton, we kids would make walls, or as we called them fortresses, out of the bigger dirt clods and have war games by throwing dirt clods at your enemy and whoever got hit was out. I got very good at dodging.

That talent carried me through many dodgeball victories in school gym class. I was usually the last on my team to get hit. And only then because the opposing team had five or more guys all throwing at the same time at me. Oh, and the farmers were none too happy to come around and find a big pile of dirt they had to knock down in order to plant their crops. So, naturally, we had to wait until they were gone before we built our fortresses.

In the fall we would have war games also. The rolling hills along the drainage wash grew some kind of tall stalk plant. We would pull those up and swing them around a couple of times until we got a good speed going and let go while aiming at the enemy hill. It hurt badly if you got hit; especially if you left a big chunk of dirt on the roots. It was really funny when anyone on either side got hit in the face. It not only knocked you flat on the ground but you came up spitting and gaging on all the dirt you had in your mouth from yelling as it hit you and your eyes and nose and ears were full of dirt as well. What can I say, that was fun, and it toughened you up to life and its many injuries!

We didn't have a lot of toys. Our surroundings furnished a great many things you could make work for you in the entertainment department. All it took was your imagination and the will to try.

This brings me back from my future remanences into my past to the present remanences of my life story in my past. Got that?

In other words, let me finish my story of why I was waiting for dad.

My friend and I had wondered about the neighborhood in search of any activity worthy of our attention. It was near to absolute boredom that we found ourselves outside of the general store. The summer was gone pretty much and the weeds had grown tall and were dry as daddy after a hard day at work. I had my hands in my pocket and noticed a box of matches. I can't even tell you how I had acquired such a thing. But there they were, just crying out for attention. I pulled them out and stared for a minute. What could I do to entertain myself with these I wondered? Then it dawned on me where I was standing. Right in the middle of a bunch of dry weeds.

Now I didn't have any thought of real harm with the matches, I just thought why not throw one down and before the weeds get too out of hand, I could stomp out the fire. That intrigued my friend as well. Two morons in agreement, what could go wrong?

I lit a match and threw it down in a small patch of weeds and it started flaming instantly. We both jumped on the fire and quickly put it out. What exhilaration, what absolutely thrilling fun.

I gave my friend a match and he threw it down. The same thing happened and we stomped it out. We were hooked now. This game had all the earmarks of one for the books. A game to record for posterity.

Now it was my turn again. I lit another match and tossed it into a bigger and taller patch of weeds. It went down to the base and once it started flaming up it went crazy. I had no idea it could grow so big so fast. We both tried as hard as we could to put it out but it was beyond our meager attempts to squelch it.

We both panicked and ran to our own homes to hide from the trouble we knew we would be in if we were ever found out.

I ran into my house just to see my dad standing there. He looked at me, breathing hard from the run I had just finished, and the obvious, by the many times before, guilty look, I didn't seem to ever be able to hide from him. He asked me what was wrong? I couldn't just outright tell him and so I stammered and mumbled. Tiring of that he went outside and looked down the street. He saw the big billowing plume of smoke that was a dead giveaway. He came back, looked at my guilt-ridden face, and not saying a word went to the bedroom and grabbed a blanket. He got it soaking wet and ran out the door toward the general store.

Now we are all caught up to the present moment of my story. I am simply waiting for dad to come home and give me my punishment. He has been gone a long time and quite frankly I was getting worried about him.

He eventually showed up covered in soot from the fire. He had obviously put in great effort to extinguish the fire. He didn't say a word to me, he just stood there and looked at me for a long time.

I could not tell you why he didn't lay into me right then and there. He had every right to send me to the next life after that bonehead move. But I never even got a spanking. Just him looking at me the way he did and seeing the disappointment on his face was a worse punishment than I had ever had before in my life or since.

I remember he once told us we all mess up sometime in our lives, some more than others as he looked right at me. But as long as you don't dishonor the family name, I can live with it. That was the "Cardinal Rule," don't put shame on the family.

Though I can't remember just how but I later learned, dad had told his version of what happened that day.

Here is his recollection.

"My youngest son came running into the house to beat the band. He was up to no good as usual just from looking at him. After getting nowhere trying to get him to confess which never worked anyway, I looked outside and saw what I thought at the time was the general store going up in flames. I knew instantly my son had some hand in it.

"Truthfully, I didn't want to go, but since my son was probably the cause, I felt honor-bound to try and help put it out. So, I ran down with a wet blanket and helped the few folks that were there trying to put out the fire.

"The biggest and most fearful time of it all was when we were deciding whether to high-tale it out of there because the flames were surrounding the fuel tank and it could have exploded at any time. I think I would have run with the rest, but I knew my son was the cause and I felt obligated to stay. The store owner and I were left to put out the fire from that time on. Lucky for us the tank did not go up. Though I really could not tell you why. I guess the good Lord was watching over us that day.

"After we had the fire out, the store owner asked me why I stayed when everyone else ran for the hills. That was the bravest thing he had ever seen.

"I had to be honest and tell him, sir I said, I would have been right on those other folks heels myself if not for the fact I believe my son caused the fire.

"He looked at me for a minute and quietly asked," "the young one?"

"I answered yes."

"He grinned, as he plainly thought back to his own recollections of my son and grinned.

"He just said, "thought so."

"Then he added, "don't be too hard on the boy. He has learned a whopper of a lesson today, and frankly, this was mostly my fault for letting the weeds get so out of hand. I saw the problem I could have if this very thing happened, and I was just too lazy to clean it up. Your son saved me the trouble in a way. The store is undamaged and the property is cleaned up so all is good in the world. But I thank you for helping anyway. I still think you're a brave man."

So that is my story. I never realized until I had heard his side of it just how close I had almost come to causing my own fathers' death. It left an indelible mark on me of his courage and dedication to the family.

Dad did have a cure when no one would tell who among us kids had done something wrong or confess to it. He would simply line us all up and give us each a spanking. That way he was sure to get the right one, one way or the other. And, the guilty party would have to live with the guilt of having to watch the rest of us get the licking he or she had coming. As it happened a few times, apparently that someone didn't care about the rest of us all that much, you reckon.

I do have a serious but kind of funny story of dad and myself.

He had bought me a 410 shotgun as a young teen. Thirteen maybe. He wanted to take me with him hunting pheasant or quail.

We were in a rolling hills grassy pasture type land.

One of his rancher friends had given us permission to hunt on his property. So, we went out early one morning and started walking together on the property. For some time, we had not seen anything so dad said he was going to go to the left and I was to keep straight ahead. No problem, right?

He was soon walking out of sight behind a hill and for five more minutes, there was still nothing around.

Suddenly in front of me, I saw a bunch of pheasants fly up and were heading off in the direction of dads' location. I really didn't know where he was nor did I care at that moment.

I just knew my moment was at hand. Immediately lifted my new shotgun and aiming at the birds I let go with a round. The next second, I heard this scream come from over the hill. I wondered what that was all about. Then a few minutes later dad came toward me from the other side of the hill. When he got closer, I could see he had little red spots on his face. He came up to me and said very gruffly, "why did you shoot me?"

I had no idea I had done that. I told him I didn't know the pellets would hit him. I was shooting at the birds flying away.

He thought for a minute and admitted, this was his fault for not teaching me how to hunt properly, and separating was a no-no to start with.

He did not suffer any lasting effects as the pellets had lost their power and had just descended on him, peppering him with spent buckshot that just put little holes in his skin deep enough to make them bleed a little. He was lucky they didn't get him in an eye.

We hunted regularly after that and he taught me how to be a good hunter. I rarely missed. I was apparently a natural shot.

As I grew up, I found I was good in any sport that had me directing an object into something. From my early days with the bees to later with guns and sports like baseball, badminton, volleyball, tetherball, soccer, pool, foosball, ping-pong. Everything I tried.

***

There was one last story I want to impart before I go to another topic. I was always doing things that got me into trouble a lot of times. It was just because I was defending myself from bullies and the school always took my self-defense as aggressive behavior. So be it. I never backed down to a direct threat to myself. I knew where that would lead. I know the ways of bullies.

I had one instance where a bully decided to hit me in the back of the head with a spitball from his straw in the auditorium before school started. I of course retaliated with my own barrage and of course it was me that went to the Principles office. They had a flat wooden paddle that was used on many occasions on me for a multitude of offenses. I was a problem child because I didn't take any guff off of anyone. I finally got smart and took the fight to someplace off school grounds where I settled things once and for all.

I had a Sherriff in a small town I lived in who apparently took notice of my actions and after talking to me for a while decided to teach me some judo. I was never to use it in any fight or he would stop teaching me.

Now that was some deal, right? I was forced to fight guys to defend myself and he was teaching me to defend myself but I was unable to use what he taught me. What a crock. But I did as he said and he would hear of my fights and holding to my honor to not use what he taught me and he was pleased. Go figure.

One bully, I had to fight had big rings on every finger. Now I admit, that had me worried. He was one of those guys that failed a grade or two and was a lot bigger for it in my class. He was at least 6 inches taller and much bigger. I, on the other hand, had been fighting for a while at other schools so I was no beginner at this game.

I beat him by ducking and dodging for a while trying not to get hit by all those rings which I knew would be a bad thing.

After a few cuts to my hands from blocking his rings, I decided to heck with this and it was time to finish it. He was obviously not as good as I was at fighting.

Most big guys aren't. They just like to intimidate the smaller people into doing their bidding. I was not that guy. I was eventually able to land a straight shot at his mouth and he dropped to his knees.

Blood was pouring out of his mouth. I wanted to just pour it on him but I was always a gentleman when fighting. I always fought fair, stupid as that was. I waited for him to get up.

After he stopped spitting blood and cursing me, I could tell he had endured enough because he wasn't even trying to get up again. So, to give him an honorable way out, I suggested calmly to him that he should heal up and we could go at it again at a later date.

I could tell by then he did not want any more of me. I had already shown him he was no match for me. He took the bait and said ok.

I waited for a couple of weeks and he showed no signs of wanting further action so I went and sat down next to him in the bleachers in gym class and we began talking.

Soon, as always happens with bullies. he wants to be my friend. I always go with that.

Sub Chapter 3

It is Just an Ability

My time serving in the army was more of a long holiday for me than a duty. I was one of the lucky ones. I did not have to go to Vietnam. I was sent to Germany for my tour of duty; just a luck of the draw as they say.

While in basic training I still had a bit of mischief in me from my younger days.

Right off on the first day, I was last in line to get my obligatory buzz haircut. The barber asked me how I wanted my hair cut and I was surprised I had been offered a choice seeing as how all the others had been basically scalped with no power to resist.

Being a rebel at heart I decided to push the limits as I had always done and told the barber to leave about two inches on top. When he was done, I saw a lot of hair and I knew I was going to be challenged by my drill sergeant, but I had to try. That is what I do best.

I also told them to leave a small mustache in place. That made it all look nice.

I went back to the barracks and sure enough, the first person I ran into was my Captain looking over the men. I came in, went to my bunk, and stood at attention.

I could see the guys on the other side of the aisle giving my hair the once over and looking at me with smirks, like, buddy you're in for it.

The Captain soon came around to me and stood looking for a minute. He shocked me with what he said next.

He said, "I like your look and if you had cut it to just an inch long, I would let you keep it. But it is just too long for this part of your training. I will let you keep your mustache though. Get out of here and get it done."

I could see the drill sergeant taking mental notes of who I was. I guessed he was looking at me as a possible troublemaker.

I came back bald like the rest of my company but I had a mustache. You have to take your victories where you can.

We had to learn to spit-shine our boots. We didn't actually use spit that day, just water, but when you're in the field that is what you did. I couldn't seem to get the shine I knew they wanted and the lieutenant was talking us through the way to do it.

Of course, I saw an opportunity and jumped on it.

I said "Sir, I just can't get the shine to come out right," as I held up my boot for him to assess.

He looked at it, then at me, and took the bait.

He said, "all right, everyone gathered around." He took my boot and began demonstrating for all to see how he shined the boot to perfection. After he was done, he said, "Ok, you all got that?"

We all said, "Sir, yes Sir."

He handed me back my boot and walked out.

I thought one down and one to go.

I started on the other one and soon the Captain came in. He was looking at our progress and when he came up to me, I looked at him.

Should I? That was a stupid question. Of course, I should.

I said, "Sir I am having trouble getting a good shine on this boot. It just doesn't want to cooperate it seems."

He looked at me and then at the boot. He took the boot and said, "watch closely."

He began polishing my other boot. The guy in the next bunk looked at me. I shook my head at him. I had hopefully made myself understood with my limited gestures for him to mind his own business.

After a while, the boot was done and the Captain gave it back. He said, "now I expect you to have the brightest boots in the company.' He left and the guys all came around me and started saying I was either a total idiot or had more you-know-what's than were allowed on any one man. Someone commented I probably hauled them around in a wheel barrel. If the word got out that I had both the Captain and the

Lieutenant shine my shoes I would shudder to think of my short life span after that. I did worry for a while about someone snitching on me, but it turned out ok. I guess they all thought that was cool, stupid, but cool.

I continued to impress my fellow comrades with different exploits and shenanigans for the fun of it.

When I finally got through basic and MOS training I ended up in Heidelberg, Germany.

I started acting like I was a martial arts expert by practicing here and there with different moves I had seen in the movies. I would practice leg kicks and roundhouse kicks while showering and once in a while a guy would come in and catch me. I would stop immediately and deny I was doing anything. I would practice hitting things hard with a chopping motion. A few would catch me doing that and I just said I was keeping my hands hard and ready.

The word soon got around that I must be some kind of martial artist that did not like attention drawn to it.

That came in handy when I was confronted one time when a guy, I had embarrassed, wanted to beat me to a pulp. I knew he could do it as he was a monster bodybuilder, both in size and build. But he refrained from doing so up until then because he had heard I was some kind of expert in the arts.

He came into the room where a few of my friends were hanging out and said, I heard you know some fancy stuff. Why don't you show me what you can do? I could tell by his demeanor that his intentions were not friendly and I was in for it. I knew he was feeling me out to see if I could be beaten before he stepped in it. This was not my first encounter with violence.

Let me interject for a moment from the story and explain.

I had moved from school to school while growing up, not spending more than a year or two at the most in any location. That meant to me that in each school I had to fight a bully or group of bullies to be accepted and left alone. It was universal as a situation I encountered in every place we moved, so I became very good at fighting. It was always a bigger than myself opponent.

Bullies never picked on someone their own size it seemed. But I was smart and very quick and learned the hard way to avoid getting hit. *I never lost a fight; that is no brag, just a fact.*

I don't know why but after I beat these bullies in the fights, they all wanted to be my friend. Anyway, back to my story.

I just stood up, faced him, and stared him straight in the eye, and slowly as a gunfighter would when confronted by a challenge said menacingly, I don't think so. That told him that if he wanted to know what I knew he would have to find out the hard way. Then I asked him what was this all about?

He told me about the insulting way I treated him a few days ago in a bar. I remembered that moment and I told him as I became completely relaxed and put my hand on his massive shoulder, trying to defuse the tension and save my bacon, I am sorry for that, I said with total honesty and sincerity. I was feeling no pain that night and I do admit to running my mouth out of turn. You had a right to be mad and I apologize again.

That took him by surprise and he relaxed and said, thank you for that. You're not all bad.

We became best friends.

I had learned a long time ago that psychology trumps brawn most every time. If you can convince someone to believe it is in their best interest to avoid a conflict then you have already won. That is why I developed the martial arts image of myself. I was tired of fighting and as I said, brains trump brawn, most every time.

I had no other need to fight after that. Everyone kept a friendly attitude toward me. I had beat the biggest man there without a single blow.

I had one prank I remember well among the many I did that I want to share.

I had bought a string of firecrackers and wanted to share with everyone but they were all in a room in our barracks on the bottom floor having a party. I was on the second floor in a room I had gone into. It was not my room. I had gone into the room looking for some friends to help fire off the firecrackers. I noticed the party and an idea hit me.

I looked out the window and saw the window below was open. I did what I usually did when a fun idea comes along. I don't think it through, I just do it.

So, without any more delay, I excitedly went back to my room down the hall and got some string, and came back to the room. The party was going strong, the music was loud and pleasing. Everyone was talking, laughing, and having a great time.

I tied the firecrackers to the string and measured out the length I calculated the string needed to be to reach down to the window below. I calculated the timing of how long it would take the firecrackers to start going off after I lit them from the winding I did of the fuses. I was ready.

I did a few practice swings to get the feel of what I had to do and lit the fuse.

I quickly tossed the firecrackers out of my window and when they were out far enough, I stopped them from going father and let the string swing the firecrackers into the open window below.

I had executed a perfect swing as I watched the firecrackers going into the room. They started going off just as they were entering the room below. I heard complete pandemonium as everyone started screaming and yelling as the firecrackers went off. The cussing was getting to a fever pitch then and that was when the reality of what I had just done hit me.

As I said, I don't always stop to consider the consequences of my pranks before I do them. What fun would that be? Anyway, I decided I had better get out of Dodge before I was found because the crowd below was getting to be hostile sounding.

After the firecrackers stop going off and the guys in the room calmed down a minute, I distinctly heard a few say let's get that {expletive deleted) and I could hear the sounds of them running out of the room.

I quickly ran to my room and grabbed a book and was just pretending to read it when my door burst open and a couple of guys stood there looking at me. They yelled; did you hear or see anybody just now? I looked at them casually and said calmly, no, and added with a hint of concern, what's going on?

They said, some SOB just threw a bunch of firecrackers in our window and scared the (expletive deleted) out of us, we thought we were being attacked.

One guy said, I was sitting in the window when they came through and they started going off right in my face. If I catch that (expletive deleted) I am going to kill him.

With that they left, continuing the search. I thought to myself, this trick was a little dangerous to my health. If they had caught me, I would have a lot of explaining to do, if they had let me. Not only to them but also to the Captain the next day, possibly even having to face a court-martial. I never until now, confessed to that prank.

I also cut out any really bad pranks from then on.

Sub-Chapter 4

OLD AGE

Sitting on this park bench feeding the birds; I once again begin to reevaluate my life. I do these self-reflections every ten years or so, just to satisfy myself that I still am relevant and vital to society at large.

So, how old do you have to be before you're truly old? I am almost seventy now and still do not consider myself old.

Sure, my body feels and shows many years of wear and tear. But my brain says I am just as vibrant as I ever was. I just don't think bungee-jumping would be a good idea any longer. Is that rational' coming from old age or common sense?

Am I now trying to find things I always wanted to do but never did a challenge to accomplish, like a bucket list of sorts before I pass, or am I seeking to get things done before I can no longer physically do them?

Are my priorities changing due to my lack of energy to do them or my acquiescence to the fact I no longer wish to strain so hard to get them done?

I can hire someone else to do menial labor and chores. Does that mean I don't want to do them any longer or that I can't do them due to my age? I think a little of both now.

When I was younger, I thought I would be labeled lazy if I watched some other person do the lawn, or the dishes, or paint my house. Now I have no problem with it. I might even give instruction to a missed spot or a certain way of doing a thing without any guilt for saying it.

I find I now freely give my opinion to any and all around me whether solicited or not and do so without regard for whether they even wanted it.

I consider my acquired knowledge a benefit to others if only they would listen.

It is funny how people always say age is just a number until they get to a high number themselves. Perspectives begin to change and attitudes and tolerances to many things once accepted now succumb to intolerances of past behaviors of others.

Little effort or lenience is exuded in the blind charitable acceptance of foolish ideas from younger and less experienced individuals. In other words, hogwash is denounced blatantly and with satirical candor.

I admit to being on both sides of the issue as far as voicing my opinions and also debating with less knowledgeable individuals. I let others think they are convincing me on a particular subject just to have peace and tranquility for a while. I know they are wrong but see no sense in a constant argument over a subject in which beliefs will never change. Discussion is futile to many who have solidly committed beliefs.

Once again, I deem myself worthy of value to humanity as I have demonstrated the cognitive abilities needed to teach and guide future generations.

Chapter 11

THE WISHING WELL

I understand that many believe when you use magic it always comes with a price. So, when I found a bubbling watery looking, I guess you could call it a doorway or a channel that grants a magical gift transference when you passed through it, had appeared in my home, I was surprised, to say the least.

It was not a gift you could pick on your own but was a wish-fulfillment the anomaly opted or maybe chose to do for you from the desired initial wish you had asked for. It was like it knew better than you what your real wish was.

But I hadn't figured out any of this at this point in my story. That came later after I was able to study it better. But I figured I should give you some sort of heads up to what I was dealing with in advance.

I could not tell you at that time why it had appeared in my home or if it was magical or anything about it. It just showed up one day while I was at work. And when I came home, there it was, just seemingly floating in the air in the middle of the living room.

Of course, I was a bit upset at first but it did not attack or show any sign of violent tendencies so, I calmed down and began looking it over more closely.

I began to walk around it and in describing it, it looked just like rolling bubbling water as it would appear if you saw it on the ground looking at it from above with a geyser fountain effect, only it was flat. Almost invisible from the side as it was so thin. It covered a circle of about seven feet in diameter.

I grabbed a cane and stuck it into the center of the,---, I didn't know what to call it. Enigma? unidentified anomaly? Calling it a "Thing," did not seem appropriate.

The cane simply went through the aberration with no noticeable effect. The cane did not show any signs of distress to its form or condition. No coating of water which, from the look of the spere, I would assume was wet but was not.

I tried waving the cane back and forth through the oddity sideways. Still no perceivable disturbance. I could see the cane going through with no disturbance or distortion of the flow of the visual effect of the apparition? Illusion? Dream?

I began to wonder if I was imagining this physical or manifested disturbance as somehow compensation for something going on in my life. Maybe I was having a breakdown. Losing my mind. I was thinking all kinds of crazy things trying to justify this "unexplainable presence" in my home.

Soon, giving up on the notion I was nuts, I began to think of things to rationalize its existence.

I thought the most supportive logical explanation, with my limited knowledge of such anomalies, was to think it had to be magic or some gateway to another dimension. Both were unbelievable and yet it had to be something.

One thing was certain. The only way to prove any one of the ideas was to step through the thing. There, I had said it. It was a thing. Something tangible, a reality.

Now the next step after deciding it was real was to figure out what to do about it. Should I call the police? Yea, that would be just my luck. If I called them and told them I had this thing in my living room and described it, I could imagine who would show up with a nice white coat to wear. Especially if the thing disappeared before they showed up. Or worse if it was still here and I was the only one who could see it.

Now that was a thought to consider. Am I the only one that can see it? I should test that theory if for no other reason than to know if maybe I really was bonkers. But who could I get to share this discovery with that I could trust to keep quiet? After all, I didn't know what this was myself. And here I am trying to find someone else to share in the secret. That might get a little risky. I mean who really knows how someone will react to such a strange apparition. I even had a few dicey moments when I first encountered the thing. The only reason I didn't run screaming out the door was that this was my house. So, I stayed to maybe protect it in some silly custom of bravado.

I saw that nothing happened to the cane but I was not about to step through the thing myself before I tried it out on something else living first to see if it did anything to it. So, I went down to the pet store and bought a hamster. I figured if nothing happened to it, then probably nothing bad would happen to me.

I took the cane and hooked it through the cage handle. Then slowly put the cage through the thing. It went through without even a glimmer of anything out of the ordinary. But I did set the cage down and quickly went to the fridge and got a big carrot and hurried back to give it to the hamster.

I had not even thought about it; I just did it reflexively. But why? It felt like the most important thing in the world I needed to do.

Well, that was an eye-opener. If I followed the logical conclusion with my limited input so far, I could extrapolate a hypothesis that the anomaly had somehow willed me to manifest for the hamster his wish for a carrot. I concluded with little more than a feeling it must be a wishing well of sorts.

To tell you I was excited would be putting it mildly. I was jumping and yelling and having moments as I have never felt before.

I was ready for the plunge as it were. I wanted my wish as well.

It was strange how I felt perfectly comfortable in my analysis or was I deluding myself and jumping to conclusions not yet warranted?

I stopped and considered the ramifications of doing this. Remembering the saying all magic comes at a price I debated with myself.

Not only did I need to consider the consequences but also what would be my wish if this were truly a wishing well.

All the wells I had ever known to be had been those that you threw money into while making a wish. This one I had not tried that as yet. This one appeared to be, from my limited experience, where you went through it to be granted your wish.

I grabbed a quarter and tossed it through. Oh, shoot I scolded myself. I forgot to make a wish. I grabbed another quarter. This time I said "I wish I had a million dollars. Go big or go home I thought. And tossed the coin.

I waited in anticipation. Nothing so far. I called my bank and yep, I still had the same measly amount in my account. So, this was not that kind of wishing well.

I decided to go for broke and go all-in on a wish. If I was walking through the well, I needed to make it count. I gathered my courage and my wish on my lips and stood at the well.

I wish I had a million dollars. I then stepped through with the wish deeply ingrained in my thoughts.

As I stepped to the other side, I waited for something to happen. I had not felt nor had seen anything going through except a slight shimmer from what I perceived was the slight thickness of the portal.

Then after about ten minutes, I heard the doorbell ring. I was so excited. I just knew the wish had come true and I was going to see someone ready to hand me a million bucks at the door.

I rushed to the door and when I opened it there stood my ex-wife, Riley. I froze.

That was the last thing I had expected to see at my door. Not that I wasn't glad to see her. I never wanted the breakup in the first place. She had found someone else to fall for and run away with while I was busy working my butt off. But there she was in all her magnificent beauty.

I stood flabbergasted and wondering why she was here.

Coming right to the point, Riley said, while humbling herself, "I know you don't have any reason to take me back but I have come to realize my big mistake in leaving you. I am asking with all my heart if you could forgive me and take me back? I will make sure you never regret that decision if you can only forgive me. I will show you my love in a million ways."

That last comment hit me like a ton of bricks. A million ways? Was this my wish come true, as decided by the will or within the limits of the wishing well?

Any way you cut it I was all for it. It was my million-dollar wish come true.

Without saying a word, I opened the door wide and held my arms out for her and she came to me.

There was no way to hide the well from her if she could actually see it. I was still not certain others could as yet, but I figured chances were that it could be seen.

So, I decided to tell her all about it before letting her in the house as the well was right there in plain sight for all to see. I didn't want to freak her out by just surprising her with the anomaly.

Riley didn't know what to think and I couldn't blame her at this point. I just said finally, "come in and see for yourself. Don't be frightened."

I am sure she was having doubts about my sanity at that moment but Riley had come home so she pretty much had to go along for now.

Riley walked slowly into the house, with every muscle ready to turn and run in a split second. She got to the living room and saw it. It was true. It was real. There was something there. Not only was she relieved I was not crazy; but so was I. I now knew this thing existed for sure.

Riley walked around it in amazement as I had done and finally asked me, "what is it?"

I said, "I don't know for sure but I think it is a wishing well."

She looked at me puzzled. You could see the, maybe I was a nut-job after all, written on her face.

I had to quickly explain my limited knowledge of what I did to test it and the hamster experiment also. I left out the part of my wish. I wasn't too sure how she would react to the idea my wish might have brought her back to me. And honestly, I wasn't totally convinced it was the well doing that myself. Maybe it was simply timing that had occurred, a coincidence. No need to cause a problem if none existed, right?

I was also beginning to wonder if there was a time limit on how long the well would stick around. If that were a factor, I should try more wishes. I didn't want to push my luck in asking for too much, if that was even a problem here, there were a lot of unknowns.

I decided that I should play it safe for a while. After all, I had received the best wish I could have asked for already.

I asked Riley if she had a wish to fulfill. That way she could test it and I would also have a way of verifying my theory the well was what I thought it was through someone else's wish. To prove once and for all it was not a fluke.

I did inform her of the, all magic comes with a price, warning. I also told her that I wasn't sure this was really magic or something else entirely. It was all too new at this point to speculate or quantify.

Riley was a little apprehensive, to say the least. But you could see she was also getting a little excited in thinking of the things she could ask for.

Riley decided to not wish right now. She wanted time to think about it. "What if you only get one wish," she said. If she was going to do this, she wanted to make it worth her while.

I thought that was very mature and logical. Even I didn't think it through to that level.

I wanted to confess to her my wish and how it came to me in a much different fashion than I had asked but I still could not because of the possible repercussions. So, I just let her do her thing as I had done and hoped for the best for her. All she had to go on was my story with the hamster so she was very limited in her actual knowledge of how it all worked.

I did finally give her some advice in that sometimes a wish might come in a different form than you actually wished. I hoped that would help her decision-making better.

Maybe we could get more than one wish, that would be awesome.

I told her that I wasn't sure how long the well would stay here and that maybe she should think about asking before it was too late.

Riley saw the wisdom in that and decided to try one.

She said I should go first since it was my wishing well.

I was stuck. I hadn't thought she would point that out. Now I was going to have to try another wish so she could trust that the well was safe. She had a point. She was not aware I had gone through it already and she wasn't going to be the first to try walking through such a strange apparition. She was no dummy. Riley was simply saying you go first, buddy.

I had already been thinking of my second wish and stepped up like a real hero and said, ok.

I moved to the structure and thinking of my wish I walked through again.

I did not make it to the other side this time. As I completed my step through the portal, as I now thought of it. I was in a misty sky-like environment. Like I was floating in the clouds. The swirling mist was all around me, up, down, sides. Where had I been transported, I wondered? I felt no pain or gravity. I was weightless.

As I was trying to get some kind of bearing when I heard voices. They sounded familiar, like something from my past.

Slowly the mist began to dissipate revealing a scene I had never known about before. I knew who the people were but I also knew it was impossible for them to be there and looking so young.

I saw my mother in a hospital bed holding a newborn baby and my father was standing over her leaning down also look at the baby. Both were smiling and saying what a beautiful little boy he was.

I was stunned. I was looking at my first moments on earth with my parents. Or at least that was what I was feeling and sensing from the connection I had in watching the images. How is that possible? But there it was right in front of me. The moment of the most powerful love ever between a couple and I was witnessing it. There were many disappointing times later I could recount that I gave my parents, but this moment was sacrosanct. The bonding happening here was immeasurable in its intensity. The joy, the happiness, the love.

Then it dawned on me. I was experiencing the gift of the well. It, as I finally acknowledged, had to be a wishing well for love. Everything was pointing toward that analogy.

As I watched my parents, I could hear them discussing what name I should have. They decided my first name should be my Fathers choice and he picked David. That was his favorite name. He had always wanted to be a David. Mom picked Lee as her choice for my second name. She said it flowed well with dad's name and it was her grandfathers' name as well.

As I saw them kissing, the clouds began to blur my view once again and I was left with a great disappointment. But also, there was a wonderful feeling that I had witnessed my parents and had a connection if only for just a brief moment to them once again.

I had missed them so much since they had passed in that horrible car crash. It gave me a sense of closure and sustenance money could never buy. I had been deprived of saying goodbye to them and somehow this kind of gave me that. It was nourishment and relief for my grief-stricken soul.

I suddenly found myself back in the room standing right where I would be if I had stepped through the portal. Which I had apparently done.

Riley said, "so how long do you think it takes before you get your wish?

I turned to her still full of all the emotion and wonder of what I had just witnessed and felt.

I stated in a choking voice, barely able to speak; "I have already received it."

I told her of my journey through the well and she was flabbergasted.

Riley said," but you just stepped through and I saw nothing happening?"

It was as if everything I witnessed had happened in that split second of stepping through.

Riley asked seriously," are you pulling my leg?

Then she saw the tears running down my cheeks. Those had not been there when I passed through the well. I had somehow gone through an obviously emotional ordeal.

She asked me, "what did you wish for?"

I said, "I wished my family would spend more time with me. We have all moved farther apart since my parents passed away and it hurts a lot. I guess that is what the well picked up on and gave me just what I needed not what I wanted. That must be how it works.

This gave my wife and me much more to ponder in how we should approach the well for wishes. It had a mind of its own in selecting our wish fulfillment. That was not entirely a bad thing. So far, I was one-hundred percent on board with the outcome of my two wishes.

Riley was anxious now to try it. She had seen me and my wish come to pass and was ready now with her own desire. She stood in front of the well and thinking of her wish stepped through.

Just like all the other times, it appeared that Riley had simply stepped through the wells gateway. But she was smiling with a huge ear-to-ear grin.

She looked at David and without any explanation said, "now we wait."

In ten minutes, the doorbell rang. Riley said, "that will be for me," and went to the door.

David could hear talking going on for some time and was about to go see for himself what was happening when Riley came in followed by the man she had run away with.

What the blazes David exclaimed. He was caught completely off guard by this turn of events. Had he been played a fool once again by Riley? His mind was racing with all kinds of different and unpleasant explanations or enlightenments he was sure would be coming.

Riley, facing me, just said very quietly, "David please keep quiet for a moment." She turned to face Bob, who was staring at the well. "Well, I'll be, he said stunned. You were right. This is just plain weird."

Riley said all you have to do is think of a wish and step through to make it happen.

Now I was just beside myself with anger and hurt. She must have wished for Bob to come over to get back together with this jerk and also get more wishes to start their new life again. What a fool I have been.

I started to say my piece when Riley anticipating my reaction put her hand out and said pleadingly, "I asked you to give me a moment, please!"

I was so angry that I just sat down and kept quiet. I was afraid at that point of what I might do if I didn't.

Riley said, "Ok Bob, are you ready to wish?"

He looked at me and how she had handled me and with a grunt of satisfaction said, "sure babe, let's do this."

He asked, "ok how do I play this machine?"

Riley said, "just stand next to it, make a wish and step through, that's it.

Your wish will come true."

Bob said with confidence, "got it, see you on the other side," and stepped through.

But he didn't step through. He just disappeared. As he went through, he never came out the other side. What was going on? I had no clue that could happen.

I jumped up and went around the well looking for any sign of Bob. Nothing. He was just gone.

I turned to look at Riley. "Do you know what just happened? Did you have something to do with this?"

She was smiling at me.

Riley said, "I just received my wish."

I said, "ok, it's time to explain this."

She looked at the well and said, "thank you."

Riley took my hand and we both sat on the couch. She began her story.

She said, "I knew that Bob would come looking for me after I left him. And I also knew he would come looking for me here. He said he would never give me up and I would regret coming here. So, I knew I would have big trouble with him. He was a bad guy and I just didn't see it until it was too late. I had been thinking about the well as a fix the whole time. If I could get the well to help, then all would work out for you and me.

"For my wish, I asked for some way to get Bob to leave and never bother us again.

"While I was going through the well with my wish on my lips and in my heart, I met a lady that was waiting for me. She was standing in a flower garden. The most beautiful of which I had never seen before. She very gently asked me if I was truly in love with you? I said yes, I had been a fool to be swayed by Bob and his constant phony charms.

"She said, since I had asked for love and not money, she would find a way. She would not hurt Bob because that was not their way. But Bob would find what he was looking for and would never desire to try finding you again. He will get, not what he wants, but what he needs.

"I knew the theme of the well by now and was in agreement with the lady. I said thank you very much from the bottom of my heart.

"Then I was standing on the other side of the wishing well again."

I was astonished, Riley had done that for me. She had proven her love for me was real. I was speechless. All I could do was look her into her eyes, wrap my arms around her and hold her close for a very, very long time.

When we finally moved apart, we looked at the well. It was gone. I really wasn't surprised and neither was Riley. It had done what it had come for. It brought love back to our home.

We assumed it was off to another location to do what it does best. I was just glad it had sought us out to help.

Riley said thoughtfully. "Oh, and that wish you had to get your family together again? We can work on that. And also, maybe, saying shyly, we could work on starting our own."

BIOGRAPHY

David Lee Henley, born in West Memphis, Arkansas, grew up while moving from place to place. He spent three years in Germany in the Army and has worked many jobs starting at age twelve.

Such diversity has allowed a great deal of interaction with society and given him many encounters from which to draw life lessons in his writings.

In his debut book {POEMS, LYRICS AND DIVERSE THOUGHTS}, he imparts a particular moment in time, that everyone can find within themselves which should awaken a memory they have at one time lived. The lyrics in this book are from the songs he has written.

Other books by David Lee Henley are:

{THE LAST RIDE IS FREE} is his first thriller fantasy novel about three people and their adventures in the world of criminals and honest society. A journey from the dark side of humanity toward a more enlightened, soul-searching encounter.

{THE LAST RIDE IS FREE: BOOK TWO} is his continuation of a fantasy thriller novel in a series about the Malone family. It is packed with the same nonstop action as the first book. It has also brought their son into the fold as an agent working alongside his parents, Mario and Julie.

{THE LAST RIDE IS FREE: BOOK THREE} is the final novel in the series of the Malone Family. It brings the whole family full circle.

As usual, it has many adventures and missions but also has secrets about the family that even they were not aware of all finally brought to fruition.

Made in the USA
Middletown, DE
31 October 2024

63123231R00144